UNDER THE CINDERTIP

Under the Cindertip

Nigel Paul Morgan

Published with the financial support
of the Welsh Books Council

ISBN: 1-84527-142-4
978-1-84527-142-8

Cover design: Sion Ilar

Published in November 2007
by Gwasg Carreg Gwalch,
12 Iard yr Orsaf, Llanrwst, Wales LL26 0EH
☎ 01492 642031   🖷 01492 641502
✆ books@carreg-gwalch.co.uk   Website: www.carreg-gwalch.co.uk

To the memory of my mother,
Elaine Francis Morgan, 1936-1994:
she was a Queen Bee; and to the memory
of my father, Dennis Haydn Morgan, 1931-2003:
a south Wales miner.

Biography

Nigel Paul Morgan was born in Swansea. He worked as an electronics engineer before graduating in history from University of Wales, Swansea. He subsequently trained and worked as a teacher, and has been Head Teacher of a Swansea primary school since 1997.

Passionate about history, Nigel is a re-enactor with the American Civil War Society, commanding the 69th New York Volunteer Infantry, 1st Regiment, Irish Brigade. He is fanatical about music, football and all things Celtic, and tries to live a life that combines all three, and dreams that as many young people as possible living in Celtic countries grow up with a sound knowledge and understanding of Celtic traditions and culture.

Acknowledgements

I drew inspiration from Cymdeithas Dic Penderyn; Professor Gwyn Alf Williams; the town of Merthyr; the city of Swansea; the work of Alexander Cordell; the stories of The Mabinogi; the work of JRR Tolkien; Professor Peter Stead; Professor David Howell; The Mediaeval Baebes; Within Temptation; the wonderful children I have taught; the heritage, culture and character of Wales, and finally, but not least, from Richard Lewis, known as Dic Penderyn, whose legend and spirit will always be with me.

I am indebted to Dr Jasmine Donahaye – a wonderful and challenging editor – for her guidance, support and constant encouragement; Gwasg Carreg Gwalch for giving me this opportunity; Jan, Richard, David, Gemma and all my family for their belief; Jan Griffiths for all her work and patience; Val Holt for her advice on the clothing of 1831, and the children and staff of Danygraig Primary School for their enthusiasm.

Historical sources and select bibliography:
Home Office Records – HO 41/10
Home Office Records – HO 17/128
Reports of the Children's Employment Commission, 1842
The Cambrian, 1831.
David Egan, People, Protest and Politics – Case Studies in Nineteenth Century Wales (1987).
Gwyn A Williams, The Merthyr Rising (1978).
JeanMarkale, The Celts (1976).
Thomas Rolleston, Myths and Legends of the Celts, 1998
The Mabinogi (various editions).

8

Chapter 1

Daydreams and nightmares

'You told her what?'

'Well I didn't think you'd mind.'

'We've spoken about this Zoe: we can't have a dog, we're out at work and you're at school all day.' Zoe sighed and stopped listening as her mother went through her usual arguments. 'It's out of the question I'm afraid. It's just not practical,' she was insisting.

Why do mothers have to be so practical, Zoe thought. 'But Mum,' she persisted, 'Sarah's mum says that if they don't find homes for the pups they'll have to take them to the Dogs Home – and you know what might happen then . . . ' Zoe drew her finger across her throat.

'That's enough!' her mother snapped.

'Don't nag Zoe, there's a good girl,' her father said calmly.

'But Dad,' said Zoe, turning to her father, 'I've already told Sarah that we'll have the little one with the white paws. Oh Dad you should see him . . . he's so cute.'

'I had a little dog when I was a lad,' Zoe's father began but his wife abruptly interrupted:

'David! Don't encourage her.'

'Oh Mum . . . '

'That's quite enough,' Zoe's mother said firmly.

'But Mum . . . '

'I don't want any more talk of puppies until after our visit to your great gran.'

'So that means we can talk about it later?' Zoe asked hopefully.

'Maybe . . . when we get home.'

'Yes!' Zoe shouted.

She lapsed into a satisfied silence, her thoughts drifting. She imagined rolling around with a playful bundle of fur. *Patch* she'd call the puppy, she thought, and pictured walking him in the park. Her mind turned to school or, more accurately, to her friends. Earlier she'd had a text from Kelly inviting her to the cinema that evening. Zoe had texted her back, explaining that she couldn't go because of the family trip to Merthyr. Kelly had sent another text telling Zoe that Sarah and Nicola would also be going . . . and that they were going for a pizza before the film. Zoe had pleaded with her mother to be allowed to go, and told her she would be able to sleep over at Kelly's. Her mother wasn't having any of it. 'This is a family visit,' she'd insisted, 'and besides, you haven't seen Nan for a long while.'

Zoe smiled to herself, thinking of her great grandmother. She'd always called her Nan. It had been a family understanding – an unwritten rule . . . Dad calls her Gran and I call her Nan, Zoe thought. She could just hear her great grandmother's voice: 'Dere 'ma cariad, come to Nan, there's a good girl.' And it was true, she hadn't seen her Nan for quite a while, but . . . why did it have to be *this* weekend?

Loosening her seatbelt, Zoe struggled to get her mobile phone from her jeans pocket. She flipped the phone open and looked wistfully at the text messages as her mind went back to the morning's battle of wills . . .

'But Mum, it's just that—'

'I don't think a sleepover is a good idea,' her father had interrupted. 'Don't forget, you have homework to complete tomorrow because Monday is a Bank Holiday and we're going to Oakwood Park. Mrs Anderson told me you need to get a move on with your history assignment if you're going to meet the deadline. There'll be other weekends for the cinema and sleepovers. This weekend is for family . . . and homework!

'*Great!*' Zoe had muttered. There were times when she hated the fact that her father was a teacher. Even worse, when he's a teacher in *my* school, she thought. Still, at least he was popular. Most pupils considered him to be a good laugh, but Zoe avoided him at school as much as possible. Normally she liked his company and they got on very well, but he was Dad, and this was school . . . Most of Zoe's friends were amused by the situation and would often pull her leg about not being able to pretend that she didn't have homework. Zoe chose to take the bus to and from school with her friends rather than have a lift with her dad, in an effort to be seen as an ordinary pupil and not Mr Davies' daughter.

Zoe fidgeted, adjusting her seatbelt, and sighed loudly at the thought of what she would be missing.

'Problem, Zoe?' her father asked over his shoulder, his eyes fixed on the road ahead as he drove.

'No, Dad, just thinking about things.'

'Like homework perhaps?' he chuckled. 'Wow, did you see that low-flying pig?' he added facetiously.

'It nearly hit the car!'

'Ha ha,' Zoe replied. 'Don't give up the day job, Dad.'

'Don't forget though, Zoe,' her father said softly a bit later, 'if you want me to look over any of your work at any time you only have to ask.' There was no reply from the back seat. He looked in the mirror and saw Zoe staring sightlessly ahead. She appeared to be in one of her trances again.

When Zoe had been younger they had often called her 'Dolly Daydream' because of her tendency to lapse into this trance-like state. In those days, he recalled, when Zoe had been in primary school, she would be amused by being called Dolly, and would describe imagined adventures and fantasies with great enthusiasm and theatrical flair, enjoying entertaining people with her vivid stories.

Just recently he'd been marking books in his classroom during lunchtime with the window open, and he'd heard Zoe's voice from outside. She was talking to her friends Nicola, Sarah and some others, and was describing her favourite passage from *The Lord of the Rings*. 'What?' Nicola had asked, 'have they written a book about *that* film now?' The others had roared with laughter when Zoe had said, 'You might be one of my best mates Nic, but if you had a brain you'd be really dangerous!'

Zoe was popular with her school friends, largely because of her sense of humour and sharp wit. David chuckled to himself again as he remembered her description of her friend Kelly, who was often the centre of attention, especially with the boys, because of her looks and her unswerving pursuit of fashion. Zoe had called her a 'weapon of mass distraction', and

12

even Kelly had laughed at this and was really quite proud of the label.

David glanced again into the rear-view mirror and recognised the signs of his daughter's daydreaming.

Zoe had, indeed, drifted into one of her trances but her father might have been surprised to know that she was thinking about her schoolwork. The day before, Nicola, Sarah and Kelly had asked her for help with details for their history assignments and Zoe was happy to have been able to offer suggestions.

'How come you know so much?' Sarah had asked.

'Don't know really,' Zoe replied. 'Maybe it's because of all the things my Dad has told me, or the places we've visited. You know what my father's like for history . . . ' Zoe paused, and then she began again. 'Perhaps I've absorbed the details,' she said dreamily, 'but it's as if I can see things happening . . . hear things, smell things . . . ?' After a few moments of silence, while her friends waited, Zoe whispered, 'It's as if I'm really there – a fly on the wall of history!'

There was another pause; the girls looked at each other. With her fingers spread out wide Nicola had slowly moved her hands back and forth in front of Zoe's face and said in a slow, deep, trembly voice: 'You have been hypnotised and brainwashed by a mad professor father, oooooooo!'

Zoe had grinned and playfully hit her friend. Now, remembering, she closed the phone and pushed it back into her pocket and reached forward to press the button to open the car window. It was very warm in the car and the sudden rush of air through the open window felt refreshing on her face.

* * *

Emma Lewis, a police officer, sighed and drummed her fingers impatiently on her steering wheel as she waited for the traffic lights to change. This road is ridiculously busy, she thought, as she looked at the gridlocked vehicles on both carriageways. The junction, with three sets of traffic lights and two slip-roads always seemed to be congested because of the new Superstore, which was on the edge of a large shopping centre, behind a long row of Victorian terraced houses. Emma considered the houses, as she always did when she was stuck at the lights. They looked out of place to her: their front doors opened directly onto a narrow pavement beside the road. There had once been houses on both sides of the road, but the others had been demolished to make way for the dual carriageway that now served as the main route into town.

The lights changed and Emma drove her blue Volkswagen convertible into the left-hand lane, towards the regional police headquarters car park. She waved to the security guard, drove slowly under the raised barrier and pulled into a parking space behind the row of houses. With their slate roofs, ornate ridge tiles, intricately carved wooden front door surrounds and bay windows, they seemed so out of place between the plain modern, practical architecture all around – a time slip; a bygone memory standing still in a world moving rapidly forward . . .

Dropping the car-keys into her bag she strolled briskly along the path from the car park to a grey building with large, rectangular smoked-glass windows. The warm early summer sunshine cheered her and she stopped briefly to watch a large honeybee buzzing busily amongst the flowers in a carefully tended bed next to the footpath.

'You look happy in your work, little fellow,' she smiled. After watching it for a few moments she straightened up and muttered to herself: 'May the First tomorrow – the start of summer . . . I really love May.' She breathed in deeply. It's far too nice to be working in here today, she thought, as she ran up the steps and through the large double doors, under the sign that read *Gorsaf Heddlu - Police Station*.

* * *

The space fighter hurtled over the craggy mountain peaks and sped downwards towards the crater-ridden surface of the hostile planet. Within seconds two bright red rebel space command vehicles were following in hot pursuit. The tip of the fighter's wing disintegrated in a blinding flash as a blue-white laser ray leapt from a forward gun of the leading rebel spacecraft. The space fighter immediately started to spin, losing control, rolling violently from side to side. The control console joystick was pulled hard back as the pilot desperately struggled to gain altitude and pull the fighter away from the planet's surface and certain destruction. 'Come on, come on . . . YES! That's it my little beauty,' he yelled in triumph as the wings of the fighter levelled and the craft started to climb steadily away from danger. 'Now for my final throw of the dice,' he breathed softly. The rebel jets were closing in rapidly. He skilfully rolled his almost crippled spacecraft from side to side, successfully dodging the flashing laser rays of his pursuers. Large building structures appeared – towers and gantries, nestling below a series of rugged mountain peaks. With rapidly increasing speed the vehicle hurtled towards the dark buildings and mountains, the rebel fighters still close behind. The shapes ahead grew larger and larger as the digital speed meter continued to increase. "Steady, steady . . . ' A mass of large buildings lay directly in his path. "Now!" he yelled, and the fighter rose sharply and turned through ninety degrees onto its side, narrowly missing the buildings and roaring through a small gap between two sheer cliff faces. 'YES!' the space pilot roared triumphantly.

'You're not paid to play games,' Emma remarked lightly. 'And that computer,' she pointed out in a sterner tone, 'is official police equipment.'

'Yes, Sergeant,' the young detective constable grinned.

'What are you playing anyway?' Emma asked.

'"Invasion Mars" and I've just scored . . . '

'Never mind that,' Emma interrupted, 'lots of paperwork to do. Boring, I know, but we need to make a start.'

'Okay Emma, you're the boss.'

'Yes I am,' she chuckled. 'And by the way, we're on duty – it's "Sergeant" to you.'

'*Yes* Sergeant,' he barked, standing rigidly to attention and saluting.

Emma laughed, pushed him playfully and walked over to the desk and a pile of waiting paperwork. 'Oh, by the way Ian . . . ' she said, looking up from her desk and throwing a paper bag in his direction. 'You have a choice. Cheese, or . . . cheese!'

Ian smiled, sat down behind his desk, and took out the roll.

'Detective Constable!' Emma snapped suddenly.

'Yes Sergeant?' Ian sighed.

Emma leaned forward in her seat and fixed him with a

menacing glare. 'Milk, no sugar for me, and that's an order,' she said slowly.

Ian laughed, screwed up the paper bag and threw it at his boss. 'You really are pushing your luck Emma Lewis!'

*   *   *

The family car hummed as it sped along the smooth monotonous lanes of the motorway. The scenery, however, was now not quite so monotonous. As the car headed eastward Zoe stared thoughtfully at the massive metal structures of the chemical works and oil refinery, with their towers, pipes, gantries and chimneys that had belched out thick grey smoke for as far back as she could remember. Zoe had always thought of it as a space city, a futuristic landscape; in her imagination she saw it as a frontier settlement in some far-flung corner of the galaxy. Soon she saw not a futuristic space scene but a landscape of the past, full of ghosts and shadowy images. She remembered the thick, hazy clouds of smoke that for years had hung over this area – from the hills, with their stark, chemical-damaged trees, to the sea nearby, with its busy traffic of ships to and from the nearby city port.

The road climbed, and it seemed to Zoe that the car had reached the top of the world. Here too the landscape might have been of another planet, or another time: the hills stretching in all directions, as far as the eye could see, seemed so barren, so desolate. In the distance there were green hills covered with woodland, but those nearer to the road were yellowish, light brown and black. They were menacing, yet at the same time sad. What stories did they have to tell? Why on earth should people want to come and live in such a place? she wondered. The answers, she knew, were there in the landscape, and there in her mind, the memories of her father's history lectures: old workings, quarries and industrial waste tips. In some places she could see the natural outcrops of what had once been the very lifeblood of this faraway planet. The veins ran through the land, under the hills and the very roads on which they were now travelling. This was coal, known in times gone by as *King Coal* or *Black Gold,* she could hear her father saying, because it was coal that had ruled over the lives of those who flocked to live in the hills and valleys of south Wales. *Coal was fuel. Coal was power.* It was the ample supply of coal, wood and water that had brought the iron and copper masters of years gone by to Wales. She remembered how when she was little she'd imagined how these masters had looked.

Zoe's idea of Wales was of a bright, lively seaside city with swimming and surfing on the Gower coast, riding, cycling and, of course, computers . . . but this barren landscape, with its scars and remains . . . She shook her head.

Her thoughts drifted back to her friends. The day before had been a beautiful, warm Friday, with the fragrance of freshly mown grass hanging in the air. The sounds of early summer were all around like a carefully arranged musical composition, the low buzz and hum of insects providing a bass drone, the shouts, chants and laughter of people giving the rhythm, and the high pitched songs of birds adding the melody. As the group of girls were walking by the tree-lined school playing fields, Zoe had been thinking about the vivid dreams and visions that she experienced so often. Her friends knew about her imagination of

18

history, but not the down side . . . Ought she to tell them, she'd wondered. A few paces ahead the girls had laughed and giggled as Nicola wolf-whistled at a group of boys strolling off the field. They froze for a moment when a tall, good-looking lad in immaculate cricket whites grinned at them, winked, and then swaggered away with his bat slung over his shoulder. Then they shrieked with laughter.

'Oh . . . my . . . *God*! Did you see *him*?' Nicola gasped.

'Well I think he was winking at you, Sarah,' Kelly teased. Sarah blushed and giggled as her friends chatted excitedly. Zoe smiled to herself again. She and Sarah were very close. They shared secrets and yet . . . Zoe frowned as she thought of it: she could tell them about the coal masters, this landscape a hundred years ago, but she had never told any of them about her nightmares . . .

Bethan Davies also noticed that her daughter appeared to have lapsed into one of her daydreams. She asked Zoe what film her friends were going to see and, getting no response, glanced towards the back seat. She recognised instantly the glazed look on Zoe's face. Bethan looked at her husband and gestured with her eyes towards Zoe. David shrugged and sighed but said nothing. As parents they were naturally worried. Daydreaming wasn't so much of a concern, but the nightmares . . . The most recent, Bethan recalled, had been the previous weekend. She shuddered as she remembered the terror and disorientation of being woken suddenly from sleep by Zoe's shrill screams. David was already sitting up at her side, also trying to orientate himself after coming so quickly out of a deep sleep. And then, in a split second, they both scrambled from their bed and ran towards the pitiful sobbing that was by then coming from Zoe's bedroom. Bethan wrapped her arms around Zoe. David switched on the bedside lamps and looked on as his wife comforted Zoe, and wiped the perspiration from her face. David touched his daughter's arm tenderly and whispered, 'I'll get you something to drink.'

A little later he walked back into the bedroom where Bethan and Zoe were sitting against the headboard with their arms around each other. Above them, the faces of Che Guevara, the Manic Street Preachers, and the actors from Twin Town looked down from Zoe's posters, next to an autographed Swansea City F.C. photograph.

Zoe rested her head on her mother's shoulder as Bethan talked to her soothingly. She sipped the glass of water David had brought, as her parents looked on patiently, not pushing her to talk. She put down the glass and after a little while started to speak. Her voice was quiet and shaky. 'It was the same thing again, and . . . and . . . ' She stared at the curtained window at the far end of the room and chewed her lip nervously.
'Shush now, you don't have to say a thing,' Bethan reassured as she held Zoe's hand tightly.

'It's okay Mum . . . but I *am* frightened because it's always the same thing. Why, Dad? What does it all mean?'

David put his arms around his daughter. 'I don't know, cariad,' he sighed. 'I really wish I knew. Perhaps it's just a phase, a part of your growing up.'

That had been nearly a week ago. On the Monday morning Bethan had spoken to her friend and colleague, Doctor Rhian Walsh. She worked as a community nurse at the local Health Centre where Rhian was a doctor. Bethan liked Rhian's down-to-earth manner. During a break on that Monday morning she told Rhian about the nightmares and her growing concerns. 'Would you be able to see her, Rhian?' she asked. 'Zoe is registered with this practice.'

Rhian thought about it carefully. 'Doctor Morgan is far more experienced,' she said. She paused for a moment and then added, 'Or perhaps Zoe needs to see a specialist.'

'But she knows you, Rhian,' Bethan pleaded. 'I'm sure she would feel more at ease with you . . . at least for an initial chat . . . Please?'

'Okay,' Rhian agreed, 'but you'll have to make an appointment, to keep everything above board.'

Seeing Bethan's worried expression Rhian touched her hand reassuringly. 'I'll see what I can do. I did some work on child psychology during my time in Med School. I'll give it a try. I'm sure things will be fine and there'll be a fairly simple explanation. If I have to refer Zoe to someone more specialised then so be it. We'll have a chat first and see where we go from here . . . '

Zoe sat in a chair at the side of Doctor Walsh's desk as her mother brought in three cups of tea. At first she had been reluctant to see the doctor about her 'problem' but her mother had reassured her that it would be very informal and that it needn't go any further if that was what she wanted.

Zoe had met Rhian on several occasions, but this was the first time that she had seen her as a doctor. She felt a little nervous and self-conscious but responded to the doctor's gentle prompting . . .

'It's very, very dark. I . . . I'm frightened and I can't breathe properly. I can't see a thing but I can feel . . . no, *sense* . . . I can sense walls nearby. There's not much room and the walls seem to be moving closer. I'm trapped, *trapped*! Then, in the darkness, I can hear something. It starts quietly . . . always starts quietly, then it gets louder.' Zoe closed her eyes and gripped the edge of the dark wooden desk. She was breathing quickly and was shaking slightly.

'Go on Zoe; tell me about the sound you can hear,' Rhian said.

'I can hear a child crying,' Zoe continued. 'It is so, so sad. I can't see a thing. Everything is so dark . . . I can just hear the sobs and I start crying myself . . . ' Tears began to roll down Zoe's face.

'What next Zoe?' the doctor coaxed gently, handing her a tissue.

Zoe blew her nose, dried her eyes then took a deep breath. "It's lighter then. There are crowds of people pushing against me, hurting me. I can see their faces but I don't know them. They are angry . . . and frightened. They make me feel afraid. Then . . . " Zoe's voice dropped to a whisper, "there are explosions and everyone starts screaming. I feel panic; my head is hurting. I close my eyes and put my hands over my ears and in the blackness I can hear the child crying again, sobbing, alone . . . and I feel the most terrible sense of dread!" Zoe put her hands to her face and shook her head.

'Is there anything else Zoe?' the doctor asked.

'No, Doctor.' Zoe's voice was hoarse. 'That's when I wake up. It's always at the same point that I wake up.'

'And how do you feel when you wake?'

Zoe thought for a moment. 'I feel confused and . . . a

terrible dread, just like in the nightmare. I feel that something really horrible has happened.'

'Not that something horrible is *going* to happen?' Rhian asked.

'No. I always feel that something really bad has already happened. I feel very upset . . . and sad, really really sad.'

The doctor questioned Zoe about her general health, and about the daydreams and trances, making many notes as Zoe answered.

'Nearly finished now Zoe,' she said. 'Do you have any questions?'

Zoe thought for a moment and then said, 'Yes. What's wrong with me?'

Rhian smiled. 'Well, that's what we're trying to find out and . . . '

'But why is it always the *same* nightmare?' Zoe asked, her voice raised.

'Zoe,' her mother said warningly.

'But why, why . . . *why*? Zoe asked, losing control. *'What is wrong with me?'* she screamed, standing up and bursting into tears. 'I don't understand. How can I see things that other people can't see? What does it all mean? Why can't I be normal? *Why . . . can't . . . I . . . just . . . be . . . normal?'*

Later, at the end of evening surgery, Rhian called Bethan from the doorway of her consulting room. 'Come and sit down Beth,' she said, gesturing towards a chair.

Bethan sniffed and pulled out a tissue. 'I'm so sorry about earlier,' she said. 'I just didn't expect . . . ' She slumped in the chair and started to cry. Rhian handed her another tissue and said softly, 'Try not to worry too much, Beth. Zoe is confused, and she's frustrated because of it. We have to try to help her unravel her feelings and allay her fears.'

'Yes, but how can we do that if we don't know what causes the nightmares?' Bethan asked. 'And what about the daydreams, the trances and the vivid imagination? Are they all part of it?'

Rhian sighed. 'Look Beth, I don't have the answers at the moment but let's take it one step at a time,' she said. 'Now, about the nightmares and the feeling of being trapped and in the dark . . . We have no evidence or history of claustrophobia. Is there a film that might have particularly disturbed Zoe?'

Bethan shook her head. 'Not that I am aware of.'

'Obviously we can explore diet and Zoe's behaviour patterns before she goes to bed. That might shed some light on the nightmares . . . but . . . ' Rhian looked through her notes as she spoke to her friend, 'the thing is Beth, I *am* a little concerned about Zoe's tendency to slip into trances, daydreams, call them what you like. Zoe is aware of this condition and is able to describe how she feels during these episodes.' Bethan sat in silence, her head bowed as Rhian continued. 'You say that you and David have also noticed that Zoe is able to vividly describe, with incredible empathy and minute detail, events from various times in history.'

Bethan nodded.

'Can you give me an example?' Rhian asked.

Bethan thought for a moment. 'I know that lots of children have imaginary friends,' she said, 'but Zoe's fantasies went way beyond that. Once, she told us she was a Celtic servant girl working in a Roman household. It went on for weeks and David was amazed by the accuracy of her descriptions and her knowledge of the workings of the house – she even used terms, so David said, that were historically correct, and went through elaborate rituals at mealtimes.'

'She probably picked up the details at school,' Rhian said. 'Children are like sponges when it comes to absorbing knowledge, especially if they are particularly interested in something.'

'Yes, I know but she was only six years old at the time,' Bethan said.

'Zoe's an exceptional child,' Rhian commented, 'so that doesn't really surprise me.'

Bethan looked at the doctor. 'There was another episode only two years ago when she talked continuously about her friend Ginny,' she said quietly. 'She talked about events on a farm, and in a small town in Pennsylvania. She seemed to be in a trance as she spoke and described things as if they were happening at the time – she seemed to be really living it. She told us it was 1863, and over a period of days she became more and more frightened and agitated. She described, as if she were looking at the scene, how wounded soldiers ran through the streets away from rebels, and how cannons were being put up on the hill near her farm, and around the town's cemetery. Then, one morning she became absolutely distraught and told us Ginny was dead – she'd been killed by a rebel soldier's bullet.'

Rhian frowned. 'What was that all about?' she asked.

'David explained that it was the Battle of Gettysburg in the American Civil War,' Bethan said.

'Could it be that Zoe had read the details in one of David's history books? Rhian probed.

'Possibly, but that's not David's area of interest,

Bethan answered. 'He has very little on American history, but she does watch the *History Channel* a lot and *you* know what she's like for films. But, there was more to it than that. David did a bit of research and discovered that the only civilian to be killed at the Battle of Gettysburg was a young woman called Mary Virginia Wade, known to her close friends as Ginny. And,' Bethan continued, 'the events at Gettysburg took place from the end of June until the third of July, the exact dates that Zoe went through her fantasy.'

Rhian was silent for a few moments. Then she said, thoughtfully, 'It almost seems to be a form of self-induced hypnotic regression, if we are to believe that such things are possible.'

'*What?*' Bethan gasped. She looked amazed and shocked. 'Is that when people are hypnotised and they claim that they can remember living in a previous life?'

'Yes, something like that,' Rhian said, 'but what is more probable, however, is that Zoe is simply able to retain details of stories in her subconscious and recall them in her daydreams.' Rhian looked at her friend and sighed. 'I'm sure everything is fine. Zoe is a well-adjusted young person . . . and she *is* normal. Growing up is difficult . . . Talk to Zoe and David and, if you wish, I will refer her to a specialist, just to explore things a little further and, I hope, to put your minds at rest. It's up to you, Beth. Let me know what you decide.'

That had been Wednesday, Bethan remembered, as she sat staring ahead through the car's windscreen. Zoe, distraught and exhausted after her visit to the doctor, had slept all that afternoon and right through to Thursday morning. During the evening, Bethan and

David had talked over and over what to do, sharing their anguish while their daughter slept.

The next morning Zoe had gone to school and by teatime was behaving as if nothing had happened. Bethan remembered getting in from work and hearing peals of laughter coming from the living room. Looking round the door she had seen Zoe and Sarah sitting together watching *Scooby Doo*.

'Hi mum,' Zoe had said brightly. 'Dad's in a year-group meeting, he'll be home by six.'

As the car turned right, passing a sign for Merthyr Tydfil and Georgetown, Bethan glanced over her shoulder and noticed that Zoe was still staring in her customary trance-like state. What *are* we going to do with you Zoe, she wondered. Why is this happening to you?

Chapter 2

Nan

'Nearly there now,' David called, breaking into Zoe's thoughts.

The car sped down the hillside road. I wish I'd brought my bike, Zoe thought. 'Or my roller-blades,' she muttered under her breath.

To her right, through the car window, she could see a wide valley stretching away. At the nearest point there were the buildings and houses of a town. Somehow Zoe couldn't imagine this place as a dark, dirty centre of human suffering, but this was Merthyr now, not the Merthyr that her father sometimes talked about – the Merthyr of nineteenth-century industry . . . masters of iron and things like that. Whatever, she thought. That's Dad's stuff. She was far more interested in older history, ancient stuff . . . I'd love to have been a Celt, she thought – following Boudicca or Madryn or some other warrior Queen into battle . . . *Princess Zoe*, with woad symbols of the horse Goddess, Epona, painted on my face . . .

Within a few minutes Zoe could see the houses and shops of Georgetown. As they'd driven down the hill, passing some rows of very old houses, her father had commented 'Workers' cottages.' They were small low buildings, packed together into a tight terrace. Zoe smiled at the thought that she'd actually noticed the buildings. Her friends never seemed to notice things like buildings – well, not historical buildings anyway. They'd notice a Pizza Hut or McDonald's or a cinema. She thought, amused, how Nicola would say, 'There's something wrong with you, girl. Get a life!'

Zoe looked up at the large, majestic building of Cyfarthfa Castle perched high on a green hill. It seems so different, so out of place, she thought.

'Here we are Zoe,' her mother said. 'We'll be at your Nan's in a couple of minutes.'

The car headed up a small hill and passed a row of shops and new houses. Zoe thought that the layout of most of the streets of Georgetown looked like this, all the same: new estates of redbrick houses. Number 3, Davies Row was her great-grandmother's house.

She stood back as her father greeted his grandmother warmly. She was eighty-two years old but Zoe thought she didn't act or move in the way you'd expect from someone of that age. Her small wiry frame zipped this way and that, taking the coats and sitting her visitors down. She chatted excitedly, flitting between Welsh and English: 'Now sit down, eisteddwch plis, I'll just put the kettle on. You must be dying for a cup of tea. Well, well Zoe, you look all grown-up.' She smiled at Zoe. 'Sut wyt ti?' she asked.

'Fine thanks Nan,' Zoe replied.

'Yn Gymraeg os gweli di'n dda,' her great-grandmother scolded.
Zoe smiled. Her Nan always insisted that she speak at least some Welsh.

'Wel?' her Nan repeated, 'sut wyt ti Zoe?'

'Da iawn diolch Nan,' Zoe replied, smiling broadly.

'Good, good – dyna welliant!'

Zoe giggled at the way her Nan managed to speak a mixture of Welsh and English in the same sentence. She smiled again as she thought of her father's opinion on the subject . . . 'My grandmother,' he'd once said in mock exasperation, 'has brought a whole new meaning to the term bilingualism: the language of Wales according to Mrs Rose Davies!'

For years her great-grandmother had lived in an old cottage on this very site. Zoe could just about remember the old house on the steep hill of Georgetown Street – misty images of an ancient, stone building with a low, grey slate roof, small, square windows and a green, wooden front door. It was funny, she thought, how *clearly* she could remember the flaking green paint of the front door. She must have been about four when the new house was built and she remembered Nan living with them in Swansea while the work on her new home was being carried out. Number three, Davies Row was a new house in a road with a new name . . . but on the same site and the same steep hill.

Tea was served – best china of course, brought out from the wooden dresser in the kitchen. Zoe watched her Nan as she organised the tea. She noticed that she was dressed in old-fashioned dark clothes, and *that*, she thought, is an *old lady* shawl. The dark brown shawl contrasted with her Nan's white, fluffy, candyfloss hair. Her animated hand movements and fast, singsong-like speech made her seem much younger than eighty-two. She was certainly lively and chatted about everything non-stop, wanting to know all the family gossip and eager to tell of the goings-on of people whom she assumed Zoe knew . . .

Zoe got up, smiling, and walked over to a dark,

ornately carved sideboard, wondering if her Nan ever stopped for breath. She picked up a small, framed, black and white photograph of a young man and woman. 'That's your great grandfather and me,' her Nan called over. Zoe already knew this; she'd seen the photograph many times before. 'Nearly sixty years ago,' she continued, 'duw, Ernest was a handsome man . . . and I could turn a few heads too. Mind you, my hair was the colour of shining copper in those days. I was a *bit of a looker*, I can tell you . . . Is that what you say these days Zoe bach?'

Zoe chuckled. 'No Nan, it's *well fit* now.'

'Well then,' her Nan said, 'I think you are *well fit* too Zoe.'

Zoe screeched with laughter. 'Nan!' she said, *'you're* not supposed to say that; it's what boys are meant to say to girls, or girls to boys.'

'Bobl bach, what?' her Nan spluttered. 'Are girls allowed to speak to boys like that these days?' She shook her head as Zoe, Bethan and David collapsed with laughter.

Later, while her Nan showed her parents the garden, Zoe sat at a table and flicked open a copy of the *Radio Times* and quickly got engrossed in an article about a new television drama called Mysteries of a Time Traveller.

Startled, she jumped at the sudden sound of a voice saying her name. She'd been sitting at the table staring into space and had lost track of time. She glanced down at the Radio Times still open at the page she'd been reading. She hadn't noticed her Nan coming in and sitting down beside her. 'Sorry Nan, I . . . I didn't hear you come in,' she stammered, blinking rapidly.

The old lady was looking at her in a strange way, her eyes searching.

'Beth sy'n bod, cariad?' she asked Zoe gently.

'Nothing Nan, honestly . . . just daydreaming,' Zoe smiled apologetically.

'And what about nightmares?' Her Nan leaned in closer, her eyebrows raised knowingly.

Zoe nodded slowly. 'Mum and Dad have told you then.'

'Oh, they've hinted at things, but you know what it's like, they don't want to worry the *old girl*.'

Zoe smiled.

'But, Zoe bach,' her Nan continued, 'they didn't have to tell me.' She paused and sighed. 'Your old Nan knows a thing or two about dreams and nightmares . . . and a lot more besides.'

'Really?' Zoe was surprised by this revelation. 'Do you have nightmares and . . . daydreams?' she asked excitedly.

'Not for a long, long time now . . . but when I was a girl . . . ' her Nan said, and lapsed into silence. Zoe saw that her eyes were staring, as if remembering things from the distant past.

'What are you saying Nan?' she asked. 'You mean you used to have strange dreams and nightmares . . . just like me?'

'Of course I did,' her Nan replied, 'it's in the family. Mind you, cariad, it doesn't seem to affect the men . . . ' She smiled at Zoe and patted her hand. 'Just us women. I had three boys and grandsons, and they were all as right as rain. You, Zoe, are the first girl in the family since me.'

Zoe's mind was buzzing. 'Nan,' she said hesitantly, 'what did you mean by . . . *and a lot more besides*?' 'Did

I say that?'

'Yes, Nan, you did,' Zoe said, desperately eager now, but before her great-grandmother could answer, they were interrupted by her father, who came in carrying a folder of photographs.

With her parents and Nan engrossed in the pictures, Zoe excused herself and announced that she was going to take a stroll to the shops at the bottom of the road.

'Now you won't go up the hill, to the site of the old tips will you good girl?" her Nan called. "It's nice up there now, with grass and trees, not like it used to be in the old days, but it can still be dangerous if you're on your own, especially if it starts to get dark.'

'Okay Nan, diolch. Pob hwyl everyone – see you later.'

Zoe walked down to the shops and went into the newsagent, where she bought a magazine and a Pepsi. Outside the shop she stopped and looked across at a group of children playing on wasteland, just the other side of the river. Nan's always telling Dad stories about this part of Merthyr in the old days, Zoe thought. The small patch of wasteland, near to a new, large office block and a supermarket car park, had once been a densely populated part of the town. Somewhere nearby, according to her Nan, there had been huge cinder and slag tips, where ashes from the ironworks' furnaces had been dumped, together with rubbish from the iron-ore smelting.

Zoe imagined the mountainous waste tips, like those that had once been behind her Nan's house, towering above a landscape of terraced houses and casting shadows over a grim industrial scene . . . Fantastic, she thought; what a great setting for a film. She wandered slowly towards the main road, which led to town and ran parallel to a river. Must be the Taff, she thought, remembering what she'd studied for her last geography exam, and how the Taff wound its way down from the mountains, through Merthyr and eventually away to Cardiff to the southeast. Zoe chuckled as she remembered catching her mother's yawns as her father described how the river, along with the canals, had once been a major supply-route taking iron and coal from the iron-works and mines of Merthyr to the coast . . . and to the world. Merthyr might have been a nineteenth-century centre of world trade, Zoe thought, but her mother obviously hadn't been enthralled and had snapped, 'For goodness' sake, David, can we just get to Tesco!'

Zoe sat in the late sunlight, propped against the sign for Dynevor Road, flicking through her magazine. Wow, she thought as she turned a page and saw the tour dates and a preview of the new album by the *Mediaeval Baebes*. Now this is the sort of world trade that I'm interested in.

She looked up as the sounds of children playing drifted across from the wasteland beyond the river. She closed her magazine. The children were now out of sight and it became quiet. "I wish I *had* brought my roller-blades now," she sighed as she ambled slowly across the river-bridge, stopping for a moment to drop stones into the fast flowing water. She paused next to the rough waste ground at the other side, the Bethesda Street end, and pulled her mobile from her pocket. The girls will have been for a pizza by now, she thought. Shall I text? No, they're probably in the cinema . . .

She put her phone back into her pocket and leant against a wall, idly sipping her Pepsi. As she dangled the can from her hand a bee hovered around, attracted to the sweet stickiness of the drink. Zoe stepped away from the wall but the bee followed.

'Get off, go on, go away!' she said, shooing it with her hand, but the bee continued to hover, buzzing around the can.

Her voice rose. 'Go on, clear off . . . ' she said, alarmed, but still the bee buzzed, settling finally on the top of the can. Zoe swiped at it, yelping 'Shoo, go on!' The bee flew up and buzzed loudly around her face. Zoe flapped her arms, spilling the drink. 'Go away!' she screeched, hitting out, and then she felt a sharp pain in the back of her hand. She waved her stung hand about, whimpering. Losing her balance, she fell against the nearby wall. The sky started to spin and she felt sick. Everything blurred, cleared slightly then blurred again. A terrifying noise began to build in her head. The sound became deafening, like the wind and sea in a raging storm. She wanted to clasp her hands over her ears but her arms felt numb and wouldn't respond. She staggered forward and stumbled to her knees, dropping her magazine and the can. She watched, as if in a dream, as the Pepsi can seemed to hit the ground in slow motion, the black liquid shooting up like a fountain before falling back and fizzing onto the grass in a creamy foam. Her legs, like her arms, felt lifeless and numb. She managed to crawl a few inches, feeling weeds and rough grass between her fingers. Her vision blurred again, the noise continued to scream in her head but somehow she was able to pull herself up and stagger forward again. With her head spinning she felt her way along a wall. She was hot, so, so hot, and was sure that she was going to faint: her legs buckled and she knew she could do nothing to keep herself from crashing to the ground.

35

The spinning sensation in her head stopped; the noise faded away and Zoe gradually became aware of hands gripping her arms . . . She had been saved from a fall.

'Slow down, slow down. Are you unwell?' a voice asked.

The feeling of sickness subsided and her vision cleared slightly. She panted, her hair plastered to her forehead with perspiration.

'There, there. Feel better now?' the voice asked again.

Zoe nodded gratefully and took a deep breath. There were two of them – a man who stood a few feet away and a woman who now held her and looked at her closely, frowning with concern.

'Here,' the woman said, 'drink this – it'll make you feel better.'

Zoe, still in a state of confusion, drank from the small silver flask, but instantly spluttered and coughed as the liquid burned her throat. She looked up at the woman and noticed, for the first time, her unusual appearance. She wore a dark cape around her shoulders, and a hat . . . a bonnet, Zoe thought, tied around her chin with a wide, blue ribbon . . . and a dark blue skirt, which was full and bulky and reached to the ground. The man was dressed in baggy brown trousers and wore a waistcoat over a dirty white shirt. He looked, Zoe thought, like an old fashioned farmer.

The man stood a short distance away with his back to them. Once or twice he glanced over his shoulder, but seemed more interested in peering down a dark alley as if waiting for something or someone.

Zoe couldn't speak. She *wanted* to speak but felt confused and disorientated. She saw a small boy run out of the alley's gloom and say something hurriedly to the man. The boy's appearance seemed to Zoe even stranger than that of the grown-ups: his face was dirty, he was dressed in rags, wore no shoes or socks, and his feet, like his face, were blackened with grime.

I must be dreaming, Zoe thought, or I'm ill and having hallucinations. I can see things and hear things, but they don't seem real . . . this doesn't *feel* real . . . I am dreaming again. She shuddered violently and slumped forward into the woman's arms.

'Now's our chance,' the man hissed.

The expression on the woman's face changed suddenly. She glared at Zoe. 'Come on,' she snapped. Then, roughly, she grabbed Zoe's arm in a hard grip.

'Who? . . . What?' Zoe stammered.

The man and boy ran off and Zoe was whisked almost off her feet, into the alley and through to a narrow street of small, shabby houses.

'Keep a look out, John Wylde,' the woman called to the boy, 'learn your trade and earn your keep. This one's ours. She's not for the streets of Pontystorehouse or the other gangs. She looks fit and could be useful to us.'

What is she talking about? Zoe wondered, still trying desperately to make sense of things. Is she talking about me? I've had dreams and . . . and clear images of things before, but I've always been on the outside looking into a scene. I've never felt myself in something like this . . . '*What's happening*?' she cried out suddenly.

* * *

'Zoe, Zoe?' Bethan called up the stairs. She turned to her husband. 'Have you heard from her, David? She's been gone for over an hour. I've phoned her mobile and I'm getting a 'number unavailable' message.' She walked to the front door, looked up and down the road, and walked back into the living room. 'You try your phone David,' she demanded.

'There's probably no signal here. She'll be back soon,' he said.

'Just try her number please,' Bethan said sharply.

'Okay, okay,' he said, taking out his phone.

His grandmother looked on, bewildered. 'Have you *all* got those things?' she asked.

'Yes, Gran,' David said, frowning as he pulled up Zoe's number.

'Couldn't be doing with one of those fiddly things,' his grandmother muttered. 'I'd probably lose it anyway . . . I can never even find my glasses!'

'Mmm,' David mumbled, looking at his phone screen. 'It's the same as yours Beth – "number unavailable". Strange . . . Hey Beth – she went down to the shops. She probably got talking to some kids down there; you know what she's like.'

Despite David's upbeat manner Bethan was not reassured. She paced up and down the room, looked at her watch, sighed loudly, walked to the front door again and stepped out onto the pavement. She looked towards the bottom of the road but there was no sign of Zoe. She walked back into the house and cut abruptly into her husband's conversation: 'We'll have to go and look for her,' she said.

David looked a little exasperated. 'Beth, she'll be okay. She's probably . . . '

'*Now*, David. I . . . I've just got a feeling . . . ' she pleaded.

'Relax Beth, you know Zoe,' David said, but Bethan interrupted:

'David, *please*!'

David looked in surprise at his wife. He spoke quietly now, reassuringly: 'I'll go out and get her. She can't have gone far. Keep trying her mobile.'

'I'll come too,' Bethan said as she reached for her jacket, and was already on her way through the door.

Zoe's Nan watched, frowning thoughtfully, as David and Bethan hurriedly made their way down the hill towards the Georgetown shops.

The shop assistant in the newsagent had seen their daughter; he had sold her a can of Pepsi and a *Rox* magazine, but that had been over an hour earlier. 'She's not been back since – well, as far as I'm aware, anyway,' the assistant added.

They had no luck in the chip shop either. Nor could a group of youngsters on bikes remember seeing anyone of the description they gave.

David rubbed his chin as he looked all around. 'Look Beth, perhaps she's back at the house,' he suggested. 'You go back, and I'll take a walk down towards town.'

'I'll have a few words to say to that young madam. I . . . I . . . I'll . . . ' Bethan warned.

'Beth!' David put his hands gently on his wife's shoulders. 'Come on Beth, that won't help. You go back. She's probably there by now . . . Beth?'

Despite his calm words, he was sweating, and Bethan saw that he was as worried as she.

'I'll carry on looking,' he said in a quiet voice.

Slowly, he started to walk away from his wife but stopped, turned and cleared his throat as he looked at her. Unspoken, the fear of their worst nightmare as parents lay between them: *abduction*.

'Keep trying her phone, okay Beth?' he said quietly,

'I'll do the same, but if . . . if she's not back at the house . . . phone the police, just in case.'

Chapter 3

The Bristle Gang

Dazed and bewildered, Zoe was pulled by the woman through dark, narrow streets. The small boy ran ahead. The man muttered and pushed people out of the way as they followed. Zoe was confused but she forced herself to take in details. Where am I? she wondered. I don't know this place; I've never seen it before. I must try to remember; I *need* to remember so that I can find my way back . . . what *am* I thinking about, this isn't real . . . well, I don't think it's real . . .

They ran through another dark passage between houses and turned left. Zoe was dismayed to see that it looked just like the other alleys and streets. The houses on either side were very close together and were all built out of the same drab, grey stone. The wooden doors were low and narrow, mostly unpainted and some quite obviously rotten. The window frames were small with cracked or broken glass, and all caked in thick black soot and dust. Some windows had rags or paper stuffed into holes, and some had filthy, ragged blankets draped over the outside.

Zoe gasped for breath as she was almost dragged, at running pace, through the scattered litter, bones and puddles of the street's pitted, dirt surface. The woman's fingernails dug roughly into her arm, hurting her, although the situation was so surreal that Zoe hardly noticed the pain.

As they ran, she began to experience a growing sense of claustrophobia. She felt trapped, not only by these terrifying people, but also by the closeness of the buildings, the deep, dark shadows, and the stifling heat . . . This *is* a nightmare, she thought, it must be, please . . . I *want* it to be. With a growing sense of panic, she looked at the woman at her side and screamed, '*Stop! – I want to wake up.*'

The woman looked startled and released her grip. Zoe stumbled on the uneven surface and lunged forward, sprawling onto her hands and knees. For a few moments she felt nothing, as if she'd fallen into a black void and her senses had, mercifully, shut down . . . but then, gradually, she became aware of an ache in her head and the pounding of her heart as she gulped air into her lungs. One by one her senses seemed to snap back into action. The clamour of voices swirled around, shouting, laughing, babbling – the voices of children and adults speaking in English and in Welsh. Zoe opened her eyes, her face only inches from the ground. The fingers of her right hand were resting in a pile of cinders and red ash, and her left hand was partly submerged in a pool of grey, scummy water. What *is* that smell? she wondered; it's absolutely disgusting, just like when our drains were blocked. She groaned as a feeling of queasiness swept over her, and she started to retch. Instinctively she lifted her hand from the puddle and put it to her mouth, but the putrid smell from her hand made her retch violently and she was sick onto the dirt and ash. Turning her head aside, she saw just a few feet away a channel, about a foot wide and running along the centre of the street. This, too, was filled with filthy water and sewage. Then a rapid movement caught her eye . . . a rat. She gasped in horror as the rodent scurried from the sewage channel over to the rotting remains of what looked as if it might once have been a small dog.

The back of Zoe's sweatshirt was pulled roughly and once again she felt the grip of a hand on her upper arm as she was yanked to her feet. Despite her confusion and terror she lashed out with her free hand. Her face was hot and she felt anger rising, overriding, for the moment, her other emotions. She hit the hand away and pushed at the woman, who seemed astonished by Zoe's reaction.

Zoe trembled as she said to the woman, through clenched teeth, 'Don't . . . touch . . . me.'

'Why you little . . . ' the man snarled, as he lunged towards Zoe. Without thinking she jumped to the side, her foot splashing into the channel of sewage. The man pounced again but Zoe quickly stepped back out of his reach. She was aware, however that a crowd had now gathered and was moving in around them and, again, she felt trapped.

'Stop!' said the woman firmly, glaring at the man. 'Leave this to me . . . Now,' she said, turning to Zoe, 'there's no need for this. Be a good lassie . . . I'm not going to hurt you.'

In desperation Zoe looked to the faces of the people who now surrounded them and pleaded, 'Help me . . . do something. Please . . . don't let them touch me . . . someone call the police . . . please, please.' She was shaking uncontrollably and her teeth chattered. No one moved or spoke: they just gawped at Zoe as she turned in a slow circle, whimpering. 'Please, p . . . p . . .

please,' she implored. 'Please, someone . . . help me,' her voice now a whisper between sobs as she lost hope.

Suddenly a small, thin girl reached out, tugged at Zoe's sweatshirt and then pulled her hand away as if she'd had an electric shock. She stared in wonderment, her eyes bulging, looking at Zoe as if she were a strange animal. Zoe noticed that the girl was wearing a plain dress of rough, sack-like material. The dress reached to the girl's ankles and Zoe could see that her bare feet, like her face and hands, were engrained with dirt. Her long dark hair was matted and filthy and there were several large sores around her mouth. As the details started to register in her mind Zoe looked at the other people and noticed, too, their strange appearance. Where on earth am I? she thought. What *is* going on?

'Come on lassie,' the woman said softly, 'time to get going.' She took Zoe's arm and pulled her forward. They followed the man and the young boy out of the narrow street and through a small, square courtyard packed with rowdy people who were fighting, shouting and swearing. The boy was small enough to dart between people but the man had to push past brawlers to clear a path for Zoe and the woman.

They stopped suddenly at a small flight of steps that led down below the level of the street. Zoe was bundled down the steps and as she was shoved through the door into a dark room, she cried out in terror: '*Stop, stop, please* . . . no, oh please no, where are you taking me? What are you going to do to me?'

The door was slammed shut and Zoe slumped to her knees on the rough dirt floor. She rolled onto her side and then pulled herself into a tight ball, with her knees up to her chest and her arms covering her head

– something she'd not done since she'd been terrified by a large, ferocious dog as a young child. Her mind frozen in a state of shock, she was unable to speak. She began to realise that the soft, pitiful sobs that echoed in her head were her own. She *knew*, now, that this *was* a nightmare. She could feel the familiar sense of dread that always accompanied her nightmares but, in a strange way, she was comforted by the fact that very soon it would all be over and that her mum and dad would be there to help make the bad feelings go away. The sobbing child in the nightmares, she thought . . . must have been me all the time. Then she thought of the man and woman who had pulled her through the streets . . . the boy . . . the thin girl and the crowds of people . . . and . . . and being pushed into a dark room . . . and now the sobbing. This *is* my nightmare, she realised. She shivered even though she was very hot. Her face felt damp and clammy as she tried to brush strands of hair from her mouth. The air was stifling and there was an overwhelming smell of . . . cabbage? Yes, she thought, it *is* cabbage. She opened her eyes, moved her head slightly and felt, in the darkness, cold, damp earth against her cheek. She started to panic. Oh come on, she thought, it's time to wake up now, I've *had* my nightmare. She felt herself being lifted to her feet, and sobbed with relief. "Mum?" she cried, but as her eyes grew accustomed to the dim light she gasped and stared in disbelief. It was not her mother.

'You're in no danger lassie,' the woman said softly. 'You'll be safe with us sure enough; far better than trying to survive alone in those rat infested streets.'

'Please,' Zoe whispered, 'tell me this is not happening.' She covered her face with her hands and screamed, '*No, no, no, no* . . . ' She slumped forward and was caught by the woman who guided her to a hard wooden chair.

'Tom, quickly,' the woman called. 'Get the wee colleen a drink, would you.'

Despite her terror and desperate disappointment, Zoe's mind was taking in details: the room was small and was lit by a single candle that stood on a table. She noticed, for the first time, that there were several other people sitting in the shadows around the room.

'Will you hurry, Tom,' the woman said, and Zoe was able to place her accent: Irish, she thought; the woman is from Ireland.

The lad, Tom, offered a small metal mug to Zoe. 'I don't want a drink,' she started to say, trying to summon up the little courage she still possessed. 'I just want to know what's happening . . . please . . . I . . . I want to be at home, awake and . . . and not in this nightmare.' Once again she broke down, her shoulders shaking.

'Don't cry my sweet. We are here to look after you,' the woman said soothingly. 'That's why we took you from the streets of Pontystorehouse. You wouldn't have lasted long out there.'

Zoe stopped sobbing suddenly and wiped her eyes with the back of her hand. '*What* did you say?' she asked.

The woman smiled and said, 'We want to help you —'

'No, not that,' Zoe interrupted. 'You mentioned a name . . . a place. I . . . I heard you say it earlier. What did you say?'

The woman thought for a moment, then asked, 'Pontystorehouse?'

'Yes, that's it,' Zoe snapped. She was puzzled;

46

despite her terror something was nagging at the back of her mind, something that her dad talked about. Why don't I pay more attention to what he says, she thought.

'Please,' the woman said, 'have a drink.'

'Pontystorehouse!' Zoe exclaimed, ignoring the woman and talking to herself as she remembered. 'That's it, Pontystorehouse was the name of the old part of Merthyr, near to the bridge where . . . ' she looked at the woman and continued slowly, 'where I first saw you.' She gasped as a sudden thought, a memory came into her mind. She lifted her left hand and examined it carefully. It was covered in grime and dirt but just above the thumb, on the back of her hand, she could feel a raised bump that was sore. 'A bee sting,' she whispered, raising her eyes and staring at the candle flame.

The room was silent; everyone was looking at Zoe. She stood up, stepped away from the chair and announced, 'Pontystorehouse doesn't exist now.'

Everyone in the room laughed. Annoyed and confused by the reaction, she said again, 'Pontystorehouse does *not* exist. There's waste ground by the bridge and a car park, and offices and, and a . . . supermarket.'

The people in the room were still laughing as Zoe became more agitated. 'Pontystorehouse,' she continued, 'was part of old Merthyr . . . it's not there anymore.'

The woman put her hand on Zoe's shoulder and said softly, 'Sit down wee lamb, and try not to get upset.'

'But I *am* upset. Who are you, anyway? What do you want? I . . . I don't want to do this anymore,' Zoe protested. 'I just want to wake up and be in my own home.'

'All in good time, all in good time. Tell me,' the woman asked quietly as she walked slowly around Zoe, looking at her very carefully, 'where is your home?'

'Swansea,' Zoe muttered miserably, wishing she were back in the streets she knew – back in school even. 'But we're visiting my—'

'Swansea?' the woman cut in. 'Well, well . . . Swansea. Well my love, we'll see what we can do but I think it's time you took some rest.'

Too weary to protest any more, Zoe allowed herself to be led to a corner of the room where a large wooden pallet covered with dirty straw lay on the floor.

'You rest there my sweet,' the woman said, 'and if you want anything just ask Kathleen; I'll see what I can do.'

The woman turned away, and Zoe stepped after her, her mouth open to ask further questions. '*Eistedd,*' a harsh voice rasped. Shocked, Zoe reeled around. Standing to her right was a girl, perhaps a little older than herself, although her hard features made pinning an age on her difficult.

'Pwy wyt ti?' the girl hissed.

'Zoe 'dw i.' The response was automatic and it took a few moments for Zoe to register that this was the first time in this place that she had been spoken to in Welsh.

'Eistedd,' the girl repeated slowly. 'Sit down and don't make trouble! Just do as you're told . . . if you know what's good for you.'

The woman, Kathleen, turned calmly. 'Go easy, eh Nell? The wee lamb is our guest, don't forget.'

Nell stood glaring at Zoe, her dirty face,

surrounded by filthy, matted hair, distorted in a scowl. She clenched her fists, but at a nod from the Irish woman she hesitated, her eyes flickered and looked away as she stepped back towards her other companions, leaving Zoe alone in the corner.

As she sat down on the straw-covered board, Zoe tried to make sense of the situation. What was going on? Everything seemed unreal but it felt real. This straw feels real, she thought, so if it's not a dream then what exactly is happening? Have I been kidnapped? If so . . . why? And . . . who are these people, dressed in – she thought carefully – in clothes from the past? The streets . . . they called the place Pontystorehouse . . . it can't be . . . It *must* be a dream . . . or some sort of hoax, or hallucination, or . . .

The more Zoe thought about things, the more confused and frightened she became. She thought of her parents and started to cry again. She hugged her knees and rocked to and fro. Her face was wet with tears as she abandoned herself to her distress. Before long, physically and emotionally exhausted, she lay down on the pallet and cried herself to sleep.

For a moment when she opened her eyes Zoe didn't know where she was. Then, as she remembered, she hoped again that it was all a bad dream and that now she really would awaken from it . . . As her eyes adjusted to the gloom she took in the scene around her. The dirty straw tickled her arm and her heart sank as she realized that this was no dream. Instinct told her not to move but to lie still and pretend to be asleep. The only light in the room came from the candle on the table where four people sat. She recognised two of them – Kathleen, the Irish woman, and the man who had brought her to this place. The youngsters, whom she had seen in the room earlier, slept in various positions nearby, their regular breathing and snoring providing a backdrop to the quiet voices of the four people huddled together in conspiracy around the table. Zoe heard the occasional word or phrase – *Penydarren works, Cyfarthfa, cwrw bach* and *long pay* – but couldn't make much sense of the conversation. The conspirators spoke in urgent whispers. Occasionally one of them would raise his voice in anger. The argument was obviously important and, at times, became quite heated. Zoe could hear the Irish woman's soft but strong voice, and listened carefully.

'The young 'uns will find out where, sure enough, don't you worry,' she said. 'Anyway, we have a new member, the orphan from Swansea . . . '

Zoe almost jumped up at this. What did she mean by the *orphan from Swansea*? But, she reasoned, if they think I'm an orphan then this is obviously not a kidnapping. Perhaps they really *do* think that they're helping me . . .

'She don't look like an orphan to me,' one of the men remarked. 'She's too well fed to be an orphan!'

'Well she's not gentry,' another man commented. 'She ain't dressed like gentry.'

'Gentry young 'uns wouldn't be wandering alone around the cellars of Pontystorehouse,' Kathleen said. 'No, she's not gentry.' She paused and then continued, as if thinking aloud: 'Her clothes are so strange . . . she's wearing trews . . . they're certainly not the clothes of gentry.'

'Well they're not the sort of clothes that folk round here wear and she don't look like the other street urchins,' one of the men remarked.

'*Rodneys*,' Kathleen corrected him. 'The begging children on the streets of Merthyr are called *Rodneys* but don't ask me why.'

They laughed quietly and one of the men muttered mockingly, '*Rodneys*.'

'No, you're right, she don't look like the other Rodneys,' Kathleen agreed. 'And sure, you heard her,' she added, 'she's from Swansea. Strange town is Swansea. You've heard her voice, the way she speaks – in English, *and* she understands Welsh . . . ' The men mumbled their agreement.

'Aye, she's from Swansea, and from Cornish copper-folk I'll wager. Well, orphan or not, she's one of ours now,' Kathleen continued, as Zoe lay still, holding her breath and straining to hear the soft voice. 'We'll try to put her into the ore mine at Cyfarthfa – speak to Shoni about it . . . We'll be well covered at Ynysfach *and* Cyfarthfa then; one more helper for us.'

'One more spy more like it,' one of her male companions said. They all laughed quietly.

'She'll settle soon enough . . . once she gets to know our ways, have no worries,' Kathleen assured the men. 'Nell will keep an eye on her.'

Zoe was horrified: what were they planning now? What did they mean by *another spy*? And what was the fearsome Nell going to do with her?

As far as she could see, the only door in the room was beyond the four people sitting around the table. She could hardly run for it. Once more tears welled up in her eyes, and she lay in her misery, the tears hot on her cheeks until eventually, with the room quiet except for snoring, she lapsed back into sleep.

* * *

David walked from Georgetown towards the town centre, a distance of less than half a mile. Passing The Three Horseshoes pub he took the main road, speaking to many passers-by, asking about Zoe, but no one was able to help him.

He walked through the busy bus terminal asking everyone he saw, and then went up towards the High Street and spoke to a group of young people outside The Castle cinema. No one had seen anyone of Zoe's description.

'Excuse me,' David said to the young man at the cinema's ticket desk, 'I'm looking for my daughter, she's . . . er . . . she's missing.'

The young man looked blank.

'She's thirteen years old, about five foot four, with shoulder length hair . . . ' David began, indicating Zoe's height with his hand.

'Colour?' the ticket assistant interrupted.

'Sorry?' David said, looking puzzled.

The man sighed and said, 'what colour hair?'

'Er, sort of light brown . . . ' David replied.

'Any highlights or red streaks or anything?' the young man asked distractedly as he leant back in his chair and looked at his computer screen.

'Oh, for goodness' sake!' David said, agitated and exasperated by the man's casual attitude. 'Look, her name is Zoe . . . she's wearing a black sweatshirt with a sort of mask logo, like a bird's face with a pointed beak . . . small . . . white . . . and the word Ospreys . . . '

The assistant shook his head slowly, shrugged his shoulders and said, 'Haven't seen anything like that, but then, lots of people come in here.'

David took a deep breath and tried to calm himself before speaking. 'Okay, I'm sorry for getting worked

up, but this is important – I don't have time to . . . Do
. . . do you think I could speak to the manager?'

The manager was called and after David had
explained the situation and repeated Zoe's
description, members of staff were dispatched with
torches into the dark cinema.

David paced anxiously up and down the foyer.
Stop; keep calm, he thought, this is doing no good.
He stared at the plush red carpet, taking in the details
of a regular black pattern showing a small castle
above the word Odeon. He started to count the
number of castles on the first step of a flight of stairs
. . . Come on, come *on*, he thought, this is ridiculous.
The waiting seemed endless, but after about ten
minutes the manager reported, with regret, that Zoe
didn't appear to be on the premises.

David checked a nearby supermarket without
result, and tried again to phone Zoe's mobile, but still
got the 'Number unobtainable' message. 'For God's
sake Zoe . . . Where are you?' he groaned. His
stomach churned with anxiety. Guilt and bitter regret
swept over him. 'Why did I allow her to go out alone?
Why, why? . . . This isn't our town. She's just a child,'
he muttered to himself.

He jabbed at his phone again . . . 'Beth, anything?'
he asked when his wife answered. He screwed his
eyes up tightly. No news from Zoe . . . but the police
had been called. Tears welled up in his eyes and he
walked blindly, forlorn, angry and helpless as people
he passed stopped and stared at him.

Outside the town library he wondered where to
go next. The shops and the library were all closed
before Zoe went out, he thought. There's nothing else
around here that would interest her, surely. He

looked at the engraved, wall-mounted memorial to Merthyr's second martyr and read the inscription: A Martyr of the Welsh Working Class . . . 1831. That, he thought, was the year when the . . . He checked himself as he realised, with guilt and dismay, what he was doing. What am I thinking? How stupid . . . I shouldn't be thinking about historical events at a time like this.

Just then a police car pulled up. 'Mr Davies?' the young policeman asked.

David nodded rapidly. 'Zoe?' he blurted. 'Have you found my daughter?' His voice was hopeful, pleading, desperate for good news, but the policeman only said: 'We're doing all we can Mr Davies. Come on, I'll take you back to the house.'

Bethan and David paced about the small room. A few neighbours had joined them in Rose Davies' house. Everyone spoke in hushed voices as they busied themselves, trying to help, moving around from the living room to the front door or to the kitchen. Other neighbours were out searching the streets, some on foot, and some in cars. It was starting to get dark outside.

Chapter 4

Off to work

A hand shook Zoe out of her slumber. 'Come on wee lamb, time for work. You've got to earn your keep,' said Kathleen.

The room was busy with people going this way and that, carrying and fetching. Kathleen walked over to a large wooden trunk and started rummaging inside. 'Nell,' she said, 'get the girl's clothes.'

Zoe sat up in alarm as Nell quickly moved towards her. 'What are you doing?' she asked, her voice rising in panic.

Nell grabbed her arm roughly and started to pull her sweatshirt up. One of the men stood behind Nell grinning and leering. Zoe screamed and pushed Nell who, though taken aback for a moment, retaliated by snarling, lunging forward, and pulling Zoe's hair. Some of the other people in the room gathered around, laughing and encouraging Nell as she pulled again at Zoe's sweatshirt. Zoe lashed out, her arms flailing as she screamed hysterically. In the scuffle she fell back onto the straw-covered pallet and Nell pounced again and managed to pull the sweatshirt over Zoe's head. She started tugging at her vest top, and Zoe curled up in a ball screaming 'Leave me alone, *leave . . . me . . . alone . . .* ' She felt a blow to her shoulder as Nell started punching her.

'Stop!' Kathleen yelled. 'You behave like wild animals. Can I not trust you to do the simplest task?'

Nell stopped, her face contorted in anger; Zoe's hair still gripped tightly in her fist. Zoe went on screaming, her hands over her head for protection. Kathleen swiftly moved forward and pushed Nell aside, pulling the sweatshirt from her hands and throwing it onto the pallet behind Zoe. She knelt and put a hand on Zoe's shoulder.

'No, no, please, I . . . want . . . to . . . go . . . home . . . ' Zoe cried pitifully, her words hardly recognisable through the violent sobs.

'No one is going to harm you,' Kathleen said softly. 'Now sit up my wee lamb and let Kathleen help you' She put her hands on Zoe's upper arms and tried to pull her up.

'*Don't touch me*,' Zoe screamed, and hitting Kathleen's hands away she grabbed her sweatshirt from the straw and pulled it protectively to her chest. Kathleen stood back, looking at Zoe but saying nothing.

Zoe had never been so frightened and had never felt such despair. Her body trembled as she thought of what else they might do to her. As she looked at Kathleen the woman's face started to blur. She felt very hot and dizzy. A noise like the sound of howling wind started to build, getting louder and louder, making her head throb and her ears hurt. She felt as if she were spinning, the candlelight of the room whirling around at a tremendous speed. She could hear voices, like echoes in the distance and then everything went black . . . Zoe felt that she was floating in darkness, without fear or pain. It was like a blissful peaceful sleep, with no time and no sensations – a cocoon of protective darkness . . . Then she felt ripped from the cocoon and pulled downwards. The spinning returned, along with the mixture of sounds – the echo of voices, children's voices calling and laughing, the roar of engines, car horns and . . . distant music. Zoe gradually became aware of light: her eyes focused for a moment. Even though her thoughts were confused and unfocused she could see flashes of white light, like the headlights of cars reflecting on glass, and a broad, brightly-lit yellow strip with letters and words set against a dark sky.

The next sensation was pain – a sharp pain to her face, followed almost immediately by blackness and the howling sound of wind again, and then another sharp pain to her face . . . The noise died away and there was a dim light. She blinked and looked directly into Kathleen's face only inches from her own.

'May God forgive me for striking you in such a way but it seemed that the devil had taken you,' Kathleen said.

Zoe could feel the straw against the side of her wet face. She could smell the straw, and the stink of cabbage in the room.

'You were thrashing about,' Kathleen continued as she stood up, 'like a person possessed. I couldn't stop you so I had to slap your face. It was for your own good.'

Zoe lay on the straw pallet and stared at the room's dark wooden ceiling. She sensed that she had been somewhere else, but the memory and her focus on details seemed to be slipping from her mind in the way that happens to a dream when you wake. The more she tried to remember, the more blurred the memory became, until she was left only with the feeling that something had happened but she couldn't think what.

Kathleen pulled up a chair and sat close to Zoe. 'No one will harm you, I will see to that,' she said. 'Now, sit up. You *must* change your clothes.'

'Why?' Zoe asked. 'Why must I change? I don't want to be like you. I don't belong here.'

'You look . . . different,' Kathleen said. 'Other people – other gangs – will notice you. This is to help you and us, you have to trust me.'

'But I really don't know what you're talking about,' Zoe whimpered.

Kathleen raised her eyebrows. 'Some of the other gangs would take young girls like you for all sorts of unholy purposes . . . you'll be much safer with me,' she said.

'I still don't know where I am or what you want with me,' Zoe said. 'Why am I here?'

'All in good time my sweet, all in good time,' Kathleen replied. 'Now, there's work to be done and you have to put these clothes on.' Kathleen picked up some clothes and handed them to Zoe. 'Be quick about it,' she said firmly. 'I've given you a shift, a bodice, a skirt, an apron and a shawl. Now hurry.'

'Well, make *them* go away,' Zoe pleaded, pointing to a few of the others who were standing close by and looking at her.

Kathleen turned sharply and glared at her companions. They walked away obediently. 'I'll go away and let you dress,' she said, 'and if you need any help just ask.'

Resigned to the task Zoe turned to the wall, picked up the clothes and quickly sorted through them. This must be the shift, she thought, looking at a simple, long dress made of soft cream coloured material. She threw it down onto the straw, making up her mind not to wear it. She pulled on the plain white shirt that Kathleen had called a bodice and tugged it down over her own vest top, and then pulled the skirt on over her jeans. It was made of a heavy wool material and as far as she could see in the dim light of the room, was an almost mustard colour. She fastened the thick wooden button and, without thinking, pulled the skirt around so that the button was at the back, and then tightened it with the fabric tie that ran through the rough waistband. Finally she tied the apron about her waist and draped the shawl over her shoulders. She picked up the unused shift and folded it neatly. Where's my sweatshirt? she wondered, looking around the pallet. It was nowhere to be seen. I bet that Nell's got it, she thought. Somehow, despite the strangeness, she was acting as though this was normal, instinctively almost, and her concerns about her missing sweatshirt seemed to distract her mind, momentarily, from the whole bizarre situation.

Kathleen walked over to examine Zoe and, smiling, said: 'Sure, don't you look quite the lady.' She handed Zoe a black ribbon. 'You can tie your hair back, and when you're old enough you may have a pretty bonnet.' She looked around and asked, 'And where are your trews?'

'My what?' Zoe asked.

'Your trews,' Kathleen repeated. Zoe looked puzzled. 'Your trews . . . for your legs,' Kathleen said, 'though I don't know what you were doing wearing trews.'

'Oh,' said Zoe, 'you mean my trousers . . . Please . . . let me keep them on,' she pleaded, starting to become agitated again.

Kathleen sighed. 'As you wish,' she said. 'Now, it's nearly time for work.'

She hasn't mentioned my boots, Zoe thought, and I'm not going to bring it to her attention. The skirt reached the floor, and she hoped no one would notice them.

The others came back in and Kathleen handed a small plate to Zoe. 'Here,' she said, 'eat this.'

Zoe stared at the small offering of a piece of bread and a small lump of cheese. The last thing she felt like doing was eating but she suddenly became aware of the eyes of the other youngsters burning into her, looking from Zoe to her food.

The door opened and the man from the day before came into the room. Behind him came a giant of a man with a mop of red hair and a bushy beard. The new visitor was so tall he had to stoop to get through the doorway.

'And the top of the morning to ye Shoni,' Kathleen said brightly. 'And sure, what an honour it is to have the Emperor grace our humble abode.'

The large man laughed along with Kathleen and made a sweeping gesture towards the door with his hand. 'Behold, madam,' he said theatrically, 'Pontystorehouse – more beautiful, mysterious and exotic than the land of China itself. A man could not wish for a richer empire.'

Kathleen chuckled at the sarcasm. 'Pontystorehouse . . . China? I know some people are calling it that . . . Hell on Earth more like it!'

Something stirred again in Zoe's mind. China, she thought. Yes, that's it – the stories of old Merthyr, I remember now; my dad called the place China or Pontystorehouse.

The man looked around the room, and his eyes

fixed on Zoe. "Is that the brat?" he asked, nodding in Zoe's direction. He didn't wait for an answer but continued: 'It's all fixed up. Number two workings. She'll be with Nell.' He grinned. 'And mind you don't forget old Shoni Sgubor-Fawr's cut when the pickings come in,' he added, laughing. 'Talking of pickings,' he called out, 'John Wylde, you're with me today my fine young fellow. I dare say there will be a few pockets lighter after our visit to the market place.'

The small boy, whom Zoe had first seen the day before, trotted dutifully after the giant who had disappeared back through the doorway. Just like a little dog, Zoe thought. 'Patch' she murmured, suddenly remembering, and the tears rolled down her face once again.

Kathleen crossed the room quickly and smiled sweetly at Zoe.

'You're lucky,' she said. 'We've found you some work so you can pay your way. Good pay mind you . . . And Nell will look after you.' With this she turned and glared at Nell but her face quickly turned back to a smile as she spoke to Zoe again. 'All we want from you, in return for our . . . hospitality, is a wee bit of information. If you hear anything about where the "Long Pay" is to be given out, just tell us. So, don't forget, keep listening. Nell will take care of you . . . Oh,' and her expression suddenly changed, her lips tight thin lines: 'If you have any ideas about running away, Nell will know how to deal with you.' The smile returned. 'Now off you go and earn your keep.'

Nell and two boys walked towards the door. One of the boys, the taller and older of the two, was the lad called Tom who had brought Zoe a drink the night before. The other boy was much younger, perhaps only seven or eight years old. 'Come on, let's go,' Nell called, gesturing to Zoe.

She followed, not knowing what else to do. Outside, a thick drizzly fog greeted them. It was dark. Was this morning or still night, Zoe wondered, as they trudged through the narrow alleys. Tom was quiet, but seemed sincere in his occasional attempts to help her. Zoe kept close, realising that she stood little chance of escaping in these dark, terrifying, rabbit-warren streets. After a few minutes the sound of rushing water could be heard as the road dipped before them. A river, Zoe thought. Is that the River Taff? If so, I can probably find my way back to Nan's.

Sure enough, it was a river. They crossed a bridge that looked familiar, not unlike the one she had crossed recently on her stroll from her great-grandmother's house. But it couldn't be the same, surely, she thought. The gloom and fog made it difficult to be certain. Ahead, she could just make out large dark shapes rising steeply skywards – the foot of a hill or mountain perhaps? Could this be near Nan's house, near Georgetown Hill? The road seemed familiar. Zoe felt that she had walked here before. The bridge, too, had seemed familiar, but . . . No, it couldn't be. Then directly in front, Zoe saw through the gloom a glowing redness in the sky – or what was probably the sky; it was almost impossible to tell in the dense fog. Against the glow were tall, dark shapes: buildings perhaps, but it was difficult to see clearly. As they walked towards the shapes and the red glow, she saw occasional bright flashes that emphasised even more the looming black forms. Despite the red light in the sky, everything below was still in darkness. The road was uneven, muddy and wet, with potholes everywhere, making it treacherous to walk. The hem of her skirt felt heavy with water and mud, and her feet were soaked and cold inside her boots. The bottoms of her jeans were also wet, making them very uncomfortable. She shivered and pulled her shawl in tighter.

She could see now that the huge black shapes were, as she had suspected, buildings – but they did not look at all like what she had expected: in the flashes of light she could see that they were almost like castles with towers, and there were a number of enormous chimneys. The red glow came from several massive fires inside openings at the bottom of the buildings with chimneys. As they drew closer she could see the shapes of people moving around close to the fires. Zoe began to feel nervous as she wondered what lay ahead. With every step the noise level grew and she stopped suddenly as a deep roar, like thunder, shook the ground. A brilliant white flash lit up everything around them. The noise, the total din, and the light here was startling and awesome – a complete contrast, she thought, to the pitchy darkness and near silence of the pre-dawn sky behind them.

Zoe and her companions were quickly ushered through a large gateway. She could hear the sounds of metal wheels screeching, grinding and clanking over tracks and she began to wonder if they were near a railway station. There were many people around them, all hurrying and busy. Zoe could see that this was quite obviously a large factory of some kind – but why were they here, she wondered. She suddenly remembered Kathleen's words: *we've found you some work so you can pay your way.*

They walked past a row of enormous stone, horse-shoe shaped arches. The arches were constructed, Zoe noticed, of massive stone blocks and she guessed that they had once been huge, open gateways through which large equipment or machinery had been taken into the buildings. What had probably been archway openings were now solid inset walls of stonework with just a metal doorway, perhaps two metres high, at the base of each. Some of the doors were open and Zoe could see the red and yellow glare of huge fires inside. She could also feel the tremendous heat, and stopped for a moment to enjoy the sensation of warmth on her damp clothes and hair. The people working nearby were black with grime, and their faces were soaked with sweat. She felt a sharp prod in her side and turned to see Nell's scowling face.

'Hurry up, don't stop in front of the furnaces. If one of them blows we'll all catch it,' she shouted above the noise.

They walked down a slope, away from the fires, over a footbridge spanning a stream, and crossed a number of metal rails. As the dawn sky gradually lightened and the fog lifted Zoe could see that they were in some sort of quarry, with working areas cut into the rock face and supported with thick wooden props, like tree trunks. The ground was covered with coiled ropes, piles of rock, large boulders, logs, shovels and picks. There were rails everywhere, and lots of small trolley-like trucks full of stone. People were arriving at the quarry: men, women and children. They were all dressed in a similar way to Zoe and her companions: they looked like people from times gone by. Some of them were dressed in rags.

The noise level rose as people started their work. Men swung picks against rocks and Zoe watched, fascinated, as women picked up large chunks of stone and threw them into trucks nearby. Some of the women sang to help their work along, and Zoe detected from their accents that, like Kathleen, they were Irish. Some were old, others much younger. Some were just girls like Zoe, but in appearance nothing like her – their hands and faces were blackened with grime, and most of them smoked peculiar thin pipes. Zoe was surprised that the songs they sang were really rude. That's *disgusting* she thought, covering her mouth to suppress a laugh, but at the same time she was astonished that these women and girls were openly singing such things.

She stood mesmerized by the whole scene, as it became a hive of activity. This is bizarre, she thought, shaking her head and laughing to herself . . . This must be some sort of hoax. Her eyes widened as an idea came to her. That's it. It *is* a hoax, she thought, and she trembled with excitement as the notion grew: I've been brought onto a film set . . . Yes, that's it; my dad has set this up because he knows what I'm like for films. They even got me to dress like this. She laughed and looked around hopefully for the camera crews, make-up people, technicians . . . and her parents. Hope soared. Her heart beat fast with mounting relief, and she was suddenly embarrassed to have been taken in.

'Okay,' she said to Nell and the two boys, 'I've sussed you, the joke's over.' She expected that at any moment now people she knew would jump from behind rocks and shout 'surprise'. 'Is my dad behind this, or was it that daft lot from school?' she asked, laughing, a mixture of relief and elation sweeping over her. 'So where *is* everyone?' she added, looking around excitedly. 'Those rails,' she said, pointing to the tracks, 'I just knew . . . they're for those trolley things that carry the cameras for action shots . . . '

The three youngsters stared back at her, open-mouthed.

'Oh come on guys,' she said, 'I've played along, and I have to admit I fell for it . . . '

The three continued to stare in bewilderment.

'*Guys?*' Zoe said, becoming slightly exasperated. 'You were good, very good. Are . . . are you professionals or extras? What film is this?' she babbled. 'I have to admit, I was frightened, absolutely terrified, you really had me going . . . '

'*What are you talking about?*' Nell shouted at her.

'All this,' Zoe said, 'A set up, and –' but before she could finish the sentence Nell had dived at her and pulled her hair viciously. Zoe yelped in pain and tried to push her off.

'Look out, look out, here's the Gaffer,' Tom warned, as a large man with a red face and huge, rough hands clenched into hammer-like fists, strode towards them.

Nell let go of Zoe's hair and quickly stepped away. Zoe stood alone, her mouth open, wide-eyed, incredulous and shocked.

'New loader,' Nell snapped abruptly, pointing to Zoe.

The man looked Zoe up and down. 'So, a new brat eh,' he growled. 'Don't look to me like you've seen a day's hard work! Been in service with a gentry lady have we?' he said mockingly. Then he grinned broadly, showing just one blackened tooth in his whole mouth. 'Still, we'll soon put some muscles on you . . . Now,' he yelled ferociously, 'get to work. Mr Crawshay, God bless him, don't pay you for nothing.'

With that, Zoe was pushed roughly towards a pile of rocks. Dazed and bewildered, she watched as women dumped the rocks into trucks and then pushed with their backs to the load, their bare feet sliding in the mud between the rails.

'What are you waiting for?' Nell snapped, as she too started loading a truck. The Gaffer moved towards them, cracking his whip as he walked.

'Quick!' Tom shouted. 'Start loading.'

Still shocked and confused but in fear for her life, Zoe began the backbreaking task.

Chapter 5

Déja vu

'Evening Sir,' Sergeant Emma Lewis said as she opened the front door to Detective Inspector Bowen.

John Bowen, a short, stocky man in his early fifties was a senior investigating officer in the regional police force. Earlier that evening he had been informed that a young girl had been reported missing and immediately set about coordinating a search operation.

He nodded to Emma and her colleague, Ian Dixon, and asked in a hushed voice, 'So, what's the score?'

'The parents are in there, Sir,' Emma said quietly, gesturing towards the room. 'We've checked all the obvious things – her friends back in Swansea, buses and trains. We're just getting a few details; building up a picture, that sort of thing.'

'Okay,' the Inspector said. He studied a sheet of paper for a few moments. 'David and Bethan Davies, from Swansea . . . and their daughter's called Zoe. So, what were they doing here?' he asked.

'This house belongs to David's grandmother, Mrs Rose Davies. They were visiting,' Emma replied.

John Bowen nodded. 'We'll go in and have a chat, but I want you to run the show locally. You know the procedure. Just keep me up to speed,' he said.

The police officers stood in the hallway for a

moment and looked through the open door into the living room . . . Bethan and David were clinging to each other, sobbing, as they stood in the middle of the room. Rose, David's grandmother, sat in her chair, a handkerchief to her red, puffy eyes. Neighbours sat on either side of her. No one said a word. No one knew what to say.

David whispered something to his wife and picked up his coat. 'I feel so useless and helpless here,' he said to Alison, a young policewoman Rose Davies had said looked barely older than Zoe. I think I should go out and look again."

'Everything possible is being done Mr Davies,' Alison said softly. 'When you feel ready perhaps we could go through a few things again – see if we can get a full picture of what Zoe likes, where she might go . . . '

'But she doesn't know anyone here,' Bethan sobbed. 'My baby . . . ' She stopped as the three detectives walked into the room and introduced themselves. John Bowen explained that he would be co-coordinating the search for Zoe and repeated what PC Jenkins had stated – that everything possible was being done.

'I'll be in charge of the whole operation,' the Inspector said. 'Detective Sergeant Lewis and Detective Constable Dixon will be leading the search locally; talking to people, making enquiries . . . that sort of thing.' After talking for a while with Bethan and David, he left things to the younger police officers.

Rose snorted and muttered, 'More children doing grown-ups' work.'

Neither of them was in uniform, and Emma was wearing a short black skirt and pink high-heeled boots. Rose looked Emma up and down. 'You should put on some warmer clothes, good girl,' she said. 'You'll catch your death dressed like that.'

Ian Dixon covered his mouth to suppress a chuckle. Rose immediately turned on him. 'And what about you? In my day policemen had decent, tidy haircuts,' she exclaimed.

'I think I'll have a chat with Mrs Davies senior, and a few of the neighbours – see if I can tap into some local knowledge,' Emma whispered to Ian. 'We'll go to the kitchen; you stay here with the parents.'

The kitchen was turned into a temporary interview room. Emma sat with Rose and two of her neighbours. 'Can you think of anywhere that Zoe might have gone?' she asked.

'Well,' Rose began, 'there's the old tip at the top of the road. It's lovely up there now mind, all grass and trees, but you could easily get lost if you didn't know your way around.'

'And do you think, Rose – sorry, do you mind if I call you Rose?' Emma asked.

'I don't mind, love, and these are my friends Edith and Gwen . . . Anyway, I told her not to go up there; I told her it's dangerous,' Rose said.

'We have people searching that area now,' Emma said, as she wrote a few things in her notebook. 'Have any of you noticed anyone acting suspiciously, or behaving in an unusual manner in the area? Any new faces around?' she asked.

They shook their heads.

'Is there anyone around here who causes you concern . . . for any reason at all?' she probed.

'Well, only Dai Twp,' Edith said, and Gwen nodded her agreement.

Rose tutted and glared at her friends. 'Tom is harmless; leave him alone. Duw annwyl, druan a fe,'

70

she said, scolding her companions.

'Who are you talking about, and what are your concerns?' Emma pressed.

'They mean old Tom,' Rose explained, 'Tomos Silford. They call him Dai Twp around here but he's not as daft as he looks, and he's harmless.'

'Well he's not right in the head if you ask me,' Edith persisted, 'he's a real loner; never mixes with anyone, and the children don't like him – frightened of him they are. I wouldn't let my grandchildren near him.'

Rose cut in. 'Frightened? It's he who should be frightened, with the kids around here taunting him, Duw help . . . and don't call him Dai Twp, it's not nice.'

'Rose, where does this Tomos Silford live?' Emma asked.

'Dai Twp,' Edith said, folding her arms defiantly. 'You can say what you like Rosie Davies, but I still say he's a nutter.'

'Shame on you Edith Bentley, and you a chapel girl and all,' Rose said, tutting again.

'Yes, thank you ladies. Now, can we get back to the facts?' Emma said. She looked at Rose. 'Where, exactly, does this Mr Silford live?' she asked.

Rose reluctantly gave the address, and as Emma wrote the details in her notebook Edith chipped in. 'It's near Cyfarthfa Castle: small cottage, lovely garden mind you, apart from those blessed bees that he keeps, ach y fi, I couldn't stand those horrible things myself . . . I mean, if you want honey you can get it from Tesco . . . '

Rose sighed loudly, glared at her friend and said, 'Edith, shut up.'

Emma went back into the living room, but just then PC Alison Jenkins' radio crackled into life loudly. She got up quickly and left the room as she spoke into it. A few moments later she popped her head around the door. 'Sergeant Lewis, could I have a word please?' she said to Emma.

Emma followed her out through the door. When she returned she spoke directly to Bethan and David. 'One of our team has just found a Pepsi can and a magazine on some waste ground, just over the bridge near Bethesda Street.'

Bethan gripped her husband's hand in both of hers. Her knuckles were white, her eyes frantically searching the face of the young detective sergeant.

'We believe . . . ' Emma continued softly, 'that they are the items Zoe bought earlier this evening.'

Bethan and David took the news badly.

'There is no reason to believe that finding these items has any great significance,' Alison Jenkins said encouragingly. 'It's certainly not, as far as we can see, a sign of bad news. Zoe might simply have thrown them away; discarded them, as people do. She might have been distracted by something and simply dropped the can and magazine.' Although Alison tried to remain positive and optimistic, she was starting to feel the strain of the situation. It was now getting late and Zoe had been missing for several hours.

Bethan and David had been told that a full search was under way and they were continually being reminded that 'everything possible was being done', but they were unaware of the extent of the operation. The questions continued, and the weary and distressed couple answered over and over again, assisting the police in their attempts to piece together every minute detail of events leading up to Zoe's disappearance.

Off-duty soldiers from Brecon barracks had joined the search of the surrounding hills. A mountain-rescue helicopter swept over the whole area, its experienced crew scanning the landscape for clues. A missing-person alert had been sent to police headquarters in Aberdare, Bridgend, Swansea, Cardiff, Newport, Bristol and to other towns and districts further afield, London and Birmingham included. Police in Swansea were on particular alert in case Zoe decided, for whatever reason, to return to the city. The family home was being watched and Zoe's friends had been contacted.

Emma decided that Bethan and David should not be told, at this point, that police were considering bringing in divers to search the river.

A forensic team had examined the Pepsi can and the magazine when the shop assistant had confirmed that these were the items Zoe had bought.

Emma and Ian sat in the kitchen and compared notes.

'We'll just have to wait now,' Emma sighed. 'We have very little to go on, apart from the items that forensic have, and comments about a possible nutter,' she said.

'Let's hope the search turns up something positive . . . What's this about a nutter?' Ian asked.

'Just something the three amigos were arguing about,' Emma whispered, 'something about an old guy who's a bit of a loner . . . Kids don't like him apparently, but Rose reckons he's harmless.'

'Any reason for suspicion?' Ian asked.

'None at all, but I've got his details; something for us to check out,' she replied.

'So, what's next?' Ian asked.

'Well, if she hasn't turned up by morning then we start house-to-house enquiries,' Emma said. 'But I hope we won't need that.'

'Well, if you ask me, someone knows something,' Ian said. 'I think we *need* to start asking lots of questions. I don't believe she's just lost – not after this length of time. I think this is going to be a lot harder than I first thought it would be.'

Emma nodded. 'Yes, I think you're right. Come on, let's talk to Bethan and David again,' she said.

'I'm sorry if this is difficult, but do you think we could go through a few points again?' Emma asked, sitting beside Bethan. David was pacing the room. 'Did you have a quarrel or any other form of disagreement?' Emma said.

David shook his head. 'No, nothing like that.'

'Was there anything at all that might have upset Zoe? Did she give any indication that she might be thinking of running away?'

Once again Bethan broke down into uncontrollable sobbing. 'The puppy,' she said, gulping. 'She wanted a puppy but I said we'd have to talk about it another time. But that wouldn't have . . . it couldn't have made her . . . '

'Come on Beth,' David said, interrupting her. 'That wouldn't have made her run away.'

'But we argued about it . . . and we stopped her going to the cinema . . . ' Beth cried helplessly.

David looked at Ian and gestured towards the door. 'Could I have a quick word?' he asked quietly.

The two men walked into the hallway, closing the living room door behind them. In a whisper David explained about Zoe's visit to the doctor during the week. 'It might be something or nothing,' he said, 'and I don't want to worry Beth any further, but . . . I think it's something to think about . . . '

'It seems,' Ian explained to Emma as they walked back to the kitchen, 'that Zoe's been having problems with recurring nightmares.'

'Y-es?' Emma murmured. 'Go on.'

'Well, Bethan and David have been sufficiently concerned recently to have taken her to the doctor. David also mentioned trances and daydreams.'

Emma walked across the kitchen, switched on the kettle and picked up a jar of coffee. 'There's nothing unusual about daydreams and nightmares,' she said.

'Yes, I know, but *trances*? Bethan is a nurse, and she's clearly been worried about Zoe's condition. Apparently the daydreams and trances are frequent and the nightmares very bad,' he explained.

Emma made two coffees, handed a mug to Ian and asked, 'Are you suggesting Zoe might have a problem with her state of mind – depression or something, or do you think she's a little unbalanced maybe?'

'I don't know,' he replied. 'She *could* be depressed. Something specific might be causing the nightmares; I think it's worth having a chat with the doctor.'

'Yes, you're right.' Emma agreed. 'Make sure you get David's permission . . . and make sure the doctor is aware of the consent, otherwise we'll be wasting our time: the doctor won't talk.'

'So, what were you whispering about with that policeman?' Rose asked David.

David jumped; he hadn't noticed his grandmother standing behind him in the hallway. 'Oh Gran, you startled me,' he said.

'Well?' she asked again, 'What were you talking about that you couldn't say in front of Bethan?'

'Nothing really,' he answered, evasively.

'Well, I know it wasn't *nothing*,' she persisted, 'it must have been important.'

'Gran . . . ' David said, searching for the right words, 'it's just that I don't want to cause Beth any more distress, or give her any false hopes. I just wanted the police to think about a few things . . . a few possibilities.'

Rose looked at him and said softly, 'David bach, I'm your old Gran, you can tell me.'

David explained his worry about Zoe's condition, about the doctor's uncertainty and about the possibility of their needing a specialist's opinion.

Rose put her hand to her mouth and sat down on the nearest chair, next to the small telephone table. 'Oh David bach,' she said, 'what's the matter with me? I'm a silly old woman . . . I've only just remembered . . . I was talking to Zoe earlier about her nightmares . . . I can see now, it's happening again.'

'What Gran, what do you mean, it's happening again?' David asked, puzzled and frowning.

Rose quickly explained that she too had had dreams and nightmares when she'd been a child, that she'd been told it had happened to other female members of the family before her. 'Duw, it's all coming back to me now,' Rose said slowly. 'I went missing once. Caused a right fuss it did.'

'What?' David gasped, 'this has happened to you?' He knelt in front of his grandmother and looked into her eyes. 'What happened Gran? Tell me exactly what happened,' he implored.

'Well bach, I can't remember how old I was – a bit

76

younger than Zoe, I think . . . I was lost . . . for a few hours, well all day really; no one could find me . . . 'she began.

'Where were you Gran, what happened?' David interrupted impatiently.

'That's the strange thing,' she said, 'I can't really remember anything about it; like when you know you've been dreaming but you can't remember details.' She paused for a moment then added, 'I eventually turned up safe and sound but couldn't remember a thing. The doctor told my mam and dad that I had that am – . . . *am* something.'

'Amnesia?' David suggested.

'Yes that's it. They said I'd lost my memory and was probably wandering around not knowing where to go or who I was,' she explained.

'Gran, why haven't you mentioned this before, and why didn't you say something earlier?' David asked in exasperation.

'Bobol bach, it was a very long time ago and, like I said, it wasn't until a few minutes ago that I remembered about going missing . . . now it's all starting to feel . . . familiar.'

David shook his head, 'Gran, really . . . I wish you'd remembered this earlier . . . Come on, we need to talk to the police,' he said.

He rushed into the kitchen and repeated his grandmother's revelation to the two detectives. Rose was called in and, with David's prompting went through it again.

'This *is* interesting and useful,' Emma said. 'It's probably a coincidence of course but who knows.' She turned to Ian and said, 'Get in touch with DI Bowen; let him know about this, and make sure the search teams are aware of it too.' She quickly ushered Ian through the door into the hallway and whispered urgently, 'Zoe might still be wandering around somewhere with amnesia. Try the hospitals again . . . she could be anywhere, or she . . . someone could have taken her.'

'We're already in touch with the hospitals,' Ian said. 'I think we need to concentrate on the other possibilities.'

Emma nodded. 'We need to double our search efforts,' she said, 'this is a critical time – if it's amnesia, or a mental crisis, Zoe could be anywhere. If no one's got her, she could be wandering around or just sitting somewhere in a state of confusion. If she's not found soon we'll need to talk to her doctor . . .and if she is wandering about with amnesia I want to make sure we find her first, because she's going to be very vulnerable if someone does try to take advantage.' Ian nodded in agreement. 'Okay Ian, let's go,' Emma said decisively, 'and make sure you get house-to-house enquiries underway as soon as possible. And a list of registered offenders . . . '

Chapter 6

Help is at hand

The sun was high in the sky – a hot, burning summer sun. The early morning mist and fog had long since dispersed. Zoe's vest and bodice were soaked with sweat and clung to her skin. She was beginning to regret her decision to keep her jeans on under her thick skirt as it felt as though sweat was running from every pore of her body making her skin itch and prickle unbearably. Her arms, legs and back ached. Her fingernails were broken, her knuckles grazed and bleeding, her palms blistered and torn. She wanted to rest, but she was aware of Nell's ever-watchful eyes, and of the Gaffer striding up and down the tracks, bellowing, cursing and cracking his heavy whip.

With a mighty heave she hurled a large chunk of ore-filled stone into one of the trucks, which the others called 'drams'.

'Away number four,' the Gaffer's gruff voice boomed.

Number four, that's me, Zoe thought with dismay. She'd lost count of the number of loads that she'd been forced to push up the incline to the kiln furnace and ovens, where the drams that she and the others were filling with ironstone converged with those full of coal and limestone, which were also pushed up by women and children.

Each truckload nearly crippled her. By the time she reached the top of the slope her body was wracked with pain, her head spun and she gasped for breath as the sweat poured down her forehead and stung her eyes. The superhuman effort was the result not so much of will power as the threat of the menacing Gaffer and the icy, threatening stare of Nell.

In the middle of the day they took a short break and Nell gave Zoe, Daniel and Tom some bread, cheese and a weak beery drink. Zoe felt almost too tired to eat and soon she was back at the quarry tracks, lifting heavy rocks and pushing drams. She had long since got over the shock of rock-blasting which brought down tons more of the ore-filled stone. The first blast had come without warning and had almost made her jump over the dram she had been loading at the time. Since then the firemen, as they were called, had set off a number of ear-shattering explosions. Zoe noticed that even before the dust settled, the miners were hacking away at the boulders and the exposed iron-seams with pick axes, and the women and youngsters scurried about like ants, picking up ironstone to load into the waiting drams.

Zoe was quickly learning what everything was called and how it all worked. The kilns and furnaces, she thought, were like ravenous young birds in a nest, waiting to be fed, but hungry for iron, swallowing up the ore as fast as it was delivered, which was very fast thanks to the threats of the Gaffer.

Despite her exhaustion Zoe noticed how the others worked. The women, girls and boys loading the drams did so in an efficient way, obviously quite accustomed to the task. She had grown used to their singing of rhythmic working songs, which were encouraged by the Gaffer who often made his own rude contributions. The rhythms were fast and were designed to keep up the pace of the relentless toil. Zoe noticed the grimy, bare arms of the women loaders, which were muscular, scarred and marked, and shining with sweat. Their language, just like their singing, was also very unladylike. The miners, stripped to the waist, worked without a break. They were paid, Zoe learned, by the amount of iron-ore mined and the number of drams loaded.

Zoe stole glances at the others while she worked. She noticed that a miner working nearby kept looking in her direction, and she was aware of the look of concern on his face. As he caught Zoe's eye he winked, his dust-covered features breaking into a broad smile. There was something about his manner and appearance, she thought, that was naturally cheerful and attractive. His eyes seemed to sparkle in his grimy face and his teeth gleamed white as he flashed his radiant smile.

Everyone worked hard and with urgency – they had little choice. Most of the workers were bad tempered and argumentative and Zoe avoided looking at them. She noticed that in contrast this miner seemed full of energy and life, and was constantly calling out to workmates, smiling or laughing heartily . . . And, she thought, he's not bad looking . . . *well fit* in fact. Frequently, as she worked, she found herself wanting to look over to where he was working. Every time she glanced in his direction he seemed to be looking at her – always with that concerned expression – and she would look away quickly.

As she struggled to lift a large chunk of ironstone

she stumbled onto the dram track. In an instant, the miner was at her side, helping her up. 'You take it easy now girl,' he said. As he helped her to her feet he chatted continuously in a mixture of Welsh and English that immediately reminded Zoe of her Nan.

'I . . . I'm okay now,' she croaked. 'Diolch, thank you.' She became aware of Nell almost breathing down her neck. Nell and the miner glared at each other for a moment before he turned away.

Nell scowled at Zoe. 'Get on with it,' she hissed through clenched teeth.

The backbreaking task seemed to Zoe to go on forever. More blasting, more hacking, more lifting, loading and pushing. Every inch of her body ached. Her hands were bleeding. Her mind was numb, aware only of the severe pain. Another dram had been loaded. Zoe put her shoulder to it and tried to push. The truck was immovable; she pushed again but it wouldn't budge. It was probably no heavier than previous loads, but with the hot afternoon sun and her state of sheer exhaustion it was finally too much. 'Please move, please,' she muttered.

Her arms and legs were weak and shaky and she suddenly felt as if she were going to be sick. Unable to help herself, she fell forward; the sky seemed to spin, and the ground appeared to come up towards her in slow motion. She lay there panting, unable to move, the dust and soil between the rails of the dram-track pressing coolly against her cheek.

Something moved near her and she opened her eyes slowly and stared at a large pair of boots only inches from her face. Painfully, she lifted her head and her eyes travelled upwards, taking in the large, ugly frame of the Gaffer who now towered above her limp body. His face was contorted with anger, and the knuckles of his hands, clenched tightly around his whip, were white. He trembled with rage as his voice boomed: 'What's the meaning of this? I'll teach you to lay down on the job!' The upper part of his body twisted, his right arm moved back, the whip cracked in the air behind him and shot forward towards Zoe. She closed her eyes tightly, waiting for the impact . . .

It never came. Instead a raised voice called, "Pick on someone your own size Shenko," and Zoe opened her eyes again. The cheerful young miner stood between her and the Gaffer. In height he came only to the Gaffer's shoulders and he was of a much slighter build. Despite the difference in size, the Gaffer seemed taken aback by the miner's courageous stand. He stepped back a few paces, then the anger returned to his face. Both men squared up, fists at the ready; it looked as if there would be a fight. The other workers gathered around silently in a large circle.

The Gaffer glanced nervously around the sea of faces. His fists dropped, he swallowed loudly and his tongue flashed across his dry lips. "You're a troublemaker, Lewis, always at the centre of it," he growled at the miner.

'Don't talk to me about trouble,' the young man retorted. 'You cause the trouble, man, working children into the ground. Have you no shame?'

'I'm doing my job, as well you know, Lewis,' said the Gaffer. 'These people are lucky to have jobs. The iron industry is not what it used to be – some have been laid off.'

'Lucky?' the miner said, laughing aloud. 'Crawshay lays off skilled workers, cuts our pay, and demands we work harder . . . for his profit. You call that lucky, boyo?'

Some of the other miners and women loaders joined in, criticising Mr Crawshay and the Gaffer. Seeing his predicament, the Gaffer backed slowly away from his young rival, breaking through the human circle. 'Like I say,' he called, 'I'm doing my job and you'd better do yours.' At a safe distance he glared at the miner, his eyes and voice filled with anger. 'You're a troublemaker Lewis, always have been, always will be,' he shouted.

The miner gave a cheeky smile and, mockingly, tugged his forelock: 'Diolch yn fawr Mr Shenko sir,' he said. 'If I'm a troublemaker then say a little prayer for me on Sunday. Oh, and ask that nice Mr Crawshay to pray for me too.'

The whole company laughed as the Gaffer stomped away. A large woman took the clay pipe from her toothless mouth and slapped the young miner's back. 'Good for you Dic. Now give Betsy a kiss,' she said, and flung her arms around him as he struggled and protested, while the workers laughed even louder and whistled.

'I think he'd rather wrestle with the Gaffer,' another miner called out.

As they drifted back to their work, the young man helped Zoe up.

'Diolch,' she whispered, grateful for his help, again, but also blushing and flustered by his attention.

'Duw, don't mention it cariad,' he grinned.

Cariad . . . he called me *cariad*, she thought, feeling her temperature rise and her face reddening even more. 'W . . . will, will you get into trouble with the Gaffer now?" she stammered, lowering her eyes and thinking desperately for something else to say.

'Duw, I'm always in trouble with someone,' he answered, laughing again, his shoulders shaking. 'Now don't you go worrying about me. My name is Richard, though my friends call me Dic.'

Zoe just looked at him, unable to speak, her eyes wide and her mouth open.

He chuckled and asked, 'Pwy wyt ti?'

'Zoe 'dw i . . . my name is Zoe,' she mumbled shyly.

'Well Zoe,' said Dic, 'time to get back to work. Don't worry though, I think the Gaffer will keep away from you, for a little while at least.' He winked, smiled and walked back to the quarry face.

In an instant, Nell was at Zoe's side. 'See if you can find out from your new friend where the Long Pay will be given,' she whispered slyly.

Zoe's mind raced. She was shaken, confused and flustered, not only by Dic's attention, but also by the work and the brutality of what she was seeing, and from what she was hearing from Nell. I came very close to a beating, she thought, and she doesn't care . . . If it hadn't been for Dic . . . How can this be allowed? It *isn't* allowed, I know it's not allowed. Where on earth am I? she wondered. It feels like a nightmare, but I'm sure it's not, and yet I can't think of any other explanation.

She was still trembling as she watched Nell walk away. Her mouth tasted of grit and dust from the rough ground between the dram rails. Without thinking, she felt for her pocket to find a tissue, forgetting she was wearing a skirt over her jeans. Drat, she thought, running her hand over the skirt, now how do I get to my pocket? Suddenly, through the material, she felt a small, hard object. Her eyes widened and she

85

gasped, "My mobile! Why didn't I think of this before?"

As she stood, her fingers touching the possible lifeline, Zoe's mind darted about. In an instant her despair and confusion disappeared as renewed hope surged through her. How can I use the phone? she wondered, planning desperately. Where can I go? Maybe a quick call to mum and dad . . . No, no, just 999! Yes that's it, phone 999. But where am I? What can I tell the police? What if someone sees or hears me? Calm down, she told herself. Think it through. She decided to send a text: it would be easier, and wouldn't attract attention.

'What are you doing now?' Nell asked, striding towards her again. 'Get on with your work, you can't stand there all day.'

Zoe thought quickly. 'Please, I . . . I need to go to the toilet.'

Nell stared at her in bewilderment. Zoe mimed a squatting movement. 'The privy?' Nell asked. 'Well go on then, and hurry up.'

'But where?' Zoe asked.

Nell gave an exasperated sigh and pointed. 'In those rocks over there,' she said. She put her grimy face uncomfortably close to Zoe's and hissed, 'Now move!'

Zoe ran to a large pile of grey boulders and quickly ducked behind a high rock, her heart beating quickly with excitement. Gasping for breath, and with her sore fingers shaking almost uncontrollably she yanked the skirt up, pulled the phone from her pocket and flipped it open. She was alarmed to see that it was switched on and that the battery level was low. That's strange, she thought: no incoming messages or texts. Stupid, she told herself: you would have heard them anyway if there had been any messages. But why hadn't her mum or dad tried to get in touch? She glanced nervously over her shoulder before putting the phone into 'Message' mode. Quickly she typed: *Help! Can u fone me plz? b kwik. Z.* She searched for her mother's number under 'Contacts', and then sent the message. The phone scanned, and after what seemed like a long time, a message appeared on the screen: *No network found. Message failed!* Zoe stared at the phone screen in disbelief. "What?" she shrieked.

Suddenly a shadow fell across her and before she could move, the phone was snatched from her hand. Nell stood above her, her eyes wide open in amazement as she stared at the small coloured screen. She touched the keypad with the palm of her free hand and the phone bleeped as the menu image changed. Nell gasped and jumped but still held onto the phone. Zoe leaped up and, despite her desperation to get the phone back, she found herself both fascinated and baffled by Nell's reaction. She's never seen one before, Zoe realised; she doesn't know what it is . . . or what it's meant to do . . .

'Can you text?' Zoe asked, wanting to see Nell's reaction, amazed by her amazement. Nell didn't say a word, but continued to stare, mesmerised, at the changing colours and cloud images of the screen-saver.

'Well, can you?' Zoe asked again irritably, stepping closer to Nell.

Nell didn't speak but growled at Zoe, warning her off like a dog guarding a bone.

Both girls looked at the phone, their eyes drawn to the small object as if it were a sacred relic with powerful, magnetic and magical properties.

'Please,' Zoe whispered, 'could I have my phone? Please Nell, I need it.' She held out her hand. 'Please? *Please . . .* '

Nell looked up sharply and took a few paces backwards, holding the phone closer in a protective and possessive manner. At a safe distance she pressed the keypad again and jumped with shock as the phone responded loudly. She stared closely at the screen and, very tentatively, touched the keypad once more. This time she squealed with delight at the sound.

'Nell . . . ' Zoe pleaded. 'It's my phone and I really need it . . . please?' She walked towards Nell with her hand held out, but with surprising agility Nell leaped up onto the largest boulder, still clutching the mobile.

'Nell, will you give me that phone,' Zoe yelled in desperation and fear, as she felt hope evaporating.

Nell glared at her defiantly and grinned. 'This is *my* magic light,' she said and thrust the phone into the front pocket of the dirty apron that she wore over her dark dress. Jumping off the rock she shouted at Zoe, *'Now get back to work!'*

Zoe was desperate. The text hadn't been sent and now she'd lost her phone and any hope of contacting anyone. When I get it back . . . if I get it back, she thought, the battery will probably be flat. Oh why wasn't I more patient? I should have waited for a better opportunity.

She returned, reluctantly, to the dram-loading area. Nell was working about twenty metres away to her right. Every so often Zoe noticed that Nell would put her hand into her apron pocket, carefully pull out the phone, pull it open and look in wonderment at the *magic light.*

What is she doing now? Zoe wondered, as Nell's

finger hovered over the keypad for a few seconds, as if she were plucking up the nerve to press it again. Suddenly Nell jabbed at the buttons and squealed in delight at the noises. Despite her desperation to get the phone back, Zoe had to stop herself from giggling at Nell's comical behaviour. But her thoughts returned to the puzzle of her situation. It was clear to her that Nell really hadn't seen a mobile phone before, and the idea made her panic. What is happening to me? she wondered. She remembered reading a story about children who came across a village, deep in a forest, that had been cut off from the world for centuries . . . The village was like a mediaeval settlement and the people knew nothing about modern culture and technology. Was that possible? Was that what was happening here, she wondered. How could a part of a town be cut off from the rest of the town for hundreds of years? It couldn't, she concluded . . . it just wasn't possible.

Nell suddenly glared at Zoe. 'What are you doing?' she snarled, thrusting the phone roughly into her apron. 'Stop dithering and daydreaming and get on with your work.'

Zoe scowled and bent to pick up a chunk of rock. 'What a cheek – it's *my* flippin' phone and I don't care if she's never seen one before,' she muttered in exasperation. 'I just hope she doesn't break it.'

At last the shift ended. The workers drifted from their places of work. This had been the longest day of Zoe's life. Nell quickly gathered her charges together – Tom, the younger boy Daniel and, of course, Zoe. Nell glared at Zoe and thrust her hand into her pocket as if to guard her new-found treasure.

They retraced the path they'd taken that morning; a lifetime away, Zoe thought. This time, however, they walked in the broad daylight of a summer's evening, past the arches with the fires that she'd been told were the smelting furnaces, through the gates and onto the road that led towards the river. As they approached a bridge, which spanned a canal and a river, Zoe studied the surrounding hills and saw something that made her stop suddenly. On the hillside to her left, looking out over the smoke-filled valley was the unmistakable landmark of Cyfarthfa Castle. This was something she knew . . . something real, yet on her previous visits to Merthyr she'd never noticed the iron works. How could she have missed such a sight? The feeling of panic started to grow again as she realized something else. If that's Cyfarthfa across the river to the left, she reasoned, then the hill ahead and to the right, with its rows of cottages and a huge waste tip behind . . . must be Georgetown.

Zoe found it difficult to concentrate. She felt exhausted and confused, and she'd struggled all day with a terrible physical and mental ordeal. She tried, once again, to shut out ideas that suggested she was going mad. Throughout the day she had considered one explanation for her situation after another, but all had failed to make sense, and with each one she had felt crushing disappointment and greater confusion. She was frightened, but so tired that her fear had become a deep unhappy dread. Nevertheless, she forced herself to think about what she could see, what she was experiencing and what she knew: this is Merthyr and that is Georgetown, she thought. The ironworks, the constant references to Crawshay, the people – how they look and the clothes they wear.

There are no cars or buses or mobile phone signals and, she thought, the strange way Nell has been behaving with my phone . . . I'm not in my own time, but I know that's not possible, so I must be dreaming; this *must* be one of my nightmares.

She was not, however, able to convince herself of this: she was too aware of physical pain – her knee hurt where she had banged it on the side of a dram, her legs and arms and back ached from the constant pushing of loaded trucks, and her hands were cut and torn. Also, she thought, Tom seems real enough, and so do Daniel and Nell. She looked at Tom: he was a tall, thin boy with a sad face. She noticed that he always seemed to be looking down as if he were too nervous to make eye contact with anyone.

Come on Zoe, she thought, you're not mad: *he's* real – talk to him. 'Why are you with Nell and Kathleen?' she whispered to him.

He glanced ahead at Nell nervously before answering, 'Don't ask too many questions. You'll only get us into trouble.'

'But why? Please answer me,' she persisted.

'I don't have a mam or dad, see, just like you . . . ' he said.

'Go on,' she urged, choosing to ignore, for the moment, the reference to her parents.

'My mam died of cholera when I was a baby and my dad was killed at the Ynysfach Works last year,' he continued. 'I was on the streets of Morlais when the Bristle Gang took me in . . . Just don't ask too many questions.'

'The Bristle Gang?' Zoe asked, in a slightly raised voice.

Nell wheeled around. 'What are you talking about?'

she demanded.

'Nothing . . . ' Zoe replied, lowering her eyes just as Tom did. 'What's the Bristle Gang?' she whispered through clenched teeth to the gangly boy at her side.

'Most of them are from Bristol, but they say *Bristle*,' he explained. 'They come up here when the Long Pay is due . . . '

'Hold on,' Zoe interrupted. 'What exactly is this Long Pay that everyone keeps going on about?'

Tom looked at her, and seemed a little amused by the question.

'Well?' Zoe pressed.

'Workers have to wait a long time before they get paid; surely you know that?' Tom said.

'No I don't. I wouldn't be asking if I did,' she snapped.

Tom looked flustered and lowered his eyes again.

'Sorry,' Zoe whispered, 'I didn't mean to . . . Anyway, how long do they have to wait, then, for the Long Pay? Weeks, or what?'

'Many, many weeks . . . sometimes months,' he mumbled.

'Yes, but what about us? Why has Kathleen asked us to find information? Surely we'll be told about the Long Pay at the same time as everyone else,' she said.

Tom shook his head. 'No, the pay is given to the men . . . and young 'uns like us get paid the following day at the works by the gaffers, and then we give it to Kathleen.'

Zoe thought for a few moments. 'So, what about Kathleen and the Bristle Gang?' she asked. 'What are they up to? Why do they want to know about the Long Pay?'

Tom glanced at her, frowning and seeming baffled

by her questions. 'So they can take what they can from the workers,' he said.

'You mean they *steal*?' she asked.

'Course they do, girl,' he said. 'When workers have had to wait a long time for their pay, they like to spend some of it on ale. The gaffers usually pay the wages in a bar or tap-room owned by the ironmasters. That way the money goes back to the likes of Mr Crawshay as soon as he's paid it out. Then, when the workers leave the inn, merry and singing, the gangs pick them off, one by one, and take what's left of their pay.'

'But, but, but that's theft, robbery . . . that's criminal!' Zoe spluttered.

'That's why the gaffers don't tell anyone where the pay will be given until the last possible moment. Anyway, there are far worse things in Pontystorehouse, Morlais and down at Bridge Street,' Tom muttered. 'We just help the Bristle Gang by finding out as early as we can where the gaffers will pay the wages. We tell them and they feed us and give us a home.'

'We've got to do something about this,' Zoe protested.

'Don't waste your time,' he answered. 'Life could be far worse. Listen to Tom now.'

Zoe was still trying to come to terms with the events of a horrific day and the amazing revelations that were coming to her with every passing moment. Her thoughts turned to the possibility of escape, but where would she go and what would she do? For the time being at least, she decided, she would have to stay put and wait for the right opportunity, but what opportunity? How can someone escape from time? *Am I mad*? Am I hallucinating? she wondered frantically, as she was gripped by an overwhelming, panicky sense of claustrophobia and dread.

The journey through the streets and alleys of Pontystorehouse was much the same and just as confusing as the evening before. As they walked through the streets, children and cripples begged and harassed them, only to be pushed away by Nell. Women fought and swore, and drunks rolled on the ground, dribbling and vomiting, their ragged clothes caked in mud and human waste. The smell of putrid, stagnant water and sewage was every bit as bad as Zoe remembered from the night before. These people really are disgusting, she thought – human beings living alongside the rats that scurry amongst the filth of the streets. As bad as she felt about her own plight, Zoe couldn't help thinking about what Tom had said about being an orphan. She looked at the begging children and felt an immediate heart-wrenching pity. Their eyes seemed dull and lifeless with no spark of fun or joy. They pulled at every passer-by, pleading and begging for food. Their clothes were rags and their filthy hands, feet and faces were covered with scabs and open, weeping sores. What sort of life do these kids have? Zoe thought. Is this all they've ever known? Are they all orphans, or is begging normal for children? The whole place seemed immersed in an atmosphere of lawlessness, decay and despair.

As soon as they were inside their cellar room Kathleen called a meeting. Nell's loaders were asked for information but were unable to offer anything, much to the annoyance of the other gang members who sat listening intently.

Kathleen paced up and down, wringing her hands.

'We must find out something soon, sure we must.'

'*She* might know something,' Nell said, nodding in Zoe's direction. 'She seems to have made a friend – the miner who talks about Union clubs and Friendly Societies. He's always helping someone; perhaps he can help us now.' Her grimy features broke into a crooked grin. Nell told them what had happened at the works, and how Richard Lewis had helped Zoe. The men muttered amongst themselves, obviously pleased with what they were hearing.

Kathleen turned on one of her warm smiles. 'You must find out, my sweet, from our friendly miner, when and where the Long Pay will take place . . . we're relying on you.' All eyes were on Zoe as she shuffled uncomfortably, looking from one dirty face to another . . .

After an evening meal of what seemed to be potato and onion soup, and without even thinking of undressing, Zoe lowered her aching body onto the straw mattress and soon fell into a deep, exhausted sleep.

The next day followed much the same pattern as Zoe's first at the Works. She was woken before dawn for the walk to the quarries. As they were leaving the small room Kathleen gripped her arm. 'Don't forget, my wee lamb,' she whispered, 'try your best to find out what you can about the Long Pay from your Union friend and you will make Kathleen very happy.'

At the quarry Zoe once again began the agonising task of loading drams. The Gaffer was as loud as ever, shouting, cursing and cracking his whip. She scanned the quarry face, hoping for a glimpse of Dic Lewis. He was nowhere to be seen and she felt disappointed, but a little while later, as she loaded her third dram of the day, a familiar voice called out from nearby, "You all right today girl?"

She jumped and looked up to see Dic's face, lit up, as usual, with a cheerful grin. 'Yes, yes, thank you,'she replied, feeling a strange mixture of joy at seeing him and awkwardness, as if the fact she had been sent to betray him showed on her face.

As she continued with the laborious task of loading and pushing drams, Zoe tried to listen to any snippets of conversation from her fellow workers, but she heard no mention of the Long Pay. During the short midday break the workers sat around on large rocks brought down by the morning's blasting. When they'd finished their bread and cheese, many of the workers lit their peculiar clay pipes. Dic moved around the group of people, talking excitedly.

Zoe watched his every move and at one point she heard him mention the Friendly Society. 'A little something is all I ask,' he pleaded with a fireman who was leaning against a dram. 'Just a small amount, please, to help those out of work, the widows and the orphans. Come on man,' he urged, 'better than spending it all on ale. The landlord of the Lamb gets enough from us as it is.'

'Aye, aye stop going on, Dic,' the man said. 'See me tonight, at the Lamb, after the Gaffer has been with the pay. Don't leave it too late though, boyo, or my missus will have every penny, as usual.' The workers laughed at the fireman's pained expression.

As Nell turned away, Zoe caught sight of her satisfied grin. She was glad and relieved that she would not have to betray Dic by getting the information from him, or from anyone else for that matter. Kathleen will have what she wants, she thought, and it will be Nell who will take the credit.

That evening they hurried back to Pontystorehouse almost at running pace. Nell could hardly wait to reveal her gem of information. Zoe sat back on her straw-covered pallet, stretched her aching legs and watched, distastefully, as the men cheered and grinned at Nell's words, and slapped each other's backs in excited expectancy.

Only Kathleen was quiet. She paced up and down, deep in thought. "Right, me fine boyos," she called abruptly. 'The Lamb, tonight! Listen carefully. This is the plan of action . . .'

Chapter 7

Into action

Darkness descended on the rooftops of Merthyr's Pontystorehouse as the gang filed out of the cellar room. Zoe could see the last pale patches in the sky turning to inky blue in the west until, very quickly, the eerie red glow from the furnaces of the ironworks took over to dominate the darkening sky. The streets themselves were mostly pitchy-black, the gloom pierced in only a few places by the lamplight from a window. As the gang crept stealthily through the narrow streets towards its destination, Zoe found herself imagining threats in the darkness. What, she thought, was lurking in each dark recess, in each alleyway, in each pothole in the road? Was that a pair of eyes staring at her for a moment? Did something just scurry across her foot? She shivered involuntarily.

They passed under an arch between two buildings and into a narrow alley. Zoe could hear voices from behind the doors and windows of the houses bordering it, and somewhere nearby a baby cried pitifully. At the end of the alley one of the gang, a man named O'Donnel, stopped and held up his hand. Nell gripped Zoe's arm as the company came to a halt.

'Take a look, John,' O'Donnel whispered.

The young pickpocket, John Wylde, pushed

towards the front of the group and disappeared into the darkness ahead. After a few moments he returned. 'All clear,' he hissed.

With a prod from Nell, Zoe joined the others as they crept from the alley into a more open space. The road was cobbled stone. Shafts of light fell from the large windows of a building a short distance away, which was hemmed in by tightly packed terraced houses. Unmistakable sounds of merriment drifted from the place, and Zoe could hear a fiddle playing fast tunes as an audience clapped, sang, laughed and danced, their boots clumping and thumping on a wooden floor. As they moved a little closer she could see a sign hanging above the front door – The Lamb. So this was to be the scene of the crime, she thought.

As Kathleen hissed instruction and the members of the Bristle Gang obediently took their places in nearby doorways and alley entrances, Zoe began to feel very uneasy. Nell guided her to a position directly opposite the tavern and bundled her into a dark doorway. The street to the left was narrow and shrouded in shadow, and it was difficult to see where the other gang members lurked, but from her hiding place she had a clear view of the door of the inn. Zoe could hear Nell's steady breathing at her side. Zoe's breathing was less steady: she was about to witness, or, worse still, take part in a violent crime. What was going to happen? What would she do? She jumped as the noise of laughter, music and chatter suddenly increased when the door of The Lamb opened. The light from the open doorway spilled over the cobblestones as three men emerged – three large men; miners or ironworkers perhaps. Zoe watched, holding her breath, waiting for . . . she didn't quite know what she was waiting for.

Nothing happened, much to her relief, and the three men strolled casually, relaxed and in good spirits after their evening's drinking, up the cobbled street. Nell also appeared to relax and slouched back against a wall. The waiting game continued. After what seemed like an eternity of holding her breath and peering into the roadway, the telltale noise level from the inn increased again. A solitary figure staggered from the doorway and turned towards the shadows on the left. Nell stiffened. 'This is it,' she whispered. 'Time to relieve boyo of his money.' Roughly she shoved Zoe to one side.

Panic rose in Zoe's stomach; her mouth was dry and her hands shook. Were they really going to rob the poor man? Would they injure him? Would they maybe kill him? It's now or never, she thought, and on impulse she lunged forward, pushing past Nell. 'Look out, robbers, thieves!' she yelled at the top of her voice, running into the roadway. The staggering man stopped, his eyes bulged in his startled face and for a second he stood still, his mouth hanging open. Zoe raced to the middle of the road and stopped as boots clattered on the cobbles behind her and to the side. Shouts and curses from the Bristle Gang were followed by screams of anger as the startled man came to his senses and leaped back towards the doorway from which he'd come. He pushed it open and Zoe heard him shout in Welsh, 'Robbers! The gangs are out.'

She watched in frozen astonishment as a tide of bodies poured from The Lamb, yelling and screaming as they raced in all directions in hot pursuit of the thieves. For some it seemed to be sport. Whistles were blown, and a group of men whooped as they charged down an alleyway. The fiddler, a one-legged man, emerged from the inn hopping on his good leg as he continued to play a fast tune, and another man who appeared to be blind sang loudly to the accompaniment of the fiddle.

Zoe stood perfectly still with her hands to her face as the inn emptied and its former occupants ran around her in search of robbers.

'Look out,' shouted one. 'Here come Crawshay's special constables.'

Two men armed with large sticks ran into the crowd, and in a confusion of raised voices, the situation was explained to them. One of the constables, a tall thin man with a bushy moustache, turned his attention on Zoe. With two strides he was at her side and he gripped her arm tightly, his stick upraised in his other hand.

'So, one of Pontystorehouse's orphan thieves, eh?' he snarled, as Zoe looked up at him in alarm, lost for words. 'Where's the rest of your gang?' the man continued, tightening his grip on her arm. 'You'll be sorry now. This place is swarming with ruffians like you, and the only cure is to make you suffer; show others what happens to thieves.'

Zoe suddenly found her voice. 'I'm not a thief . . . it was me who warned the man about the robbers,' she explained frantically.

'Explain it to the Magistrates, my girl, but don't expect leniency; they know how the Pay Gangs work. Urchins like you are always involved in their dirty work.' His fingers dug into Zoe's arm. She winced with pain, protesting her innocence.

The commotion started to die down and people began to gather again outside the inn. It seemed the gang had all managed to slip away into the darkness, 'like rats into tunnels,' someone commented. The fact that they had escaped clearly angered the constables.

'At least we've got one of them,' Zoe's captor seethed. 'It's only a matter of time before we get the others. Perhaps a little *persuasion* is called for.' He glared down at Zoe, and she pleaded with him, but he just grinned at her nastily. She looked desperately towards the men and women who were drifting back towards The Lamb. Then, above the general chatter, Zoe heard a familiar voice.

'Who've you got there, then, Abbott?'

'Dic!' Zoe shouted, as hope started to return. 'Tell him, tell him. Tell him it was me who warned the man about the robbers.' Dic looked down at Zoe, recognizing her with surprise. 'Please Dic, help me,' she begged.

He stood in silence, searching Zoe's face as she sobbed pitifully. At last he said, 'Let her go Abbott, she's not a thief.'

'Not likely,' Abbott protested. 'This one's going to be locked up. She can tell us where the rest of the gang members are hiding.'

'She's not a thief,' Dic repeated firmly. 'She's a child, and as much a victim as the rest of us.'

'Keep out of this Penderyn; it's got nothing to do with you,' Abbott warned. 'This is not your fancy trade union business now. We'll see what Mr Bruce the Magistrate, and Mr Crawshay have to say about it.'

Zoe noticed that Dic, for once, looked slightly nervous, and his usual grin had disappeared. 'Don't talk to me about Crawshay, and don't talk to me about trade unions,' he said quietly. 'The workers need unions to protect their rights, as, for all his talk and gestures, Mr Crawshay does nothing to protect us.

Whilst he and the other masters live in luxury in their big houses, their workers are put out of jobs to save costs. Their furniture is taken from them to pay their debts, and their children go hungry.'

Zoe squirmed and wriggled, but Abbott gripped her arm tighter as Dic moved closer.

'It's all right for you Abbott,' he said slowly. 'You have your barber shop, and Crawshay pays you well as a special constable whenever he feels the workers need to be put in their place. But she's just a child. Let her go.'

'Clear off Penderyn,' Abbott retorted. 'She's nothing but a Rodney. What's it to you anyway? This is my business. Go back to your union friends.'

'I said . . . let her go,' Dic said through clenched teeth as he pushed and prodded at Abbott. The constable bellowed as Dic's finger poked into his chest. He lashed out at Dic, his fist striking the young miner's shoulder. As he did so he released his grip on Zoe, and she kicked his shin with her heel. He yelped with pain and hopped about, clutching his injured leg.

'Go on girl, run for it while you've got the chance,' Dic shouted.

'Stop!' Abbott yelled, still hopping, as she hesitated.

'Go on,' Dic urged.

As the constable lunged forward in Zoe's direction, Dic's outstretched foot tripped him and brought him crashing to the floor. The men who had come back out of The Lamb and who were now standing around watching roared with laughter. Abbott yelled in rage as he lifted himself from the road. From a safe distance Zoe stopped and turned to look back at the scene. Dic was running in the opposite direction, laughing heartily as the constable stood up, shaking his fist, and shouting, 'I'll get even with you Dic Penderyn, if it's the last thing I do . . . I'll get you.'

Dic Penderyn? Zoe thought suddenly. I *know* that name . . . but he's Dic *Lewis*. Why did he call him Dic Penderyn? Where have I . . . ? As she stood, wondering, she saw the furious constable turn back to look for her. Faced with the choice of being caught or plunging into the unknown and terrifying maze of the town's dark streets, she took to her heels and ran as fast as she could.

She ran and ran, through narrow streets, under archways, occasionally pushing past people as she went. At one point she came through a narrow gap between buildings only to find herself in a small, enclosed square, surrounded by houses. She panted and shook with terror as she realised that the only way out was back the way she had come. With head down she retraced her steps and ran, once more, out of the courtyard. Turning to the right she hoisted up her bulky skirt and sprinted ahead. A large dark building loomed before her; a church or chapel perhaps. Zoe leaped at a low wall and scrambled over, crashing onto the paved surface beyond. She crawled on hands and knees into the shadows at the foot of the building.

Gulping air painfully and leaning against a wall for support Zoe struggled to recover her strength and her breath. She noticed the sign above the large wooden door – *Capel Ynysgau*. So it *was* a chapel. The idea of a church seemed so out of place in the midst of the filth and crime of this place.

Slowly she became aware of the sound of rushing water. The river, she thought, hopefully. The streets of the town were a confusing maze but at least the river provided some bearing. This was a landmark. She didn't know quite where she would go but at least this was a starting point.

Cautiously, she climbed back over the wall and crept towards the sound of the water and sure enough, as she passed a row of small houses, she came to the riverbank. To her right, about fifty metres away, she was able to make out the shape of a bridge, spanning the waters of the River Taff. She ran onto the bridge and then across to the other side.

The path led to a busy, built-up area, where Zoe could see and hear people walking about. Creeping forward towards a rail track she ducked behind a train of four linked, stationary drams. From the shadows she could see the brightly-lit windows of another inn – The Three Horseshoes, and just like earlier she could hear the sounds of laughter, shouting and singing drifting out into the street. There was a dark lane at the side of the inn and she watched it carefully for some time before deciding to take this route. "Here goes," she muttered.

She ran along the lane and up an incline behind a row of houses, and soon left the buildings behind. Pushing through bushes and undergrowth and climbing up the steep slope of a hill, she reasoned that from high up she would be able to keep watch for danger while she recovered her strength and decided what to do. Eventually she reached a flat, narrow ledge, and walking along it found a slight hollow in the steeper wall which would give her some shelter. She yawned as she sat in the shadows of the little hollow, sheltering from the night breeze. She realised this was an iron-waste tip – the smell was unmistakable and she remembered it well from her short stint at the ironworks. The Cyfarthfa Ironworks, she thought. What else could it be? The ashy substance of the tip was quite comfortable and soft as she lay back, resting her aching exhausted body. The sulphuric smell hardly seemed to bother her and she drifted into a relaxed doze. The exertions of a day's work at Cyfarthfa and the events of the evening finally took their toll on her exhausted body and mind, and thinking about Dic Lewis, and puzzling over the name Dic Penderyn, she fell into a deep sleep.

Chapter 8

Sunday

It was early Sunday morning and after grabbing just a few hours' sleep Emma was back on duty in the small incident room at the police station. Zoe was still missing, and Emma was told that house-to-house enquiries were well under way. She looked through the search schedules and read the notes on a pinboard. The door opened and Ian rushed in. "Morning Em," he said hurriedly, "I thought you'd want to see this straight away." He handed her a piece of paper. "One of our team has just spoken to a man on Brecon Road. He mentioned this guy, Dai Twp, Tom Silford – he says his children are frightened of the old man and that he's weird and a real oddball who won't let anyone near his house . . . "

Emma scanned the sheet of paper. 'Look at this, Ian,' she said. 'This man reckons his kids don't like Dai Twp because he tells them off if they go near his garden. And what about this bit?' she added, quoting from the statement: '"I don't know what he's got to hide . . . I just don't trust him . . ."' Emma put the paper down, looked at Ian and said, 'Well it's not much, but I think we should pay Mr Silford a visit.'

'Good morning sir,' Emma said, introducing herself to

the elderly man who was peering out through his front door, which was open a crack and still secured with a safety chain. She showed him her police identification and said, 'This is my colleague, Detective Constable Ian Dixon. We're investigating the disappearance of Zoe Davies. You might have heard about it in the news bulletins.'

'I haven't seen anything,' the man said irritably.

Emma took out a photograph of Zoe that Bethan had given her the night before. "This is Zoe," she persisted, 'Do you remember seeing her at all?'

'Like I said, I haven't seen anyone,' he said sharply.

'Mr Silford – it is Mr Silford, isn't it?' Emma enquired. The man frowned and nodded. 'We need to ask you a few questions; do you think we could come in?'

'I don't know anything,' he growled.

'Please Mr Silford, it would be really helpful if we could talk.' Emma said.

The man hesitated, but then he released the security chain and opened the front door. He showed the police officers into the back room. Emma glanced around the sparsely furnished room as she sat on a plain wooden chair.

'Do you live here alone Mr Silford?' she asked, already knowing the answer.

'Just me and the cats . . . I'm a widower,' he mumbled.

Emma noticed two grey tabby cats curled up on the room's only armchair.

She smiled. 'Now, Mr Silford, just a few routine questions. You've not seen anyone recently who you think might be the girl in the photograph?' she asked.

'Told you, haven't I,' he answered gruffly.

Emma noticed Ian looking around the room carefully, taking in every detail, peering through an open doorway to the kitchen and glancing up a small flight of stairs.

'Where were you yesterday evening between five thirty and eight o'clock?' she asked.

'I can tell you exactly,' he said without hesitation. 'I was at the supermarket. Well, I got there about six and left about quarter past seven.'

'Which supermarket was that Mr Silford?' Emma asked.

'Your Choice, down by the river, near Jackson's Bridge,' he said.

Emma looked at Ian who nodded – this was the supermarket whose carpark was right next to the wasteland where the can and magazine had been found.

'I go every Saturday for my groceries and cat food,' Tomos Silford continued. 'I always go at that time because it's quieter. I don't like crowds of people.'

'How do you get to and from the supermarket?' Emma asked.

'My car,' he replied. 'I only ever use it for shopping. I don't go out otherwise, not since my Emily passed away.'

'What sort of car do you have Mr Silford?' Emma enquired.

'A Morris Minor,' he answered readily. 'I've had it for over forty years. I keep it in the garage and it's as good as the day me and Emily bought it . . . She wasn't too keen on the colour, mind you, but it was a bargain and it served us well.' Tomos shook his head and lapsed into silence, a very slight smile on his face as he remembered happier days.

Emma glanced at Ian who took her cue and said quickly, 'Wow, a real classic. I'm a car enthusiast – do you think I could have a look at it?'

Tomos nodded, and Emma laughed. 'You boys and your cars; I don't see the attraction myself,' she lied. 'Don't be long. We have work to do.'

Tomos got the keys and led Ian through the kitchen and out to the garage, which was at the end of a large, beautifully kept garden. Emma watched through the window as they walked up the path. Very quickly she ran up the stairs. There were two bedrooms and, just like the room downstairs, they were very sparsely furnished. She rushed from one room to the next, looking under the beds and in the wardrobes, but touching nothing. She looked through the back bedroom window and could see that Ian and Mr Silford were still in the garage. She glanced up at an attic trapdoor. 'Zoe,' she called. 'Zoe . . . ' She listened carefully. Nothing. She dashed downstairs, into the front room, then sped to the kitchen. Finally she looked around the small downstairs bathroom. 'Well, there's nothing here,' she said to herself, 'absolutely no trace of Zoe.' She walked out into the garden and noticed the beehives that Rose Davies' friend had mentioned. She looked around the garden but could see nowhere that might be used to conceal a person. At the door to the garage she said, 'Sorry to spoil your fun, gentlemen, but we really must make tracks.'

They thanked Tomos for his co-operation and made their way back to Emma's beloved VW convertible. 'Not interested in cars,' Ian chuckled. 'What are you like Emma Lewis!'

'The house was clean. No sign of anyone having been there,' Emma reported as they pulled away from the cottage.

'I've got full details of the car, and I managed to have a good rummage around the garage too. Not a sausage,' Ian said. 'Top motor though,' he added, grinning at Emma.

'And, talking of top motors,' she replied, 'let's put this little beauty through its paces. We're off to Swansea. I've arranged to see Doctor Rhian Walsh, Zoe's GP.'

After the visit, and back in the car, Emma made a few notes while Ian phoned the incident room. 'Nothing to report,' he said to Emma as he put his phone back in his pocket, 'but DI Bowen wants us back in an hour for an update meeting, so you'd better put your foot down.' Dr Walsh had been surprised by information about Zoe's great grandmother, particularly her experience of amnesia, and had agreed to talk to her. But they were none the wiser about what sort of condition Zoe might be in.

When they got back to the station, Detective Inspector John Bowen stood up in front of his team of police officers in the packed incident room. Some were plain-clothed detectives, others were in uniform. 'This is a real mystery, there's no other way to describe it,' he said. He looked around the room. 'We have no leads, so what are the possibilities?' he asked. Without waiting for an answer he counted off on his fingers: 'One . . . Zoe's lost her memory and is still wandering around. Two . . . she could be injured or trapped somewhere. Three . . . she's run away and is being sheltered by someone. Four, and the most likely in my opinion, she's has been abducted, and five . . . ' John Bowen looked around the room before continuing quietly, 'five . . . murder.'

'But we don't have a body, Sir,' Emma commented.

'You're right. We don't have a body, so we don't have a murder investigation. Okay everyone, let's work on the first four possibilities. Emma, over to you, let's look at what we have so far.'

For the next ten minutes Emma went over details of the investigation, including the visit to Tomos Silford's house – being very careful not to say too much about her unofficial search. She outlined the circumstances of Zoe's disappearance, the theory of amnesia and the doctor's report, the few clues in their possession, forensic reports and an update on all police activity including a thorough search of Zoe's computer. The mobile phone network company, she reported, was monitoring Zoe's account for any calls or texts, in or out.

Emma confirmed that the case was now national news. A recent photograph of Zoe had appeared in television news bulletins and also in newspapers. Police forces across the country were in possession of details and were actively involved in the search.

When she finished her report Inspector Bowen took over. 'You now know the extent of this operation,' he said. 'We'll work on the assumption that she's still alive and that someone knows something that's going to give us the breakthrough. We have to find those people so let's get back to it.'

'You're pretty certain she's been abducted aren't you Sir,' Emma said softly, not looking at DI Bowen.

'Yes I am, Sergeant and I'm sure it's local too. I think we're wasting our time looking in London and other big cities for a runaway. No, she's been abducted and someone out there is probably laughing at us as we

112

speak. What's the score with this chap Silford?' he asked.

'He's a bit of a loner and the locals think he's strange; they call him Dai Twp,' Emma said, 'but we went to the house and had a good look around . . . absolutely nothing.'

'Have you checked him out?' John Bowen asked.

'Yes sir, Ian checked all records – no convictions, no suspicions . . . clean as a whistle,' Emma said.

The Detective Inspector sat down wearily. "I'm *sure* it's local. Go and find me something Sergeant, anything – just bring me some news. Talk to her friends again: find out if she mentioned talking to anyone on chat-rooms; hints about new internet friends, that sort of thing. It won't be easy because they'll cover for each other if they think they're protecting their mates. I think you need to be a bit more aggressive in your methods, Sergeant. I need information."

Emma sighed but bit her tongue. There was little point in arguing with the Old Man, as most colleagues called him. She picked up a folder and her car keys and headed for her office.

Ian walked into the office as Emma was flicking through a pile of papers on her desk. 'Where next, Em?' he asked.

'Back up to Georgetown, see how the house-to-house is going . . . the Old Man is expecting something soon,' she said.

As Emma drove past the Three Horseshoes pub her mobile rang. Ian took the call, and then said to Emma, 'Back to the station, quick, they've got something.'

At the station, two policemen and a forensics officer brought a large, clear plastic bag into the incident room. Emma picked up the bag and looked at the black sweatshirt inside. The small white logo on the front was distinct – a mask with two eyes and a bird's pointed beak, and the word 'Ospreys'.

'This is Zoe's all right,' Emma murmured. 'We'll have to get a positive identification of course, but I think it's too much of a coincidence. This is what she was wearing.'

Ian nodded. "This is Merthyr, Em – Cardiff Blues territory. I wouldn't have thought there were too many Ospreys fans in this town."

'You're right, this *is* Zoe's . . . Where was it found?' she asked, turning to the constables.

'A trolley collector at the Your Choice supermarket found it a little while ago,' he replied. 'He'd heard the radio reports and Zoe's description on his way into work for the afternoon shift. He was collecting trolleys at the bottom of the car park and he noticed something behind some cars, next to a wall – turned out to be the sweatshirt. Anyway,' the constable continued, 'he remembered the description on the radio and called the store manager, who called us immediately.'

'Thank you,' Emma said. 'Ian, make sure you get a full statement from the supermarket worker and get a team down there now to question the others.'

'Yes Sergeant,' he said formally, 'and DI Bowen is on his way, he'll be here in about twenty minutes and wants a full update.'

'Okay, I'll be ready for him, and Ian . . . it won't be easy, but would you go over to Zoe's parents and try to get a positive identification on this,' she said, handing him the bagged sweatshirt. She turned to the forensics officer and said, 'It's over to you then Steve.'

'We'll get straight on to it,' he responded. 'The

area's been sealed off and our team is on site. We'll bring you whatever we can as soon as possible.'

Alison Jenkins put her head around the living room door. 'Bethan, David, you have a visitor . . . a Doctor Rhian Walsh,' she said. 'Is it okay if she . . . ?'

David looked up. It took a few seconds for the policewoman's words to register. He nodded slowly. Alison stepped back into the hallway and David heard her say, 'Would you like to come in Doctor Walsh?'

Bethan was oblivious; she was hugging a cushion and rocked slowly as she stared into the glow of the coal fire. Rose Davies sat at her side, stroking her arm and whispering soothingly.

'I got here as soon as I could, and – ' Rhian began, and stopped in mid-sentence with her hand to her mouth when she saw Bethan. 'Oh Beth,' she whispered as tears ran down her face.

Bethan didn't acknowledge Rhian but continued to stare at the red coals and the low, flickering blue flames.

'Beth?' David said softly. 'Beth it's Rhian . . . '

'It's all our fault. She didn't want to come,' Bethan wailed suddenly. 'She wanted to go to the cinema with her friends, but we made her . . . Why did we have to make her? *Why . . .? Why . . .?* '

David put his arms around her. 'Shush Beth, shush,' he whispered, not knowing what to say. 'It . . . it . . . '

'Don't you dare tell me it'll be alright and she'll turn up sooner or later,' Bethan screamed, pushing her husband away. 'We won't see her again . . . My baby,' she wept, *'we . . . won't . . . see . . . her . . . ever again.'*

'Bethan?' Rhian said softly. 'You can't say that Beth. There could be any number of good reasons . . . You must be strong and keep hoping and praying.'

Bethan turned her head slowly towards Rhian, a look of disbelief and amazement on her tear-stained face. 'Do you honestly think that hoping and praying is enough?' she said, her voice quivering. 'What do you think I've been doing every second since my baby disappeared? My daughter – a teenage girl – has been missing for nearly twenty-four hours. There's been no word from her and . . . and her sweatshirt has been found in a car park . . . ' Bethan's voice rose to a screech. '*What hope is there?*'

Rhian and David took Bethan through to the back bedroom and helped her onto the bed. Despite her feeble protests Rhian gave her something to help her calm down and sleep. David explained to Rhian that when the police had called with Zoe's sweatshirt it had been a tremendous shock to them all. Bethan had become hysterical and was convinced that it was a sign Zoe was dead, and it had taken himself, Alison and the policeman who was on duty outside the front door to prevent her from rushing out of the house.

Rose made a pot of tea. She loaded a tray with cups, milk and biscuits and carried it to the kitchen table where David and Rhian sat talking quietly. Rose sat down and poured the teas.

'I had a visit from the police earlier today,' Rhian said, looking from David to Rose. 'We talked about Zoe's condition and how it might be a factor in all this.'

David shrugged. 'I hoped you might have been able to give the police some ideas, some clues . . . I don't know,' he said.

Rhian shook her head and turned to Rose. 'I understand, Rose, from what David and the police have told me, that you've experienced something similar – the nightmares, daydreams and trances?' she said.

'Tell her, Gran,' David said.

'It was a long time ago . . . and I try not to think about it,' Rose said, but with David's prompting she went on to describe her experiences to Rhian.

'And was there a particular theme with the nightmares?' Rhian asked.

'Yes,' Rose's voice dropped to a whisper. 'The feeling of being trapped . . . trapped in the dark.'

Rhian glanced at David and said to Rose, 'That's what Zoe feels . . . I also understand that you once went missing and the doctors thought you probably were suffering from amnesia.'

'It's so strange,' Rose answered. 'I can remember the day clearly but I can't remember a thing about all those hours I was missing.'

'Tell me what you remember of the day,' Rhian said.

'I was found up at the top, wandering around on the old Georgetown tip. I don't know how I got there or what I'd been doing,' Rose said slowly, and paused to sip her tea. 'It was like waking up from a deep sleep. I remember seeing a policeman and then my Mam and Dad. Duw, they were frantic. There were lots of people around town that day and there was a funfair and circus up at Cyfarthfa Park for May Day. They thought I might have been taken by the circus people, and . . . '

'What did you just say?' Rhian interrupted.

'What, about the circus?' Rose asked.

'No,' Rhian said, 'you mentioned it was May Day.'

'Yes, that's right,' Rose said.

'Well,' Rhian pointed out, 'is this a coincidence or what? Today is the first of May, and tomorrow is May bank holiday.'

117

David frowned and said quietly, 'It's just a coincidence, surely.'

'Mmm, I'm sure it is . . . ' Rhian murmured. 'Rose, can you remember anything else about that day, anything at all?'

Rose thought hard. 'Not really, bach,' she said eventually. 'I've told you everything . . . Wait a minute though, there was a little bit in the *Merthyr Cambrian*. I've got the cutting somewhere.' She got up and shuffled over to the dresser. 'Here it is,' she said after a moment, holding up an old green shoebox. She hurried back to the table, pulled the lid off the box and started rummaging through the contents. 'Now where is it?' she muttered impatiently, tipping the box over and scattering everything across the table. 'Ah, ah, here it is!' she exclaimed, holding up a very old brown envelope.

Rhian took out the small cutting and quickly read through it. It didn't say any more than Rose had already said – *After a frantic search by police and volunteers, twelve-year-old local girl, Rosemary Davies, was found near the Georgetown tips. Rosemary had been missing for over ten hours . . . She could remember nothing of her ordeal and apart from being dazed and cold appeared to be well. Police are investigating.* Rhian handed it to David as Rose started putting things back into the box. Rose smiled as she unfolded a marriage certificate. 'Now I can remember *this* day clearly,' she said. 'My Ernest was a lovely man.'

'This is beautiful,' Rhian said, picking up a small, silver bracelet. It was made of thin strands of metal twisted together and finished with two ornate loops. 'This looks like one of those Celtic torques,' she said.

'Duw, I'd forgotten all about that,' Rose said. 'It's

been in my family for generations.' She picked up the bracelet and slipped it on to her left wrist.

'I'd forgotten about that too,' David said. 'You should get it authenticated and insured. It could date back to Roman times.' Once again David checked himself for getting distracted by trivia. He thought of Bethan, lying sedated in the bedroom above, and as he pictured Zoe's smiling face a combination of grief and guilt stabbed at him.

'What's this?' Rhian asked, pushing aside a pair of gloves and a few papers, and picking up a silver pendant necklace.

'Now that,' Rose said, 'was given to me by my mother. It's not as old as this bracelet, mind you, and my Ernest wasn't keen on me wearing it – he always thought my mam was a bit strange. He said she used to talk a load of mumbo-jumbo.'

'This is a Brighid Cross,' Rhian whispered, looking closely at the intertwined strands of silver that formed an equal sided cross. 'You said 'mumbo-jumbo' Rose – what exactly do you mean?'

'I didn't say that, it was my Ernest,' Rose said.

'Yes, I know, but what did he mean?' Rhian pressed.

David looked from one to the other, puzzled.

'Well, my Ernest was a chapel man, never missed a Sunday. Deacon he was, down at Ynysgau . . . '

'Yes Rose, but what did he mean?' Rhian interrupted impatiently.

'I was coming to that,' Rose said indignantly. 'My Ernest said we should celebrate good Christian festivals and not the nonsense that my mam talked about.'

Rhian was leaning forward. 'Such as, Rose?" she asked urgently.

'I'm trying to remember now,' Rose said, scratching her head. 'Well, things like Yule, and Midsummer, and Samhain . . . things like that.'

'And Beltane?' Rhian asked quietly.

Rose stared at Rhian for a few seconds and then said slowly, 'Yes, and Beltane . . . how do you know?'

'My room-mate at college was into Celtic myths and legends,' Rhian said distractedly as she stared at the silver pendant. 'This is the symbol of the Celtic Goddess, Brighid.' She looked up suddenly. 'The first of May, Rose . . . This is Beltane. Last night, when Zoe went missing, was the eve of Beltane,' she said. 'When the veil between this world and Otherworld is at its thinnest, am I right?'

Rose went pale and cleared her throat. 'A time when spirits can pass into the human world and people can pass into Otherworld . . . into Annwn . . . ' she said hoarsely.

David shook his head. 'Zoe is *always* talking about Celtic stuff – Celtic history, myths and legends . . . tells me that *my* history is stuffy and lacks the romance and adventure of ancient Celtic stories . . . but this is absurd,' he said, 'I can't sit here and listen to this fanciful . . . this, this . . . '

Rhian ignored him, looked at Rose carefully and said, 'Legend has it that at Beltane the Queen of Faeries will venture out and try to entice people away to Otherworld. You went missing at the time of Beltane and so has Zoe . . . ' She held up the silver necklace and murmured, 'What is happening, Rose?'

Chapter 9

The honeycomb children

Zoe was awoken by the unpleasant sensation of cold water dripping onto her face. For a few seconds she felt disorientated as she looked around. Then the dread returned. She remembered the cinder tip, and how she'd got there, but thoughts of the Bristle Gang and of the failed Long Pay robbery were quickly displaced by the more immediate problem of the worsening weather. The sky was still black – apart from the deep red glow to Zoe's left, which stood like a watchful guard dog, she thought, over its precious maker and master, the Cyfarthfa ironworks.

A deep rumbling sound brought memories of early childhood fears back to her as thunder rolled along the desolate hills that surrounded the town. Memories of fear were accompanied by the memory of a feeling of security – of snuggling under her warm bedcovers and, when the fear became too much, of burrowing under the blankets between her mother and father. She had always known that the storm wouldn't harm her; her parents would have seen to that, and the sound of the rain lashing against the windowpane somehow increased the cosiness and feeling of security within. But this wasn't her nursery bedroom. She was alone now. She was Zoe and not Little Dolly Daydream.

The rolling thunder changed to a loud crash overhead, as if sensing and mocking her vulnerability. A sheet of lightning showed in the split second of a dazzling blue-white flash the ghostly silhouettes of Merthyr. The rooftops and chimneys seemed to cower as the storm raged above them.

The rain now came down hard, striking painfully against Zoe's face and hands, drenching her shawl and skirt and rapidly turning the ground around her into mud. She huddled further into the cinder hollow and was surprised to find that the blackness further back in the hollow was not solid as she had first thought, but was in fact some sort of low tunnel or cave entrance not more than a metre high. By crouching down she was able to crawl into the shelter and get out of the downpour.

She moved forward into the tunnel on her hands and knees, trying to get as far away as possible from the muddy entrance, but suddenly the ground seemed to disappear from under her, and she fell forward, rolling head over heels down a very steep slope. Frantically she tried to stop herself, clutching desperately at the ground, but she only managed to grab handfuls of loose, ashy material. She had a sudden image of the times she had tried to dig holes in the loose dry sand on a beach, and how impossible it was, like her attempts now to stop herself as she slithered down the dark tunnel slope.

She came to a halt as the ground levelled, and she remained on the soft dirt floor with the sound of her heart pounding in her ears. The darkness was absolute: she couldn't see a thing. She could never remember ever having experienced such blackness. The smell of sulphur was even stronger here. It reminded her of the smell of matches after they had been struck.

Zoe sat up, stretched out her hand and felt the ground around her. 'OK, no more crying and feeling sorry for yourself, girl,' she said out loud. 'You've got to think about getting out of here.'

This was easier said than done. The darkness was like a thick, black cloak around her. She couldn't even tell which direction she had come from. She could sense that she was in some form of cavern. The roof seemed a lot higher than in the tunnel that she had tumbled down, and she was able to stand up. What is this place? she wondered. It occurred to her that it might be part of an old mine, in which case there might be more dangerous holes or shafts nearby. For all she knew, she might at that very moment be on a ledge with an almighty drop only inches away . . . She shuddered with that terrifying thought and stood rooted to the spot. She felt very cold all of a sudden. Her clothes were wet from the rain and her body damp from perspiration, and she began to shake violently as she thought, *this is my nightmare . . . yes, this is it. It's happening*. She listened fearfully, expectantly, but she didn't hear those pitiful sobs of an unknown child that she usually heard in her dream.

Plucking up courage, she poked one foot forward, testing the ground. It seemed solid enough. With painstaking care she took another step, and another, moving forward very, very slowly, her arms stretched in front of her like a cartoon sleepwalker. After a few minutes, her outstretched hands came into contact with the cavern wall. It was solid. 'No opening here,' she whispered, 'but there might be further along.' She moved sideways, her hands feeling along the wall, until they struck something standing off the cave wall:

something rounded, like a tree trunk. It was wood. This is a mine, she thought, and this is a wooden pit prop. She remembered seeing pit props during a school visit to the Mining Museum at Big Pit. Someone had built this underground tunnel, or cave, or whatever it was, she thought, and then she realised that if the workings were under the waste tip, then it was probably an old disused mine. 'All the more reason to be careful, and all the more reason to get out quickly,' she said to herself with determination.

She continued slowly along the wall until at last she found a gap. It was a low opening. Carefully she got down on her hands and knees and inched forward into the tunnel. The floor rose immediately in a sharp incline. "Yes! This must be it; this is where I came in," she muttered to herself, and started to clamber up the steep slope. The climb was exhausting, and it was a horrible surprise and a severe disappointment when she found the ground levelling off once more. She seemed to be inside another cavern, but she was sure that she had not come through it on the way down. She realized, with despair, that she must have gone up a different tunnel to the one she had fallen down. At that moment her frustration and fear turned to anger, and she shouted, 'What have I done to deserve this?' and she kicked uselessly at the loose gravely floor before slumping down, tears once again welling up in her eyes.

For a while she sat with her back against the cavern wall, listening, in constant fear and dread of hearing the sobs of the ghostly child, but the only sound she could hear was the rhythm of her own breathing and her heart. Then she noticed something else . . . *a drip, drip, drip, drip*. This was the first sound of water that she'd come across since entering the tunnel. Where was the water coming from – an underground stream, or from the surface perhaps? If from the surface, could she follow it . . . ? With renewed hope she moved in the direction of the sound. It grew louder, and she knew she must be near just as her hands encountered something cold and wet on the floor. The water was coming from above. Standing on the muddy patch, she looked upwards, towards the source of the water, and for a moment she thought she glimpsed a small pinprick of light. Perhaps she had imagined it, she thought. No, there it was again. She focused hard, and realized that it must be a star twinkling above. It would disappear, probably obscured by clouds, then reappear again, winking and twinkling, like a friend. Zoe shouted with joy. There must be a shaft above. She reached upwards but the ceiling of the cave was too high to touch. At least when morning came there would be some daylight, perhaps enough for her to find her way out, she thought. Things seemed a lot brighter now and, feeling more optimistic, she decided to stay where she was and wait until daytime.

She settled down with her back resting comfortably against the wall. She listened to the *drip . . . drip . . . drip*, which was a comforting sound now. The steady dripping was starting to have a hypnotic effect, soothing her tired mind, *drip, drip . . . sleep . . . sleep . . . drip* . . . Then all at once her drowsiness fell away as she heard another sound. Something was moving just a few metres away. Zoe held her breath, half expecting to hear the haunting sobs. She huddled rigidly, her hands clenched tightly together over her knees. Silence, apart from the drip . . . and then: that sound again. Something was moving along the gravel floor . . . moving slowly. Her mouth dry with fear, she stared into the darkness. Her breathing returned. She was shaking, and beads of cold sweat trickled down her forehead and down her spine. The sound grew louder. Something was moving towards her, something big. Terror gripped her, but even as she opened her mouth to scream, no sound came.

A gleam of light suddenly shot across the floor and illuminated an opening in the cave wall just a few feet away. It was from this opening that the sound was coming. Zoe's eyes shut tightly as the intensity of the light increased; it was painful after the absolute darkness. Behind her closed eyelids she could see only a burning redness, and she turned her head aside. When she opened her eyes, the tunnel was brightly lit and standing in front of her was a group of people carrying burning torches. They were children. Their eyes were wide as they stared at her silently. Zoe stared back. They were dressed like most of the other people she'd seen recently. There were two girls who were perhaps only five or six years old. Zoe guessed they were twins. At the front stood a group of young people of her own age, or perhaps slightly older. One girl, in particular, stood out. There seemed to be something oddly different about her. The other children were glancing at her now, as if for guidance. She was tall, taller than the others, and wore a long green dress with red embroidered patterns on the sleeves. Draped around her shoulders was a shimmering gold-coloured shawl, which seemed to be made of beautifully patterned lace. It was quite different to the heavy woollen shawl that Zoe had got from Kathleen. Zoe stared at the girl. Her beautiful and serene face was framed by the most striking, golden-red hair that

Zoe had ever seen, and around her head she wore a band of woven summer flowers. A *dream* – this is a *dream*, Zoe thought.

At last the silence was broken. The tall girl asked calmly, 'Who are *you*?'

'Who am I? I might ask you the same question,' Zoe retorted. 'Who are you?'

A boy moved forward quickly, looking from the girl with the flowers to Zoe. 'Queen Bee will ask the questions. Be kind enough to answer,' he snapped.

'Queen Bee?' Zoe said, looking around the group. 'Who . . . ? What . . . ? What's going on . . . ?'

Her face still placid and calm, the girl turned and said to her followers, 'Bring her with us.' She stooped and quickly disappeared back into the low tunnel. Instantly the children were at Zoe's side. She was hauled up and guided towards the tunnel. They had to stoop because the ceiling was low. Everything was happening too quickly for Zoe to think, or to ask questions, but before she ducked into the tunnel she did notice in the light a number of other tunnel entrances or exits off the cave in which she had just met this strange group of young people.

They scurried along the tunnel and Zoe noticed that it sloped far less than the two she had previously been in. In the torchlight she could now see that the tunnels were man-made: they were shored up with wooden props, exactly like those she had seen at Big Pit.

Although she was hurried along, she was not treated unkindly. At one point she stumbled and sprawled onto her hands and knees. The children stopped and two of them gently helped her to her feet. The boy who had spoken earlier asked if she wanted to rest or if she would prefer to continue. Still wary of her captors but unhurt Zoe nodded and said cautiously that she was fine, so they continued their journey. They turned this way and that, climbed inclines and descended slopes. Then Zoe saw that the ceiling ahead dipped sharply. The group of children, led by the boy, slowed down and got onto their hands and knees. Zoe followed as they all crawled through a narrow, low tunnel. As the tunnel became narrower and lower, she felt horribly claustrophobic, but before long it opened into a large, spacious cave. Zoe blinked as she stood up in the brightly-lit chamber. In the centre, on a large cloth-covered throne-like chair, sat Queen Bee, who looked directly at her and said softly, 'Please come in . . . and join us.'

Chapter 10

Queen Bee

Zoe was pushed gently into the centre of the room. She saw that it really was a room. It looked as if had been carved out of the hill under the cinder tip and was a man-made chamber rather than a natural cave. The room, perhaps ten or twelve metres across, seemed to be perfectly symmetrical, and appeared to be a carefully designed living area. The walls, all the same width, joined at an odd angle. Zoe counted, turning on the spot: there were six walls, joining to make a regular hexagon. 'This is amazing,' she murmured.

Her gaze returned to Queen Bee who sat before her patiently. As their eyes met, the calm, pale face gestured with hardly a movement, other than from the large green eyes, for Zoe to sit. The other children, having also waited for a signal, sat behind Zoe in a semi-circle.

The room was lit by a number of burning torches mounted into iron wall brackets, similar to those Zoe had seen in films of castles and dungeons. Behind Queen Bee a fire glowed in a large, hexagonal metal basket and warmed the room, the hot coals red against the black of the container.

Zoe's attention was drawn back again to the gold-shawled figure of Queen Bee. Those eyes, unblinking and hypnotic, seemed to be burning into her. She felt uncomfortable and tried to look away, fearing that her thoughts were being read, but then, defiantly, she stared back. Once again her eyes flicked over the girl's odd appearance. Her long beautiful hair shone in the room's torchlight. Many coloured flowers adorned her head in a woven wreath, trails of them tumbling down into the red-gold. Her lips were starkly red in contrast to her pale, pale skin. It was then that Zoe's attention was drawn to a polished metal brooch, which pinned together the shawl. This, too, was perfectly hexagonal with a Celtic knot pattern engraved on it. Around her left wrist the girl wore a silver torque bracelet of twisted metal.

'What are you doing here?' Queen Bee asked in a calm, silky voice, unthreatening but authoritative and demanding.

'I . . . I didn't choose to be here,' Zoe said quietly. 'I fell down a hole . . . I . . . I was trying to get away from the thieves . . . Oh, and the storm. I was afraid . . . didn't know where to . . . '

'Please be easy,' Queen Bee interrupted. She spoke kindly but firmly. 'Start at the beginning and tell us your story.' She nodded to one of her companions and said, 'Bring our guest a drink please.'

One of the younger boys scurried away through a doorway, which Zoe noted was also hexagonal. Quickly, the boy returned with a metal cup.

Zoe's hands shook as she took the cup and drank. The liquid was cool and sweet. As she sipped she tried to think what it reminded her of. 'Of course,' she said aloud, 'honey!'

'Yes, honey,' Queen Bee said. 'Now, when you are ready, please tell us how you came to be here.'

The company sat, waiting patiently as Zoe started piecing together her story. Her new associates, and in particular Queen Bee, listened intently as she spoke of her journey to visit her Great Grandmother. There were murmurs and exchanged glances as she mentioned the bee sting and only Queen Bee remained impassive. Zoe told them about the Bristle Gang, and their activities in Pontystorehouse. She described her work in Cyfarthfa, and Nell's discovery of the information that had been so desperately required by Kathleen. She recounted the events leading up to the Long Pay robbery outside the Lamb public house and, hesitating for a moment, she told them how she'd foiled the plan.

It was only when Zoe mentioned the young miner, Richard Lewis, that Queen Bee showed any outward sign of interest.

'Do you know Dic Penderyn?' Queen Bee asked.

Zoe looked up sharply. This was the second time she'd heard him called Dic Penderyn, she thought.

'Well, do you know him?' Queen Bee asked again.

'Not really,' she said, "but he helped me – at the works with the Gaffer and at the scene of the robbery . . . Why do you call him Dic Penderyn?' she added. 'I know the name . . . there's something in the back of my mind, I can't think what it is . . . but he told me his name is Richard Lewis, or Dic Lewis.'

'His name is Richard Lewis, but he's known as Dic Penderyn,' Queen Bee explained.

Something was nagging at Zoe's mind. 'Is it a nickname?' she asked. 'Is he named after someone famous? I've definitely heard the name before: someone from history, but I can't think who. So, who is he named after?'

Queen Bee looked a little puzzled. 'I think his name has something to do with where he was born,' she said. 'A lot of people know Dic, but I want to know how you know him.'

Something was still niggling away at Zoe's mind. There was something about the name that she felt she should know. She just couldn't . . . She looked up and saw Queen Bee waiting for an answer. 'Sorry,' she murmured. 'Like I said, Dic helped me. Mr Abbott, the constable, wanted to arrest me but Dic stopped him and they started fighting . . . I hope he won't get into trouble.'

'Oh, he's in trouble all right,' one of the older boys commented. 'That's not the first scrape that Dic has had with Mr Abbott. A few days ago, the night of the demonstration for Parliamentary Reform, Dic was arguing with a shopkeeper who wouldn't support reform. When James Abbott and Mr Drew – he's another constable – tried to break up the meeting there was a right fuss; fighting, too, mind you. Abbott's got his eye on Dic.' The boy looked to Queen Bee when he'd finished speaking, as though it was a sign.

She nodded to Zoe. 'Please continue,' she said.

'Well, after Dic helped me, I ran,' Zoe went on. 'I didn't know where I was going. I crossed the bridge and came to the tips. I was only trying to find shelter, and to get away from that awful place; I didn't mean to . . . I mean, I . . . ' Zoe was becoming agitated.

Queen Bee came to her rescue. 'I think you've told us enough.' Her face showed faint traces of a smile. 'Welcome,' she said, 'any friend of Dic Penderyn is a friend of ours.'

Zoe was relieved: Queen Bee's words were comforting. At last she seemed to be among friends.

'Now,' Queen Bee continued, 'I think you should rest.' She turned to one of the older girls and said, 'Catrin, would you look after our friend?'

'Zoe. My name is Zoe.'

'Catrin, will look after you Zoe,' Queen Bee said, smiling. 'Now, I think we've all had enough for one night.'

Zoe looked at Catrin. They were probably about the same age, she thought. Catrin wore a simple, long brown dress made of thick wool, a bit like her own skirt, and, like most other girls and women that Zoe had seen, she wore a cream-coloured apron tied over it. Her face was bright, her cheeks rosy and her brown eyes seemed to sparkle. Catrin's long dark hair was tied back in a ponytail. As she approached, she held out her hand and smiled at Zoe. "Come with me," she said brightly.

More and more Zoe felt at ease, and sensing that she could trust these people, she obediently followed her new guardian, through a hexagonal doorway and down a short tunnel. The semi-darkness of the tunnel gave way to another torch-lit room. This, again, was hexagonal but smaller than the room from which they had just come. Around the walls were a number of hexagonal openings about two metres across and half a metre above the floor.

'This will be your cell,' Catrin said, indicating one of the openings in the wall.

'Cell?' Zoe exclaimed in alarm.

Catrin looked a little puzzled for a moment but her smile quickly returned. 'This is where you will sleep,' she explained.

Zoe stepped up to the opening and peered in. Inside lay a thick green blanket. She pulled a corner of the blanket back and was a little surprised to discover fresh cotton sheets. She chuckled with delight. 'This is a *bed*,' she said.

Catrin laughed. 'Well of course it's a bed. I told you,' she said. She showed Zoe that the sheets covered a thick mattress of canvas stuffed with straw. Zoe picked up a rolled rug that was a beautiful deep red colour. 'And this,' she said, 'is a pillow I suppose.'

Catrin seemed to take great delight in seeing Zoe's pleasure. Zoe held the rug to her face. 'Mmm, it feels so soft, and it smells wonderful . . . like an ethnic import shop,' she whispered.

'We make them here,' Catrin said. 'We weave, and we dye the fabrics with special mixtures made from plants and roots . . . and,' she added, 'Rhiannon is teaching me to embroider.'

Some of the other children came into the room and climbed into their individual, hexagonal cells. Zoe suddenly realised how exhausted she was. Catrin's manner and constant warm smile reassured her, and she pulled off her boots and shawl and climbed in amongst the soft cloth layers. The bed was really comfortable, and she stretched her weary legs and pulled the soft, rolled up rug under her head as Catrin extinguished a nearby torch. Within moments, soothed by the soft light, the comfortable mattress and the sweet smelling pillow, Zoe was asleep . . .

Her sleep was a combination of restless dreams with confusing images, and long periods of deep undisturbed blackness, and when she woke the form of Catrin came into focus, sitting patiently by her bedside and smiling as ever.

'You've slept long, although not entirely peacefully,'

Catrin murmured.

Zoe noticed that the room was still lit by torchlight. 'Is it morning or still night? I can't tell in this place,' she asked.

'It's morning, but late morning,' Catrin answered. 'Come, would you like to eat?' It was more of an instruction than a question.

Zoe climbed out of her cell bed, pulled on her boots and picked up her shawl. 'Do you think I could have a wash first, I feel really grubby . . . and I need to use the toilet,' she added.

'Of course,' Catrin chuckled. She led Zoe up an incline to a room with a number of holes in the ceiling. Zoe was delighted to see that the holes provided daylight as well as ventilation.

'Is this the toilet?' she asked. 'Where do you . . . I mean how do you . . . you know?'

Catrin pulled back one of the many coloured drapes in the room, and behind it Zoe could see a large, low pot and a taller container at its side. 'There,' Catrin said, pointing. 'And the water is in the jug.'

'Oh well,' Zoe murmured, 'I suppose it's better than having to go behind a rock . . . or in a back alley with Nell watching me.'

Catrin looked at her and added, 'You can empty it into the pit . . . just through that door . . . we use lime.'

'You're serious, aren't you?' Zoe said slowly. 'This should be an experience!'

'And when you've finished,' Catrin said cheerfully, 'you can wash in the next room.'

A little while later, and feeling a lot better, Zoe followed Catrin down to the next level, through a short tunnel and back into the large hexagonal room. She was a little surprised at the scene that greeted her.

Queen Bee was on her hands and knees, playing with the young twin girls who were laughing and gleefully jumping on her.

Zoe was taken aback. From the previous night's meeting she could hardly have imagined the majestic and statuesque Queen Bee in this very humble and ordinary activity.

The game stopped temporarily as Zoe entered. Still kneeling on the floor and smiling, Queen Bee brushed a few strands of hair from her face and spoke brightly, inviting Zoe to sit at a table. One of the small girls sidled up and, with a thumb in her mouth, sat on Queen Bee's lap, her gaze not leaving Zoe.

Catrin placed a tray on the table. It contained a metal plate of cakes. Scones, thought Zoe, or something similar anyway. Catrin waved her hand towards the food, 'Please eat . . . and drink.' Zoe didn't need to be told twice – she was famished.

'Mmm, these are delicious; what are they?' she asked.

Catrin laughed, Honey and oat cakes. It's our own special recipe.'

Queen Bee and the young twins crossed the room and joined Zoe and Catrin at the table. It was then that Zoe noticed that the table, too, was a large hexagon made of wood. Hexagonal – everything's hexagonal, Zoe thought.

Breakfast was shared and enjoyed by the five children as they relaxed, talked and laughed. For the moment Queen Bee seemed a different person; a real person and an ordinary teenager.

'Where are the others? The other children I mean,' Zoe asked, looking around the room.

'Oh, the workers you mean,' Queen Bee replied.

'Today they're all out doing their duties, in and around town.'

'What sort of duties?' Zoe asked.

'We all have our duties. The colony depends on it. We share the tasks and help each other. The workers, for instance, collect things we need such as food, clothes, wood and fuel. We also make things for our own use, or to barter with.'

'What, like the rugs on the beds?' Zoe asked.

'Yes, that's right,' Queen Bee said, 'We weave rugs and clothes . . .'

'Did you make your dress?' Zoe interrupted. 'It's so beautiful.'

Queen Bee smiled. 'Yes, I made it, and Rhiannon embroidered the patterns,' she added.

'Cool,' Zoe said. 'And what else do you do?'

'We make pots, and jewellery,' Queen Bee explained, 'oh, and we grow vegetables and herbs of course, and we take turns to prepare food and cook. Each bee has a duty to . . .'

'Each *bee*?' Zoe interrupted, incredulous.

Catrin laughed and answered the question, glancing at Queen Bee. 'Yes, we keep bees and we are like bees. We belong to this colony and work for each other.'

Queen Bee continued, 'Bees are a gift of nature. They provide us with so much, and for that we give them our blessing and hold them in the highest regard. Like the bees of nature each bee in this colony has a duty to contribute to the growing or collecting of provisions, and to ensure that cleanliness and order is maintained in our home.'

Zoe was fascinated. 'You mean . . . you live here, like bees in a colony, without grown-ups? You look after yourselves?'

Queen Bee smiled. 'We look after each other,' she said. 'We all know our place and our duties. Even Mary and Martha here have their duties. They help me tend the flowers and collect herbs, and I've started to teach them how to make pots, and how to use plants and roots to make dyes for our clothes.'

The twins jumped up and down and clapped their hands.

'Can we water the plants?' they chorused.

'Yes, in a moment,' Queen Bee laughed.

Zoe had already noticed the arrangements of cut flowers and the potted plants around the room, some of which she recognized. Many of the flowers were wild; beautiful in their variety of shapes and shades, hanging, trailing or standing proud. She looked around at their rich or subtle, bold or pastel colours, and the sweet fragrances and names conjured up vivid and poignant memories. She felt suddenly homesick: the flowers reminded her of hazy summertime walks on hot afternoons with the heat in the fields and on the dusty tracks visibly rising and shimmering, and of her family's garden in Swansea. The image blurred, and it left her uneasy.

Catrin sat silently at her side, and Queen Bee was studying Zoe's face, as if waiting for a thought process to take its course.

Zoe shook her head. 'The flowers are beautiful,' she murmured.

'This is my favourite time of year,' Catrin said. 'Everything was decorated for Beltane and we keep them here for as long as possible. I love celebrating the coming of summer.'

Zoe sat upright at the mention of Beltane. 'Wow,'

she said. 'I've always liked those Celtic stories. They're so . . . romantic and magical.'

Queen Bee leaned forward, staring at Zoe and gripping a metal goblet tightly, but Zoe didn't notice. 'Beltane!' She exclaimed. 'The festival of Beltane. I loved reading about that, especially the . . . ' She stopped in mid-sentence and looked at Queen Bee. Then she continued slowly, 'I was a May Queen once – when I was nine – at a school May Day fête . . . ' She paused and frowned as the feeling of uneasiness and confusion swept over her again. She blinked quickly, and then stared into Queen Bee's green eyes as if searching for something. Then she said quietly, 'When I saw you last night you were wearing a crown of flowers . . . you're a May Queen . . . no, no . . . you're a Beltane Queen, except this is not a school fete . . . you're doing this for real.'

Catrin laughed again. 'Of course Queen Bee is real,' she chuckled, 'and she tells us about Beltane and the other seven festivals of the year, and about growing things and about Gaia, Mother Earth." She paused, then added softly, 'Queen Bee is our mother . . . our Queen.'

Queen Bee, smiling warmly, said, 'Catrin's duty will be to look after you until you are ready to go back to where you have come from . . . or take up duties of your own in our colony.'

Zoe turned to Catrin and whispered, 'Do you think I'll ever get back home?'

Catrin looked away and said gently, 'Come on, we have work to do.'

Zoe helped her clear away the breakfast table. They went along a tunnel that led to a smaller room, which, Catrin explained was their kitchen. There were wooden tables, containers of water, knives, ladles and other utensils. At one end of the room there was a large, black stove with a round metal door at the front. Zoe could see, through the open stove door, a glowing fire inside. There was a hole in the ceiling above the stove, which she guessed was an outlet for smoke and fumes. She wondered how on earth such a bulky object as the stove had been brought to this place. Who had carried it?

Around the kitchen there were large earthenware jars and smaller pottery containers of various shapes and sizes. These, Catrin told her, were the food and honey containers. Also, there were bowls of fruit and vegetables, strings of onions hanging from ceiling beams, and sacks of flour.

The two girls chatted like old friends as they washed plates and utensils in a container of water, which had been warmed on the black stove. While they worked, Zoe's mind stacked up questions.

'How did *you* come to this place; to live here I mean?' she asked.

Catrin thought for a moment, then looked away as she started to speak. 'I've got no mam and dad, see,' she said. There was sadness in her voice, but then in a more matter of fact way she added, 'I'm just like everyone else here! None of us have a mam and dad, but Queen Bee is a mam to us. She is our mother. She brought us here see. My mam died when I was a nipper, up at Hirwaun. It was hard for her; I was the youngest of seven and . . . and Dada . . . ' She paused for a moment, her eyes misting over, staring but not seeing. Falteringly she started again. 'Dada . . . he . . . he came to Dowlais for work; puddler he was, at the iron works. He did everything for us. Mind you, there were only three of us left when we came here. Our John went to England. Sian works for a lady in Carmarthen and Joshua stayed in Hirwaun, in love he was, with a lass from the Red Lion. My closest brother, Benjamin, died of the sickness. We got by until two years ago but then things got too much for Dada.' Catrin paused. 'He went to look old. Not the Dada that I always like to remember. His face was lined and so thin; his hair almost white . . . It was too much for him on his own . . . Never complained mind you, too proud was my Dada . . . ' She began to cry quietly.

'I'm sorry,' Zoe said gently. 'I didn't mean to upset you.'

'No, I don't mind,' Catrin sniffed. 'I get like this sometimes when I think of Dada. He was so kind, always thinking of us . . . I just miss him and my home so much.'

I know the feeling, Zoe thought, but she didn't say anything. Clearly she wasn't the only one with troubles.

'Sickness got Dada too,' Catrin went on. 'In the end the pain and the cough were pitiful to see. I was almost glad to see him out of it.'

'Your father died?' Zoe asked.

Catrin nodded. 'Yes, nearly two years ago. We had to fend for ourselves then. We couldn't afford the rent and had to go out and scrape our own livings. For a week or two we stayed together, my two brothers and me that is, but it got harder. We had to go where the work was and soon we lost touch. I haven't seen them since. Anyway, I came to Merthyr and worked for a while on the barges at Ynysfach, going to the yard every morning, hoping the Barge Gaffer would give me some work. Aye, not just me though. There were

141

lots of other children and lots of fighting, mind you, to get the work. The Gaffers and Bargemen would make wagers on who would win, and then they would take on the strongest. I had to learn to fight. It was either that or not eat.' Catrin's voice dropped to a whisper. 'I fought in the loading yards on many mornings before sunlight, with the winter's frost biting into my frozen fingers, my lips cracked and bleeding, and shivering with cold. Sometimes, it was only the scrapping that kept us young 'uns warm.'

'So how did you get here, with Queen Bee?' Zoe asked.

'Well I was sleeping wherever I could, see, under canal bridges down by Ynysfach, in ditches . . . I even slept amongst the graves up at Adulum Field. The best place, mind you, was near the furnaces at the ironworks, nice and warm there. Trouble was, you had to fight for those places too. I tried to get work on the Barges down at Pontystorehouse Wharf. Life had been hard before but Pontystorehouse was like nothing I had ever known. I was frightened, and tried to keep off the streets as much as possible. I'd been warned about the gangs that roam that dreadful place. Anyway, for a couple of days, down at Pontystorehouse Wharf, I noticed a group of children watching me; just watching. They'd appear at various times of the day and just watch the wharf. Then one night as I was walking along the canal looking for somewhere to sleep, three of them stepped out in front of me. I didn't know who they were then. I thought they were a gang of Rodneys from Pontystorehouse. I'd heard of the evil things that went on and I was terrified. What could they want with me? Of course I know them now – Rhodri, Hywel and Rhiannon. They asked if I was alone. I said that I was waiting for my brothers, but they knew; they'd been watching me. Then they said, "*You're an orphan aren't you?*" I didn't say anything. Rhiannon was kind and offered me somewhere to stay. I didn't know what to do. I was tired and had nowhere to go. Before I knew it I was here. I met Queen Bee, and I know how you must have felt last night when you saw her for the first time. I felt like that too. Rhiannon looked after me . . . and I've been here ever since.'

'Do you ever go out?' Zoe asked.

'Oh yes, we all go out . . . except Queen Bee that is. We go out to collect the things we need, and also to look out for people in need of help . . . like you. Take little Mary and Martha for instance; they've been here longer than me, for over two years now. Rhiannon found them on the steps of a church one morning. They didn't know where they were or who they were. They were little more than babies. We still don't know who their mam and dad were, or why they were left. Rhiannon brought them back here and they were looked after by Queen Bee herself. She named them Mary and Martha because they had been found at the church. They were ill when they came here and they wouldn't speak, or make a sound, or eat. They just stared. But Queen Bee nursed them back to health. Now they are part of the colony, just like me.'

Catrin and Zoe were interrupted by the clamour of voices as the children Zoe had met the night before trooped into the kitchen. Catrin laughed and clapped her hands, restored now to her old self. 'And what do you have today?' she asked. 'What rich delights have you brought from the fair town of Merthyr?' The sarcasm was greeted with laughs and quips from the others. A variety of vegetables were emptied from sacks onto the tables. At once, the children started to put the new food into their designated containers. Two of the younger boys, Sean and Liam, both Irish, as Zoe had already gathered from their accents, struggled with a sack, which they emptied into a large bucket near the stove. Coal, yet more coal to keep the stove fire burning . . .

Catrin turned to Zoe. 'You've not met our workers properly have you Zoe?' she said.

'Well, I've . . . sort of . . . '

'Come on, let me introduce you,' Catrin said, taking control. 'Hywel, Rhodri and Rhiannon,' she said, pointing, 'I've told you about them, and these fine young men,' Catrin gave a sweeping gesture with her arm and pointed to four younger boys, 'are Liam and Sean, two rascals from the Emerald Isle; Peter, found in Penydarren. Oh, and here we have Will Canal. He's eight years of age and tells us he's worked on the barges since the age of four. I brought him here soon after I joined the colony.'

They all greeted Zoe warmly.

'Hi, I'm Zoe,' she said, somewhat awkward, disbelieving, but glad to have found the companionship of the Bee Children.

During that evening the group of young people enjoyed quite a feast. Catrin and Zoe helped prepare the food and the meal, like the preparation, was eaten communally. Each did his or her share and everyone enjoyed the spoils, of which there were many. Although she joined in the festivities, the songs, jokes and, of course, the eating, Zoe spent a great deal of time observing the group. What a strange collection they were, she thought – twelve, including herself, and

144

most, if not all, orphans, or at least parted in some way from their parents or family. Yet this was a family, she told herself. Everyone *seemed* happy but she couldn't help wondering what their real feelings were. And what about Queen Bee? She was such an enigmatic character. Was it she who was responsible for creating this odd colony and for excavating these rooms and tunnels? Zoe glanced around the room, beyond the circle of children. The cut flowers and hexagons were everywhere. So many questions . . . As she looked back at Queen Bee, she saw that those large, green, calm eyes in that ever-tranquil face were looking in her direction too . . .

Chapter 11

Mair Gwenyn

As the meal came to an end, the conversation around the table quietened down and gradually trailed away. Zoe looked, expectantly, at Queen Bee, who spoke now with a manner both business-like and purposeful. 'What news do you have . . . Rhodri?' she asked.

'There's unrest at the works, Queen Bee – at Cyfarthfa, Dowlais and Penydarren,' Rhodri reported.

'They say that Crawshay will reduce wages further,' Hywel added, 'and that he intends to lay more men off work at Cyfarthfa.'

Queen Bee looked thoughtful. 'Crawshay's threatened action for some time,' she commented. 'There's a slump in the industry, and less demand for iron, but there'll be trouble if he and the other masters cut all workers' wages. What do the iron workers say?'

'The Friendly Society's active, and the Union Club is calling for a meeting,' Rhiannon said. 'The members have taken an oath to stand together. They'll not accept more pay cuts. They'll take strike action against the masters if necessary.'

Rhodri shook his head. 'There'll be trouble, you'll see,' he said. 'Crawshay won't worry about it though; he'll just bring more Irish in to do the work if there's a strike . . . And the chapels are against the oath. They don't like secret oaths, and Dic says they don't like the Union Club meeting in the taprooms and Cwrw bachs – 'Dens of Iniquity', the minister at Capel Pentre calls them, and . . . 'the union clubs are of the Devil's making'– so he says.' Rhodri mimicked the minister's stentorian voice, and the older children laughed.

For the next two days, Zoe repeated her work with Catrin, while the others left to gather stores, and Queen Bee and the twins tended the flowers and herb garden. On Zoe's third day in the colony Catrin took her to the garden. This proved to be a most unexpected experience.

'We need some honey,' Catrin explained. 'Let's go to the hives.' Zoe followed her through a series of short tunnels that led upwards. Quite suddenly a tunnel opened into daylight. After so long in candle and torchlight, it took quite a while for her eyes to adjust to the dazzling sunlight, and when she'd got used to it, she could hardly believe the sight that greeted her – a garden, a real garden. Catrin explained that the garden was at the top of the hill in the oldest part of the cinder tip. The tip was continuously growing, as the ironworks spilled out its waste daily, but although the tip grew larger, they were dumping in new areas now, much closer to the Cyfarthfa works.

The sight of a garden on the top of the tip was a great surprise, but the garden itself, completely surrounded by a grass and tree covered ridge, truly amazed Zoe. Everywhere she looked she could see masses and masses of wild flowers growing in rich, dark soil rather than cinder ash. There were paths and beds, trees, shrubs and bushes. At one end there was a row of large beehives. Bees buzzed everywhere in the garden, landing on flowers and going about their industrious tasks, and birds sang in the bushes and trees. Zoe was speechless as she gazed around her. Here was a country garden *and* a wild meadow . . . at the top of an ironworks' waste tip?

After the initial surprise, she was all questions: 'Who . . . ? What . . . ? How . . . ?' she blurted.

Catrin laughed. 'I felt the same, when I first came here.'

'Yes, but how on earth . . . ?' Zoe struggled to find the right words.

'This is our garden. It's where we get our vegetables and flowers and honey. The bees are also our workers. They provide our supply of honey and wax.'

'Yes, but where exactly are we . . . I thought we were going upwards . . . and we're living under a cinder tip . . . so how?' Zoe stuttered.

'This is the highest point of the hill on which the iron waste was first dumped. The whole place is surrounded by waste. Lower down the slope, the hill is covered with a thick layer of smelted ironstone and ash from the furnaces, but underneath it was a real hill before it got covered in waste. Queen Bee has told us that this part of the tip is nearly seventy years old, and no one comes up here.'

'Yes, but this garden . . . *how*?' Zoe spluttered.

'This is the very top of the hill,' Catrin explained. 'Only parts of it were covered with ash from the original dumping, and it was a thin layer of ash at that – the works weren't very big then. Over the years, as the dumping increased further down the hill, the wind and rain have exposed the natural hilltop and trees and plants have been able to grow again.'

'Wow,' Zoe said, 'but surely you must have had

some help to develop all this.'

'Most of it is natural,' Catrin said, 'but we have lots of friends you know, like Dic Penderyn and a few other miners and workers in the town.'

'What?' Zoe said. 'Dic has been here?'

'Yes. We have to be very careful about who knows where we live, but there are those we can trust,' Catrin said.

'You mean,' Zoe persisted, 'Dic has been here recently?'

'Not for a few months, perhaps,' Catrin answered.

'Is he likely to come here again . . . soon, maybe?' Zoe asked impatiently.

Catrin looked at Zoe for a few seconds before smiling. 'Perhaps he will. He and a number of other people have a great deal of respect for Queen Bee. Now, where was I?' she said. 'The wild flowers and trees grow here naturally and, in turn, they attract wildlife including, of course, bees. Queen Bee tends the flowers, the herbs and the bees, but we all learn and help as much as we can.'

As they walked along the paths they came across a large circle of stones. Zoe noticed there were eight stones in all, each standing about three feet high. Inside the circle there was a hexagonal shape made up of smaller stones, and two fire pits, with the ashes of recent fires still visible.

'What's this?' Zoe asked.

'It's our special place,' Catrin answered. 'Each of the eight stones represents the directions, north, south, south west and so on. They also represent the eight festivals of the year.'

'What, like Beltane?' Zoe asked excitedly, glancing at the fire pits and remembering stories she'd read

149

about the festival.

'Yes, that's right,' Catrin replied.

'Wow,' Zoe murmured, 'this is awesome. So, who did all this? Don't tell me . . . Queen Bee.?'

Catrin smiled.

They sat in the garden enjoying the warm sun. Zoe found it hard to imagine the Cyfarthfa ironworks being so close by.

'Who is she . . . ? Queen Bee I mean,' Zoe mumbled, awkward about asking the question. She didn't know why she should feel that way; it was almost as if she were asking details about a sacred being. 'You mentioned earlier the respect that Dic Penderyn and some others have for her. So, who is she?'

'It's a long story,' Catrin replied, 'but I suppose you'd get to hear it anyway, so . . . '

'Come on, come on,' Zoe prompted, impatiently, 'spill the beans.'

Catrin chuckled as she looked at Zoe. 'Well, Rhiannon told me so I'm only telling you what I was told. Queen Bee's mother was a noble lady from Shropshire, even more important than gentry. The family owned lots of land in Shropshire and in Wales.'

'What was her name?' Zoe asked

'Well, we don't know, but anyway, she met a man and fell in love with him and . . . '

'Did she marry him?' Zoe asked, as Catrin hesitated.

'This is where the problem started,' Catrin said. 'The man was wealthy. He'd made a lot of money from business, iron probably, but he was from an ordinary family, not nobility like the lady, and as nobles never marry commoners, the lady's father wasn't happy, and wouldn't allow her to see the man.'

'Don't tell me,' Zoe said, 'she found out she was pregnant and . . . '

'How did you know?' Catrin gasped.

'It happens all the time in soaps.'

Catrin stared at her, puzzled. 'What do you mean?'

'Oh . . . sorry, never mind.Go on with the story.'

Catrin thought carefully before speaking. She seemed a little embarrassed. 'The lady was expecting a baby. Her father disowned her and sent her away, in shame, from the family home and she came to Merthyr.'

'Why Merthyr?' Zoe asked.

Catrin shrugged. 'Many people came to Merthyr at that time. The ironworks were growing and there was plenty of work.'

'What, you mean she *worked* here in Merthyr while she was pregnant?' Zoe asked. 'So why didn't she go and find this guy, the baby's father?'

'Because of the shame, of course,' Catrin replied. 'They weren't married.' She paused for a moment before continuing. 'It seems the man knew nothing of the lady's condition or where she was – he'd been warned off by her family. It also seems that he knew nothing of the birth of his child . . . or that the lady died shortly after the birth of a baby girl. It's probable that she died of disease from the filth of Georgetown, not being used to such conditions, or from the cold of winter, but I think she might have died from a broken heart.'

The two girls sat in silence for a few moments before Catrin took up the story again. 'In the last few weeks before the baby was born the lady was taken in by an old woman who lived in a cottage on the edge of the cinder tip, between Georgetown and Cyfarthfa. It was deep winter and the old woman took pity on her. The old woman's name was Mair Gwenyn. Some people called her The Beekeeper and others called her Mair Twp. They thought she was mad and said she was a witch. She nursed the lady and delivered the baby on a very cold, snowy morning on the first day of February . . . but sadly, the mother died.'

'So what happened to the baby?' Zoe asked.

'Mair Gwenyn looked after her and brought her up as her own daughter,' Catrin explained. 'They kept very much to themselves, with only bees and animals as their companions, and Mair taught the little girl everything she knew about bees, honey, herbs, flowers and nature. The little girl was, of course – '

'Queen Bee,' Zoe interrupted.

'Yes, Queen Bee,' Catrin said. 'About five years ago, when Queen Bee was ten years old, Mair Gwenyn died. Some people have said that Mair was over a hundred years old. Queen Bee often tells us about Mair Gwenyn and her stories of Merthyr before the ironworks were built.'

'What sort of stories?' Zoe asked, her mind buzzing. 'Give me an example.'

'How this valley had once been beautiful, or about how Merthyr got its name,' Catrin said dreamily.

'Oh yes,' said Zoe, 'the martyr Tydfil.' She thought carefully. 'I think my father told me.'

'You know the story then,' said Catrin. 'Well, when Iron came to the valley, Mair Gwenyn watched the first works start up at Dowlais . . . then the Plymouth works and eventually Cyfarthfa. She watched as the village of Merthyr grew into a town, as the noise from the ironworks became constant, and the sunny sky became hazy with smoke. The town grew and grew, as did the ironworks until, eventually, Mair's cottage and garden were surrounded by houses, the ironworks and a cinder tip. Queen Bee says Mair stood up to the threat. Her garden was the only place around here where there were still wild things. But the cottage stood in the way of the ironworks and tip. Mair refused to move. The house, you see, was her own and not rented from the ironmaster.' Catrin sighed softly and Zoe held her breath as she waited for her to continue. 'Eventually old Mair died. The Martyr Mair. She stood alone against Crawshay and the iron industry, but was no longer there to protect the old way of life and the property of her adopted daughter. As I've said, Queen Bee was ten years old at the time and wasn't able to stand up to the roughnecks from the ironworks. She was forced to leave the cottage, and had to live on the streets of Merthyr, begging and stealing like the other Rodneys. It was during that time she first met Rhiannon, another orphan.' Catrin looked at Zoe. 'Queen Bee was different from most of the other children on the streets. She was taller than the girls her age, and Rhiannon told us that her appearance made her stand out. She became a target for the gangs who take orphaned children to work for them. She was caught by one gang but managed to escape, and decided to return to Mair's cottage, but she found that the house and garden had gone, swallowed up by the tip. Queen Bee knew then that her old life had gone forever. She needed to find shelter, and not wanting to risk going back into the town she climbed up an older part of the tip and burrowed into the cinders for warmth and shelter . . . ' Catrin untied her ribbon, shook her hair free and smiled at Zoe, 'just as you did.'

Zoe waited impatiently for Catrin to go on. 'That

was the start of it,' Catrin said. 'Before long she had hollowed out a cave and, eventually, a small series of tunnels. She was careful not to go out into the town too much – only when it was necessary to get food. On one of those occasions she met up again with Rhiannon who introduced her to Hywel. Both had been living on the streets around Pontystorehouse so they joined her in the tunnels and caves and soon the colony started to grow. Other friends, like Dic Penderyn, helped build and excavate the home that we have today. Queen Bee used her knowledge of bees and flowers to build hives and to provide honey, and the colony, as you can see, is based on the way bees live in a hive . . . They soon brought in other orphans like Rhodri, Sean, Liam and the twins. At first Queen Bee went out with the others to gather food but then it became too dangerous. She is too noticeable, so she stays here. She is our Queen – that is her duty. She looks after us and organises the colony.'

'So how did Queen Bee first meet Dic Penderyn?' Zoe asked.

'It was when she first escaped from the gang in Pontystorehouse. Dic was one of the few people prepared to help her.'

Just like he helped me, Zoe thought. 'But how, exactly, did you make all the tunnels, the doorways, the rooms and everything else? You mentioned Dic and some other workers; I presume they dug most of the large tunnels, but how did they do it exactly? It all seems so fantastic.'

Catrin thought carefully before answering. 'How does a bee make honeycomb with such perfect six-sided shapes?'

'I know *why* they do it,' Zoe responded. 'It's so the

shapes will tessellate – you know, fit together easily –
but I still don't know *how* bees manage to do it.'

Catrin smiled mysteriously. 'We had help from
skilled workers, but don't underestimate Queen Bee.
There is so much that people don't understand. Look
at how ants and bees organise their lives and their
colonies. We can learn from nature, and we have.'

'Okay,' Zoe said, 'so that explains the start of the
colony, but what about Queen Bee? She's . . . different
somehow . . . '

Catrin was silent for a few moments. 'Mair Gwenyn
said that Queen Bee had special powers,' she answered
eventually. 'You know that silver bracelet that she
wears on her wrist?'

Zoe nodded. 'Yes, it's a bit like a Celtic torque. It's
beautiful.'

'Well,' Catrin continued, 'that bracelet belonged to
her real mother. It had been in her family for
generations, passed on from mother to daughter to
granddaughter. We believe it once belonged to a
powerful Welsh sorceress from Barrowmarsh in the
Marches. Mair Gwenyn told Queen Bee that she was a
special child and that she and her mother were
descended from the Sorceress of Barrowmarsh, and
that the Sorceress was descended from a special Celtic
Queen . . . a Queen with healing powers . . . a Goddess
even. Mair Gwenyn called her a *child of the Earth, the
Heavens and the elements; of times past and times to come.'*

'What did she mean by that?' Zoe asked.

'I don't know exactly, it's what Mair Gwenyn told
the Queen, and Rhiannon has told me. But Queen Bee
does have special powers. She can make things grow
easily and she talks to the bees in their hives. She
knows how to use herbs and water to heal . . . and she

also has special pictures and dreams that visit her mind.'

'*What*?' Zoe exclaimed. She felt her heart begin to beat fast. 'What do you mean, pictures?'

Catrin hesitated. 'Well,' she said slowly, 'sometimes they are in the day when she's awake and sometimes they are at night when she's asleep . . . Sometimes, she's frightened by the dreams and she wakes up.'

'Does she tell you about the dreams? You know, what they are about and so on?' Zoe asked.

'Yes, but often she can't remember the bad dreams at night. Rhiannon sits with her and we leave them in peace.'

'What about the dreams and pictures during the day?' Zoe asked.

'They are strange,' Catrin said. 'The Queen says they are pictures of things past and possibly of things to come.'

'Like what?' Zoe insisted. 'What sort of things?'

Catrin frowned, perplexed by Zoe's persistence. She chewed nervously on her fingernail. 'Well, I remember one dream she told us was about an exploding mountain by the sea, and a city of great people being buried in a river of red-hot rocks and ash.'

'Wow,' said Zoe, astonished. 'Could be Pompeii . . . Oh . . . well, there are loads of incidents I suppose. What else, Catrin?'

'Another dream was about two huge flashes in the sky at the end of a great war and many, many thousands of people were dead, injured or were very ill.'

Zoe was amazed. 'But that must be Hiroshima and Nagasaki! How would she know about that?'

Catrin chuckled. 'Then there was the very silly dream about a man dressed all in white from head to toe, jumping about and walking on the Moon!'

Zoe glanced sharply at Catrin. 'Not so silly my friend,' she said slowly.

Catrin looked knowingly at Zoe. 'To have such powers and to see such visions can, I think, be a curse. I remember your uneasy sleep . . . and . . . and the strange things you say. I think maybe you also have this curse.'

Zoe stared at Catrin uneasily. Her own thoughts and visions were becoming more mixed up and confusing with every moment that passed. Sometimes the memories of her real life with her mother and father and with her schoolfriends were vivid, and other times they seemed so hazy and unreal. She seemed to have little control over when and how these visions came into her head. She thought about Queen Bee's odd manner. 'Perhaps it is a curse, or an illness,' she said, quietly. 'But Queen Bee does seem to have power and authority over people.'

Catrin smiled. 'Yes, but remember, a queen bee in a hive has great power and influence and, yet she can be crushed so easily.' She lapsed into silence.

Zoe was stunned by the story, but then she realised it wasn't complete. 'What about Queen Bee's father, the young man?' she asked.

'We don't know anything about him, who he was, or where he is now. He might be dead for all we know,' Catrin said.

'Strange, really strange,' Zoe whispered to herself. 'I knew Queen Bee was no ordinary girl. So who, exactly, was her mother. Do you know?'

'I know no more than I've already told you. Only

Queen Bee herself knows more. She will only talk about Mair Gwenyn though. "Mair Gwenyn was my mam," is all she will say.'

Chapter 12

Questions

By six o' clock on Sunday evening, almost twenty-four hours after Zoe's disappearance, Ian reported back to Emma and Inspector Bowen. 'The store manager and workers at the supermarket have been interviewed," he said. "We've had a lot of our people down there, but no one saw or heard anything suspicious.'

'What about customers?' Emma asked.

'We've put out an appeal for anyone who was at the store from about five yesterday until closing time, and from this morning up until the time the sweatshirt was found to come forward and talk to us.'

'Good,' Emma said, 'and focus on the car park; people who used cars, especially those who parked at the bottom end.'

'And you have the forensic report on the sweatshirt?' she asked Ian.

'Yes Sergeant, it's just come through,' he replied. 'It matched the description and size perfectly. It was quite damp, especially on the inside. It's been a sunny day but it was found in a shaded spot. Forensics believe it was probably there through the night. There was human hair of two different types; one is probably Zoe's. Also, there was straw and traces of vomit . . . but no blood.'

'Thanks Ian,' Emma said. 'The lack of blood is good news . . . but if Zoe's been sick, that worries me. Anything else?' she asked.

'Steve and his team are scouring the site in the car park, and they are running DNA tests to see if anything matches up, but that will take a little while longer,' he replied.

The three detectives looked at each other. 'Are you thinking what I'm thinking?' Emma asked. The two men nodded. Emma picked up her car keys from the table and said, 'Time, I think, to visit Mr Tomos Silford again.'

'Bring him in,' Inspector Bowen said firmly, 'and make sure he knows his rights.'

Tomos Silford sat opposite Emma in the interview room of the police station, his Legal Aid solicitor next to him.

Emma switched on the digital recorder, gave the time and said who was present. 'Thank you for coming in Tom,' she began.

'What do you think I've done?' he asked immediately.

Emma smiled. 'We are not saying at this point that you have done anything. We would simply like to ask you a few questions and, hopefully, eliminate you from our enquiries,' she said.

'You've seen me once today and I told you then that I didn't know anything,' he said, agitated.

'Yes, I know Tom,' Emma said calmly, 'but a young girl has been missing since the approximate time that you were out yesterday evening. You've told us that you were at the supermarket between six and seven fifteen and that you went there in your car.'

'Yes, that's true. I've already told you that. So what?' he said.

'We've found something belonging to the missing girl, in the supermarket car park,' Emma said slowly.

Tomos shook his head and said, 'I still don't see what it's got to do with me.'

Emma considered her next question very carefully. 'Tom,' she said, 'is there anything about your visit to the supermarket that you haven't told us?'

'No, I've told you everything that I did, and after doing my shopping I came home, fed the cats, put the shopping away . . . ' he paused for a moment then continued, 'then I watched television for a while and went to bed.'

'Perhaps,' Emma said, 'you did something, maybe in all innocence, that you haven't told us about because you're afraid of what we might say.'

Tomos looked bewildered.

'What exactly are you suggesting Sergeant?' the solicitor asked.

'Well Tom,' Emma said, ignoring the solicitor and looking directly at the elderly man, 'perhaps you gave the girl a lift in your car somewhere . . . ?'

'*I haven't seen the blessed girl,*' he shouted, 'I've told you, I don't bother with people.' His hand shook as he reached for a cup of water.

'We've been told, Tom,' Emma said quietly, 'that children are frightened of you. Why is that, do you think?'

He shook his head in disbelief and slammed his hand on the desk. 'The ruddy kids around here are out of control,' he complained. 'They throw rubbish into my garden, throw stones at my greenhouse *and* at my cats . . . and when I tell them to clear off you wouldn't

161

believe the language they use.' He was becoming very agitated. 'You can't complain to their parents because they're just as bad. There's no respect and no discipline these days. If I had my way I'd bring back the cane in schools and . . . and National Service . . . the Army would sort them out.'

Emma and Ian exchanged glances.

'Tom,' Emma said softly, 'it would make things a lot easier if we could have a look at your car and take a look around your house.'

'You will have to apply for a search warrant,' the solicitor insisted, 'and I'm not sure . . . '

'Fine,' Tom interrupted, 'I have nothing to hide. Please, go ahead, search my place and you will see I have nothing whatsoever to do with all this.'

Later that evening police officers and forensic scientists searched his home, garden and garage and carried out a thorough examination of his car. By the early hours of Monday morning Emma received the report: nothing had been found. The car and the house were perfectly clean – no fibres from Zoe's clothes, no hair . . . absolutely nothing.

'What do you make of that phone call from Doctor Walsh?' Ian asked.

'A load of superstitious claptrap if you really want to know,' Emma replied. 'Okay, it is a little strange that Zoe and her great grandmother seem to suffer from a similar condition . . . '

'And they both disappear at the beginning of May?' Ian added.

'Coincidence, it has to be . . . What, you don't believe all that nonsense about Beltane and spirits and . . . and Fairy Queens do you?' Emma said.

Ian shrugged but said nothing.

'Oh come on Ian, get real.' Emma looked at her colleague, sighed and said, 'Okay, okay. Put the word around; see if there are any occult groups, or witch's covens or whatever they call them in the area . . . anything's worth a try.'

It was very late, and Emma sat behind her office desk, idly doodling on a notebook. Despite their relentless efforts, Zoe was still missing. Even with the great amount of media publicity, the endless house-to-house enquiries and the painstaking searches of the locality there was nothing to go on.

'It's an odd coincidence,' she said to Ian, who sat opposite her, his feet up on the desk, his top shirt-button undone and his tie loosened. 'You know I've been doing research recently on my family history, for the local-history course I'm taking? Well, the earliest definite record that I could find is of a Daniel Lewis who lived in the Greenhill area of Swansea. He was born in 1853. I checked the date with the parish records and,' she paused, 'I was lucky enough to find a few personal papers including a reference to his father. No names or dates, but it did say that his father had . . . *come to Swansea, as an infant in his mother's arms, from Merthyr Tydfil and shortly after the troubles at that town.'* An ironic smile lit up her face. 'couldn't find anything else on Daniel Lewis' father. Drew a blank, you see, on someone else in Merthyr with a Swansea link . . .'

Ian stood up. 'I hate waiting,' he said. 'I wish there was something more we could do.'

'I know,' Emma said as she joined him at the window, 'but I think we'd better call it a night and get some rest. We can make a fresh start in the morning.'

'Before we go Em, you might want to look at this

report you asked for – just picked it up from my emails . . . the report from the phone network company?' he said.

Emma turned to him and blinked. 'Oh yes, sorry Ian, I was miles away. Go on.'

'As you know, we've tried phoning Zoe's number, several times,' he said, 'but we keep getting a 'Number not in use' message. The network company has just sent through an updated list of outgoing and incoming calls and texts but there's still been nothing since the early afternoon of the day Zoe went missing. Absolutely nothing since then! Also, and probably more significant, is that Zoe's number is not showing up on the network, so even when we phone her number, nothing is recorded.'

'Perhaps someone's got her phone; changed the SIM card, something like that,' Emma suggested.

'Yes,' Ian said, 'well, anyway, the company will continue to monitor the account and let us know if any calls or texts appear. I won't hold my breath though.'

'It doesn't look good,' Emma agreed. 'Thanks anyway Ian. Oh, by the way, are 'uniform' still watching the family home in Swansea?'

'Yes, and lots of other places too, but sorry, nothing to report so far.'

'And,' Emma said quietly, 'I suppose Bethan and David are still at Rose Davies' house.'

Ian nodded.

'Where are you Zoe?' Emma whispered to herself. 'What *are* you doing?'

Chapter 13

Trouble brewing

Zoe worked with Queen Bee in the garden. This was to be a special day; it had been decided that she was ready to join the others in their work around town. Catrin, who had gone out much earlier to help with deliveries at the dairy in Penydarren, was to return by the end of the morning to collect her. This would be Zoe's first trip back into Merthyr since the night of the failed Long Pay robbery and she was filled with a mixture of excitement and apprehension. She thought about Pontystorehouse, the beggars and the Bristle Gang, and realised suddenly that she had not seen anyone in town who was well off. 'Do you think I'll see any of the gentry today?' she asked. 'I mean . . . like Mr Crawshay?'

'It's possible, but I doubt you'll see Crawshay,' Queen Bee replied. 'He doesn't spend too much time in town.'

'No, I suppose he sends his *slaves*,' Zoe said, scornfully.

'Servants,' Queen Bee corrected, smiling.

'Same thing,' Zoe muttered. 'It's . . . it's just that I've heard so much about him; I'd like to see him for myself. I expect he's a vicious thug but maybe he's very ordinary and . . . human . . . It makes me angry, though, thinking about him up there in his castle with his greed and wastefulness . . . '

'They are not all bad, you know,' Queen Bee said. 'A little arrogant perhaps, forgetful sometimes, even ruthless at other times. Some of the Ironmasters are sponsors of the Friendly Societies and *will* give something to help the poor of the town. Josiah John Guest over at Dowlais has had schools, a church and a library built for his workers . . .'

'Yes, I suppose so,' Zoe said, 'but there is a lot of noise about discontent, pay cuts, strikes and unions. Rhodri and the others have talked about it all.'

Queen Bee sighed. 'This really is a difficult matter, and Mr Crawshay is largely to blame, although many of his intentions were good to start with,' she said. 'The laws of this country are decided by the small number of people who are allowed to attend Parliament. To be a Member of Parliament one has to own a great deal of land. To make matters worse, only a small number of people, again wealthy landowners, are allowed to vote to decide who should be a Member of Parliament. The whole system is very unfair,' she continued, as Zoe listened. 'The Members of Parliament only look after the interests of their friends, other rich land owners. They care little for the poor and for the orphans. Parliament doesn't worry about Merthyr's poor, about diseases and starvation. Merthyr is not alone however; there are many large towns with no representatives in Parliament to look after their interests.'

'But what part does Crawshay play in all this?' Zoe asked.

'Mr Crawshay wanted to change Parliament,' Queen Bee said. 'He wanted towns like Merthyr to have their own Member of Parliament to look after our interests. He also wanted more people to be given the opportunity to vote, not just rich landowners and Lords but also businessmen, shopkeepers, doctors – the middle classes. Of course, many people started to think about this, and about their own rights, and supported Crawshay in his campaign for change.'

'What about the poorer people, the iron workers and miners and so on . . . and what about women?' Zoe asked.

Queen Bee laughed. 'Women will never have the right to vote in politics.'

'But, but . . . ' Zoe started to say, in her mind a montage of images – women waving placards and chaining themselves to railings; a woman Prime Minister. She shook her head, confused.

'Parliament won't change in our lifetime,' Queen Bee was saying. 'The rich Lords will continue to run it for as long as they can, and the workers have formed themselves into union clubs so they can protect their own interests. These unions were illegal until six years ago. Now they are allowed by law, but are hated by the iron and coal masters such as Crawshay because they give the workers the power to strike if they are not happy with the way they are treated. There are even illegal organisations called Scotch cattle.They dress in cloaks and wear the horns of a bull to scare people. They attack the homes of workers who refuse to support a strike. Recently, many workers have lost their jobs and most have had their wages cut. Shop prices remain high and many people are in debt. There is even a local court, run by Mr Joseph Coffin, which takes away the furniture of the poor people who owe money to the shops. What are the people to do? They must have food to live. The union clubs have taken an oath not to accept any more pay cuts and have threatened strike action if further cuts take place . . .'

'Well,' Zoe murmured, 'Your Mr Crawshay has really caused himself some problems. He helped start all this but now it's backfiring on him.' She lapsed into silence and then started again, 'I wish I could talk to my dad about this . . . ' She stopped abruptly, and then whispered, 'He'd be really interested . . . I wish I could just see Mum and Dad . . .' As the pain started inside her again, Zoe felt the gentle sympathetic touch of Queen Bee's hand on her arm.

They sat on a wooden bench in a small, grassed clearing just outside the large stone circle. Zoe noticed the glint of sunlight on the silver torque bracelet around the Queen's wrist. She stared at it and, once again, questions filled her mind. Who, *exactly*, is she? Sitting here she seems just like an ordinary person; she could almost be an older girl from school. Zoe went over the story that Catrin had told her about the bracelet and the Sorceress of Barrowmarsh. Does she really have special powers, she wondered. Is she descended from a sorceress and is she a witch?

'You have a very inquisitive mind,' Queen Bee said suddenly, making Zoe jump. Those large green eyes seemed, once again, to be boring holes into her thoughts.

'I . . . I was just thinking, that's all,' Zoe stammered nervously.

'There's nothing wrong with thinking,' Queen Bee smiled, 'and you want answers to questions.'

Zoe pointed to the stone circle. 'Catrin told me about your special place,' she said, 'and they look like fire pits . . . What are they for'

'We use them during our celebrations,' Queen Bee

answered. 'On Beltane night the two fires were lit and we danced between them . . . They have healing and cleansing powers.'

Zoe frowned. 'Do you really believe that?' she asked.

'Its something I've always known; something I've always done, since I lived with my old mam, Mair Gwenyn,' Queen Bee said quietly.

'You know,' Zoe said, 'I've always loved those stories about ancient festivals. In fact, I would become so engrossed in the stories that I'd have daydreams about things like living in ancient Celtic times . . . ' She chuckled. 'My dad used to say that I was away with the fairies.' She looked at Queen Bee. 'Hey,' she said, 'do you have a Maypole?'

Queen Bee smiled broadly. 'Yes, we do,' she said. 'It's a big part of Beltane.'

'And do you dance around it?' Zoe asked in delight.

'Well of course we dance around it – on the day of Beltane,' Queen Bee laughed.

'What?' Zoe gasped, 'you and the others in the colony?'

'Yes, who else do you think dances around our Maypole?' Queen Bee said.

Zoe, thinking about what she knew about maypole dancing, began to giggle. 'Do you have a boyfriend here then?' she asked.

Queen Bee lowered her eyes and blushed but said nothing

'Well, do you? You've gone all red.'

Queen Bee shook her head and smiled. 'You say some strange things Zoe,' she said.

'Never mind that,' Zoe insisted. 'Do you have a boyfriend or not?'

'No,' Queen Bee laughed, 'I don't have time for courtship,' she said.

'Oh, listen to you,' Zoe mocked. 'Courtship!'

They both laughed.

'Okay, but . . . ' Zoe began.

'Okay?' Queen Bee repeated, chuckling. 'You really do use some peculiar words.'

This sent Zoe off into more laughter. 'Okay,' she said again, wiping her eyes. 'If you had a chance to go out with – *sorry, enter into courtship* with someone . . . who would it be?'

Queen Bee thought for a few seconds, and then said quietly, 'I don't know, I really don't know.'

'Someone from this colony? Rhodri perhaps?' Zoe pressed.

'No,' Queen Bee said, without hesitation. 'This is my family . . . I'm a mother to them all.'

'But,' Zoe protested, 'you're not old enough to be their mother. You need a life of your own.'

Queen Bee gazed at the stone circle, thinking before she said, 'Once I was a young girl without concerns, now I am a mother to my children, and one day I will be a wise old woman. Three phases of life . . . like the three phases of the Moon. It's my duty to look after them: they want me to look after them. I have been given the ability to grow plants, keep bees, use herbs for healing . . . so that's what I do. Mair told me that my ancestors were great Celtic tribespeople, the Cornovii tribe. One of my forebears was the Sorceress of Barrowmarsh.'

'Yes I know, Catrin told me,' Zoe whispered.

'She was the leader of the tribe and had great powers of magic,' Queen Bee said. She lowered her eyes and added, bashfully, 'Mair said that I, too, would one day be a leader of people.'

Zoe stared at Queen Bee. She saw next to her now, not a fifteen year old girl, blushing at the thought of having a boyfriend, but a great Celtic warrior queen, with red-golden hair like the flames of a Beltane fire, and piercing green eyes . . . a new Boudicca.

Zoe stared, trance-like, as she imagined Queen Bee riding a golden chariot drawn by powerful white horses, a crown of summer flowers around her head; the Mayday Beltane queen now a Celtic warrior queen, gathering, leading and inspiring a great army.

The trance was broken by Queen Bee gently shaking her arm and saying quietly, 'Zoe?'

Zoe blinked, shook her head and looked at her companion.

'Zoe,' Queen Bee said again, 'I saw your coming.'

'Sorry?' Zoe said.

'I knew you would come to us,' Queen Bee replied. 'I didn't know who you were, but I knew a stranger, a girl, would come to us.'

'What do you mean by *I saw your coming* . . . I don't understand,' Zoe asked.

'It was on the night of Beltane eve . . . ' Queen Bee's voice was barely audible. She stared ahead as if she too were in a trance, and Zoe leaned closer to hear her words. 'It was in a dream, as I gazed at the fire. It is a time when magic is in the air; when they say spirits can cross from Annwn, Otherworld, to this, and when people can enter Otherworld, and I saw a visitor from Otherworld.' She stopped and looked directly at Zoe, her eyes searching Zoe's. 'That stranger is you, isn't it? Beltane was a short while ago . . . You've come to us from Otherworld.'

Zoe sat in stunned silence and emotional turmoil.

All sorts of confusing thoughts ran through her head. Her eyes filled with tears, and after a while she managed to whisper, sniffing, 'Otherworld? The Otherworld that you are talking about is . . . is the land of spirits and fairies. I'm from *my* world, a real world . . . although with every day that passes it seems less real . . . and I'm starting to find it difficult to remember details.' Her lower lip trembled. 'I'm frightened,' she said. 'I don't understand all this. I don't know what's dream and what's real.'

She wiped the tears from her cheeks. 'My world is a *real* world . . . I'm sure it is . . . I think,' she sniffed, frowning with uncertainty. 'But it's not *this* world.' Zoe thought about all the stories she'd read on Celtic mythology and about Beltane . . . about Pwyll, in the Mabinogi, seeing Rhiannon on her white mare at the portal to Annwn . . . about folk tales and songs of humans in the fairy world, about elves in *The Hobbit*. She looked at Queen Bee beside her and whispered, 'Is *this* Otherworld, because *my* world is real? Have you, somehow, brought me here? Sort of, I don't know, spirited me here by magical thoughts?' she asked, almost accusingly. She gasped and moved away slightly as she suddenly remembered . . . 'At *Beltane the Queen of Fairies will entice humans away to Fairyland*,' she said, slowly. 'Is that what's happened? Did I see you in one of my daydreams? Did our dreams – our visions or whatever you want to call them – get locked together in some sort of . . . I don't know . . . spiritual plane?'

'No, no Zoe. I . . . I didn't entice you . . . I wouldn't . . . I don't know . . . ' Queen Bee was becoming agitated.

'The stories say that you should not look upon the face of the Fairy Queen at Beltane . . . but if you do, you will be taken to Fairyland for seven years,' Zoe persisted. 'Is it my fault? Did I long to see the fairies in my dreams? I can remember wishing constantly as a young child to visit the land of fairies.' Her eyes were wide with wonderment as she remembered more details from a story she'd once read . . . 'Look at the Queen,' she quoted, 'and sense alone will not hold you back.'

'No, no, no,' Queen Bee protested. 'I am sometimes troubled by dreams and visions. I see things . . . strange things. Perhaps it is your world. At times I am also frightened because I don't understand. To me, what I see is Otherworld. But, Zoe,' she said, looking around, 'this world, our garden, our home, Merthyr . . . this is a real world.'

'And my world is real too. Can't you see that?' Zoe said, suddenly resentful. Seeing the look of hurt on Queen Bee's face she took a deep breath and continued more quietly, 'Perhaps there is no Otherworld . . . just one world existing in different times, but parallel – you know, at the same time?'

Zoe could see that Queen Bee was trembling as she said, 'Perhaps you're right Zoe.' She reached out and held Zoe's hand. 'My world and Otherworld . . . this is what I have always believed. It has made sense of my ability to see things and places that are strange and confusing to me, Zoe . . . ' Her voice dropped to a whisper. 'I can become frightened too, but please don't tell the others. I have to be strong for them.'

Zoe watched Queen Bee as she calmed down, and tried to imagine carrying the responsibility that Queen Bee carried. It seemed a huge weight.

Catrin returned for Zoe as arranged. They left the colony at midday and went out onto the track that led

173

to Georgetown Hill. As they walked between the rows of houses Zoe stopped suddenly to look at a low cottage with small sashed windows. As she stared, she whispered, 'Nan . . . Mum, Dad?' She ran over to the house and put her hands on the wall. She suddenly felt queasy and started to tremble as the enormity of the bizarre concept hit her. 'This is my Nan's old house, it's been demolished, it doesn't exist and yet . . . and yet I can feel it,' she said. 'What would Nan say if she knew I'd touched her house long before . . . long before she was born?' Distant memories of childhood started to take shape and come into focus. She gasped as the cloudiness in her mind disappeared and her thoughts became clear. She stared and almost expected the wooden front door to open, and to see Nan standing there smiling and saying, 'Dere 'ma cariad.'

'What's troubling you?' Catrin asked.

'I . . . I don't know what to say,' Zoe said. She looked at her dear friend, for that was how she had come to regard Catrin, even in such a short time. Dear, sweet, innocent Catrin, she thought, what can I say to her? 'I can't begin to explain. I'm not sure I can explain it to myself,' she said, thinking back to Catrin's comments about her having a gift and a curse. 'I seem to have a mixture of vivid and hazy memories about something . . . but I'm not sure what exactly.'

She didn't want to burden Catrin with the terrifying and confusing ideas that she'd been battling with, even more so since her talk with Queen Bee earlier that morning. Can you have memories of something before it happens, she wondered, or is all *this* real after all, and everything else just a premonition of the future?

'It's all to do with Queen Bee's power isn't it?' Catrin said calmly.

Zoe shrugged and nodded. 'I suppose it is,' she said.

'Come on,' Catrin said, smiling at Zoe. 'You *are* a dreamer.'

They walked down the hill, past the Court of Requests and over the dram tracks next to the canal and the *Three Horseshoes* Inn. Zoe looked around nervously as she remembered running this way after escaping from the Bristle Gang.

'Where are we going?' she asked as they stepped onto the iron bridge that spanned the River Taff.

'To the shops and the bakery in High Street; the others are working there,' Catrin replied brightly.

'What sort of work?' Zoe asked, recalling painful memories of Cyfarthfa ironworks.

'Well,' Catrin explained, 'we help the shopkeepers with chores – repairs and errands – and they give us food and other things we need . . . We don't steal, we earn everything. Queen Bee always tells us,' she continued, 'to receive a gift we must give a gift.'

A young woman approached, holding a baby in a shawl, and to Zoe's surprise she smiled and said, 'Sure, and how are the fair folk of the hills on this fine afternoon?'

Catrin greeted the woman warmly, and gently pulled back a corner of the shawl to look at the baby. 'He's growing into a fine little lad,' she said, her face beaming.

'Aye, that he is,' the woman replied, 'he's a bonny lad, sure enough, and he takes after his father.'

The woman's beautiful, dark hair shone in the sunlight and hung loosely around her shoulders, which was quite unusual, Zoe thought, as most women she'd seen were either beggars or workers with filthy, untidy hair, or women who wore bonnets or scarves, or had their hair tied back.

Catrin chatted for a few minutes and then glanced at Zoe and said, 'I'm forgetting my manners, please forgive me. This is Zoe,' she gestured with her hand, 'and this is Bridie, Bridie Lewis and young Richard Lewis, Dic's wife and son.'

Zoe was so taken aback that she stood with her mouth open. Bridie smiled and held out her free hand to Zoe who automatically reached out her own hand in response. Bridie held her hand firmly and turned it so that the open palm was facing up. She scrutinized Zoe's hand carefully and then looked into her eyes, holding her gaze for a few moments. 'Blessed be,' she said quietly, 'and if you're ever passing Ynysfach Row be sure to call on us. There will always be a welcome.' She smiled, nodded to Catrin and continued her walk across the bridge and away from the girls.

Zoe turned sharply to Catrin. 'You never told me he was married,' she said, 'and . . . *they have a baby*.'

Catrin looked puzzled. 'Why should I have told you?' she asked. 'Besides, I thought you knew, I thought everybody knew.'

'Well I didn't,' Zoe complained.

Catrin looked at her, and a knowing smile spread slowly across her face. 'Now I understand,' she said. 'You thought . . . you . . . and Dic Penderyn . . . '

Zoe felt embarrassed as her friend chuckled. 'I know, I know,' she said, 'its ridiculous . . . It's just that I . . . I . . . you know?'

'You're soft on him aren't you?' Catrin said, her eyes twinkling with amusement.

Zoe blushed. 'I know . . . I feel so stupid now,' she said.

176

Catrin put her arm around Zoe's shoulder and laughed. Zoe looked at her and also started laughing. They walked along giggling helplessly.

'My mum would have told me that it was just a crush,' Zoe said . . . *'Nothing but a silly schoolgirl crush* . . . But he is drop dead gorgeous, you have to admit,' she went on, 'and he's kind and considerate, and always cheerful, and he's my . . . my hero, and . . . ' she sighed loudly, 'and why does that Bridie have to be so pretty?' They stopped walking, held onto each other and laughed until their faces were wet with tears.

They met up with Will Canal, Rhiannon and Rhodri and spent the afternoon cleaning and sorting vegetables into baskets at a grocer's shop, and then stacking sacks of flour and sweeping up at a bakery. As she worked, Zoe thought about Bridie and how she had studied her hand. What was she doing, she wondered. Was she reading my palm? Is she a gypsy or a fortune-teller perhaps? She wished she'd asked her now.

They finished their work, and with their earnings safely stowed in sacks they crossed the bridge at Ynysgau, where she and Catrin had met Bridie Lewis earlier that day.

'Where do Bridie and Dic live?' Zoe asked.

'Just there,' Catrin answered, pointing to a row of cottages to the left of the *Three Horseshoes* Inn. 'Ynysfach Row.'

Suddenly there was a commotion: a woman was banging frantically on the front door of a cottage.

'Dic, Dic, come quickly. For pity's sake help us,' she was screaming as she banged on the door.

'Come on,' Rhodri called, and Zoe followed as they ran towards the distressed woman.

The door opened and Dic rushed out just as Zoe and her friends arrived. 'Angharad, cariad, beth sy'n bod . . . what's the matter?' Dic asked the woman urgently.

'Please Dic, you have to help us, now . . . Please!' Angharad screamed.

'Slow down, whatever is the matter, cariad?' Dic asked again, as he stepped out into the rough roadway.

'It's Dafydd,' Angharad sobbed. 'Men . . . in our house . . . animal skins, like masks . . . They've beaten my Dafydd and they say they will burn our house. Oh please Dic, for God's sake help us.' Bridie Lewis, who stood in the doorway, leapt out to catch Angharad as she staggered and nearly fell. Dic was already running down the row, shouting at the top of his voice. "Come on," he yelled as smoke started to billow from Dafydd and Angharad's cottage. Several people had come out of their houses, alerted by the commotion.

'You heard him,' Rhodri shouted, and ran after Dic. Without another thought Zoe sprinted after him and was just in time to see Dic charge through the open front door and into a wall of choking, dense smoke.

'Dafydd, Dafydd,' she heard him scream, and then Dic was coughing, spluttering and gasping for breath as he pushed on into the smoke-filled house. 'Dafydd, can you hear me?' he yelled.

From the doorway Zoe could see that the room was well alight: flames rolled up the walls towards the wooden beamed ceiling. Her stomach churned at the thought of Dic inside the burning building and, on impulse, she lunged through the burning doorway after him. She stopped and pulled her shawl over her face as the thick, black smoke swirled around and stung her eyes. There was a loud groaning through the roar of the flames, and she could just make out shapes near the open back door. 'Dic?' she yelled.

She dived forward and bumped into someone. 'Help me with Dafydd,' Dic shouted as he pulled at the arms of a man lying on the floor. Zoe also grabbed the man and together they dragged him roughly through the now burning doorway and into the small backyard. As Dic crouched, bent almost double, coughing violently, he looked up and seemed shocked to see Zoe. She couldn't believe what she had just done. Then they turned their attention to Dafydd, and Zoe was horrified to see that his face and arms were covered with blood and his left eye closed and swollen. Then, from the corner of her eye, she noticed a slight movement and turned to see an eerie figure peering over a low wall: the head was draped in brown animal hide and on top of the head were two large bull's horns.

Dic followed Zoe's gaze. 'Scotch cattle!' he gasped as the figure quickly turned and ran. A shaking hand gripped Dic's arm. Zoe looked down to see Dafydd's open eye wide with terror.

'Please Dic,' Dafydd whispered, 'Benjamin.'

Dic looked at Zoe. 'Oh no,' he said, trembling, 'the baby. I didn't think about the baby, he must still be in the house. Where, Dafydd, where?' Dic shouted as he shook the injured man.

'Upstairs,' Dafydd managed to whisper.

Without hesitating Dic hurtled through the burning back door into the smoke and flame-filled room, and once again Zoe ran after him. They tried to feel their way towards the narrow stairs but were beaten back by the intense heat. They tried again and again but the heat was too strong. A burning ceiling beam crashed down, narrowly missing Zoe. She fell to her knees and heard Dic groan, 'God give me strength.' The small room was now almost totally engulfed in flame as Dic pulled Zoe to her feet. 'Get out, for God's sake,' he shouted and he pushed her towards the back door and tried to move, once again, in the direction of the stairs. Suddenly she was grabbed from behind and hauled from the inferno, through the burning doorway and into the back yard. Rhodri and two Ironworkers from Ynysfach dived back into the house and had to use all their strength to drag Dic out as he fought and screamed to get back inside for one more rescue attempt.

Zoe saw that Dafydd's head and face were now covered with a blanket. Dic saw it too and slumped down with his back against a wall, coughing painfully from the smoke, and crying pitifully. With tears from her burning eyes streaming down her blackened face Zoe knelt and put her hand gently on Dic's shoulder.

After a few minutes he wiped his face and looked at her. 'You could have been killed in there,' he said. 'You must be mad.'

'You could have died too but you didn't give a thought to your own safety,' she replied.

'But it was dangerous . . . anything could have happened,' he said softly, 'and you're . . . you're . . .'

'What? I'm a girl? Is that what you were going to say?' she said. Coughing, she whispered hoarsely, 'I know it was dangerous . . . but I couldn't let you go in there alone, I had to try to help.'

Dic put his hand on hers. 'Diolch yn fawr, cariad,' he murmured.

Dic sat on the road, staring at the ground, as the

families of Ynysfach Row, ironworkers and furnacemen from Ynysfach and members of the Friendly Society worked to bring the ferocious fire under control. A tall man walked over to him and Zoe gasped and turned her face quickly away as she recognised the Special Constable, James Abbott.

'So, what do you know about this business Penderyn?' Abbott asked.

'I know just as much as you, Abbott,' Dic said hoarsely.

'Well it was your union people who were responsible for this . . . atrocity,' Abbott sneered.

Dic stood up and looked into Abbott's eyes. 'The people responsible,' he said, defiantly, 'are Crawshay and the other ironmasters, for cutting pay and sacking workers. That is why some men feel the need to strike, and others come into conflict with their brothers because they simply can't afford to strike. Can't you see the misery that Crawshay is causing?'

Abbott laughed. 'But it wasn't Mr Crawshay who burnt this house, it was your union,' he said.

'It wasn't the union,' Dic yelled. 'It was the Scotch Cattle as well you know, Abbott. Union members are ordinary, decent people. The Scotch Cattle are a group of thugs and ruffians. The union will have nothing to do with them.'

'You won't get away with this, Dic Penderyn. If I find that you have had anything to do with this . . . ' Abbott said menacingly to Dic as he turned to walk away.

'For God's sake man, I've just seen a friend die,' Dic cried. 'His child was in the house . . . I . . . I . . . I tried, God knows I tried to . . . '

Dic sobbed and put his hands to his face. Abbott

stared coldly, spat on the ground and hissed through clenched teeth 'Like I said Penderyn, if I find out . . . '

Bridie pushed through and ran to Dic's side. 'Take no notice. Come on, you must rest,' she said, and led her husband through the crowd of shocked, whispering neighbours. Zoe and her friends followed, and inside the cottage Bridie tore strips of linen and Rhiannon poured water from a jug into a large bowl as they prepared to treat Zoe and Dic. Apart from a few minor burns and scrapes they had both managed to escape without major injuries.

'What will happen to poor Angharad now?' Dic asked quietly. 'She's lost her husband and her child.'

Bridie was silent for a few moments, and then she spoke softly. 'It is worse I fear. Angharad was also carrying an unborn child. She will lose that too.'

Dic looked up into his young wife's sad face. 'Dafydd only did it because of his wife and child,' he whispered, as he coughed and fought back the tears. 'He refused to take the oath, and he accepted a pay cut so that he could provide *some* money for his young family. We talked about it . . . we even argued about it, but who can blame him for thinking about his family? Curse those murderous, idiot Scotch Cattle . . . and curse Crawshay, Guest, Hill and all the other masters for their greed.'

Zoe watched Dic rocking a small, wooden cradle, and turned and noticed Bridie staring at her. She looked away quickly from Bridie's gaze. Dic reached into the cradle and lifted his baby son onto his shoulder. Everyone was silent as he walked slowly around the small room singing, between coughs, a soft, melancholy lullaby:

Where have you gone you birds of Merthyr?
Where have you gone these broken years?
Leaf and life have gone together, lost in dust of
*   furnace fires.*
As I walked out one morning grey,
Upon the streets of Cardiff Town,
I thought I saw some joiners working,
The crash of hammers beating down . . .
Down, down into darkness . . .

Bridie crossed the room quickly and put her arms around her husband and baby son, and led them upstairs.

Zoe looked around at the downstairs room, which was dominated by a large open fireplace. She gazed at the smooth grey flagstone floor, at the steep, narrow staircase in the corner that led to the upper floor, and an unexpected thought popped into her mind: This is like the rooms in a cottage in . . . in St Fagan's Folk Museum.

She heard footsteps on the wooden stairs and watched silently as Bridie returned to sit with everyone around the kitchen table. Bridie said that Dic was asleep, exhausted by the ordeal. 'He doesn't sleep well,' she explained. 'For months he's been troubled by bad dreams . . . always the same dream.' She looked at Zoe as she said it.

'What sort of dreams?' Zoe asked.

'Always the same . . . always the same,' Bridie said. 'He will wake suddenly as if the devil is in him, gasping for breath and trembling, his shirt soaked in sweat . . . and it's always the same dream. He says he feels he is choking, unable to breathe, and he is falling down into blackness . . . '

Zoe sensed Bridie already knew something of her own dreams, but she didn't say anything. She was puzzled over what it was, exactly, that she ought to know about Dic. His name was well known in Wales but she still couldn't think why. I'm sure he's some sort of working-class hero, she thought. Will he become a leading political figure, a kind of nineteenth-century Che Guevara? I can't ask people what he's *going* to be because they don't know yet.

'I won't let anything happen to him,' Bridie said. 'He spends all his time helping others but, sure, I will always be here for him.'

'He's helped me, twice,' Zoe said. She looked at Bridie and asked, 'How did you meet him?'

Bridie smiled as she started to tell the story. 'It was three years ago that I first met him. I was just seventeen years old then and had come to Merthyr from Swansea with two of my sisters to look for work. Back in Swansea I had been one of a family with twelve children, living in a rented house in the Greenhill area. Some of my older brothers and sisters could remember Ireland but I was a baby when we arrived in Wales. Life was hard in Greenhill but we were a happy family – there was always someone to talk to and to share secrets and troubles with. We only moved away from Greenhill to look for work – we had no choice. I remember feeling very sad and upset at leaving Mama and Dada and all my brothers and sisters. I didn't even know then where Merthyr was,' she laughed. 'We'd all heard about the work and money available in the big, exciting Iron Town, so I set off to walk with Catherine and Molly to the *Promised Land*. The reality of Merthyr was, as we soon found out, quite different.' She smiled again and looked around the faces of her friends sitting at the table.

'So,' Zoe asked, 'did you meet Dic in Merthyr?'

'Yes,' Bridie replied, 'but he's not from Merthyr. He was born in a little cottage called Penderyn in the parish of Aberafon. He, too, came here looking for work . . . '

'Has there ever been anyone else that you know who was called Dic Penderyn?' Zoe interrupted, 'anyone from history or stories I mean . . . Is Dic named after someone?' she added, trying to explain herself.

Everyone in the room looked at each other and Bridie laughed. 'He's the only Dic Penderyn I've ever known . . . Anyway, it was at the Cyfarthfa quarry that I first saw him. I was always very slight, and Dic looked after me and helped me.' She paused for a moment then laughed and said, 'He called me his *little Irish butterfly* and told me that I was the prettiest girl in Merthyr and probably the prettiest in the whole world . . . But that's Dic for you, full of the old blarney.'

Zoe felt a pang of jealousy. She also felt slightly irritated. Why does he always have to play the gallant hero with everyone, she thought, and was immediately annoyed with herself for thinking such things . . . But she knew she couldn't help it. She also knew that whatever it was about the name Dic Penderyn, the person sleeping upstairs, the man who'd called her *cariad*, was a real person – *the* Dic Penderyn. But who was he?

Chapter 14

Old acquaintances

It was another bright May morning, and Zoe chatted with Catrin and Will as the group set off for town and their daily work tasks. They walked through Ponystorehouse, and Zoe remembered with horror her experiences there with the Bristle Gang.

Alongside the river they came across the notorious Cellars. These houses were small, cramped, decaying buildings with the lower part below street level. Peter had spent a while living here and he told Zoe that the ceilings were very low, even for a child, and that the river, with its filth and pollution, often flooded the rooms, causing disease. The Irish, Peter explained, were now the main occupants of these cellars. Zoe looked nervously at the faces of the people who sat on the cellar steps: each face contained its own story of misery, pain and suffering. No one spoke and Zoe walked on by uncomfortably.

Not all the people of Pontystorehouse, however, were resigned to defeated misery. Zoe was surprised to see street races between young urchins and men from the taprooms, with other men betting on the outcome. There were fist-fights too, ranging from out and out brawls, with biting, spitting and cursing, to more organized events, although here the rules were not much better, particularly where Welsh fought Irish. The women's clashes were worse, with people forming a circle around the fighters to prevent anyone from intervening. The women were also encouraged to inflict serious injury and to continue until one or other was unconscious.

'This is an awful place,' Zoe said to Catrin. 'It's full of beggars, criminals and drunks.'

'Yes,' Catrin agreed, 'and you have to watch out for pickpockets and wicked girls who work for the gangs and entice men so that they can rob them.'

Zoe looked at Catrin. 'So why do you come here?' she asked.

We come here to try to help people, Catrin explained. 'That's why there are lots of chapels here, too, mostly very small places, just houses really, but they go where the Church of England fears to go. Mind you, the chapels have to compete with the taprooms for singers – there's many a fine choir here in Pontystorehouse, especially after a day's shift, when throats have been lubricated by good ale. Many fine poets here too – Dai'r Cantwr for one. On a Saturday and Sunday night Pontystorehouse is the place for eisteddfodau – not the fancy ones of the gentry, but the poems and songs of working people.'

They left the slums of Pontystorehouse and walked towards the town's main square. The buildings here were taller and the road cobbled. This was where Zoe had spent the previous afternoon working. She was glad to be away from Pontystorehouse, and relieved to be in a place that seemed altogether safer and much more respectable. There were shops on both sides of the wide, spacious street displaying all kinds of goods: butchers, bakers, and a fishmonger, shoe repairers, drapers, milliners, grocers, pubs and a barbershop. Some of the shopkeepers were in their doorways talking to customers; others were carrying goods out to display on the pavement.

'Come on, this is where the work starts,' Will said to Zoe. 'Hello John,' he called out to one of the shopkeepers. The grocer returned the greeting and Zoe noticed his accent was from somewhere in the west country. In fact many of the shopkeepers in Merthyr, she learned, were from outside the town. There were many west countrymen, others from Newport, some from London, some of them Jewish. One fishmonger, known to the locals as Solly Pysgoden, seemed particularly friendly with Rhodri and asked for news.

Zoe spent the day trudging around the shops with Catrin. Some shopkeepers gave them items of food, which were immediately tucked away in the collection sacks, and others struck up deals and asked them to earn their wages. They did all sorts of jobs: tidying shelves, washing counters or windows, sweeping floors and shop fronts, and generally fetching and carrying.

Carrying their sack of earnings between them, Catrin and Zoe walked past the Castle Inn towards the place where they had arranged to meet the others, and as she peered through the window of a barbershop Zoe's heart nearly missed a beat. 'Abbott,' she gasped. Catrin glanced at her, puzzled, and then looked through the window. The barber, who was busy shaving a well-dressed gentleman and wiping his blade on a white apron, was none other than the special constable, James Abbott. 'Come on,' Zoe hissed, 'just in case he recognises me.' They hurried past the window and on to the meeting place, where they waited for the others. Rhiannon was the last to join them, having scrubbed a baker's counters in return for a small sack of flour.

It was early evening and the streets were filling with ironworkers and miners coming off shift and making for the taprooms. Rhiannon thought it might be better to avoid Pontystorehouse with their earned goods, so they set off in the direction of Ynysgau and the Iron Bridge. Zoe and Catrin stopped to rest against the wall of a cwrw-bach. Then, just as Zoe stooped to lift her sack it was torn from her grip and kicked across the street. Shocked, she looked up into an ugly, weather-beaten face. She saw a row of black and broken teeth as the man's face smiled down at her triumphantly.

'Well, well, well, if it ain't the young Rodney what squawked on us,' he said.

'Oh no,' Zoe whispered, 'please, not again.'

Catrin stood silent and frightened, as the man's eyes narrowed and he stepped closer to Zoe and pulled her towards him. His face was just an inch or so from hers and she recoiled from the stench of his foul breath.

'Please . . . no,' she whispered.

'Oh yes,' he snarled. 'You're coming with us.'

This was a nightmare-come-true, Zoe thought: they had fallen into the hands of the Bristle Gang. Before she could warn Catrin, they were both grabbed and shoved roughly through the low door of the cwrw-bach, and flung, face down, onto the floor.

Zoe felt a sharp pain as she was pulled up by the hair and pushed back against the wall. Catrin crawled over and pulled herself up alongside her. They both stood, trembling, looking around the room at their attackers. It was the Bristle Gang all right: Zoe recognised Tom, Daniel and Nell who sat with their backs against another wall. The man who had caught them stood menacing Zoe and Catrin with a long stick. Behind him sat four other men and a figure covered with a shawl. The figure stood and pulled the shawl back. It was Kathleen. She smiled softly.

Ye can leave this to me, fine boy, she said calmly. Zoe felt slightly relieved that Kathleen was there. The Irishwoman walked slowly across to them. 'Step forward please,' she said quietly. The girls obeyed. There was a sudden loud *crack* and Zoe felt a burning pain as Kathleen's hand struck her face with a vicious and terrific force. Kathleen's eyes were bulging, and her lips stretched back to reveal her clenched teeth. "You, wee lassie," she said, "are going to pay for squealing on us. No one betrays the Bristle Gang and gets away with it." She reached out and snatched the stick from the man. Zoe watched in horror as the stick came crashing down. This time the pain was in her shoulder and chest. The blow knocked her to the floor. Catrin screamed and covered her face. Kathleen stepped forward and stood over Zoe. She raised her arm high, trembling with rage as she prepared to hit her again. Tom looked horrified, Daniel buried his face in Nell's dress and even Nell winced. Zoe rolled into a ball and covered her head with her hands.

When the crash came, it was not Kathleen but the sound of a heavy stone shattering the window and sending glass and wood everywhere. The door splintered and it seemed as if an army had invaded the small room. There were screams and yells, crashes and bangs. Zoe saw fists and boots flying. She kept her head down but could hear people groaning and gasping in pain. There were sounds of breaking glass

190

and smashing furniture. She looked up again but it was difficult to see who was who as people and debris flew around the room.

Catrin suddenly appeared in front of her. 'Are you alright to move?' she asked urgently.

'I think so; I hurt a lot but I can move,' Zoe replied.

They crawled between legs, hopped over rolling and fighting bodies and made their way towards the door . . . or what was left of the door. They managed to escape onto the street where they immediately ran into Sean, Liam, Peter, Will and Rhiannon. A large crowd had gathered round to watch the sport and Solly Pysgoden had started a book, taking bets on the outcome of the brawl.

Rhiannon examined Zoe's injuries and frowned. 'Doesn't look too good, but Queen Bee will tend to you when we get home.'

Two figures darted from the cwrw-bach; they pushed through the crowd and ran into Zoe and Rhiannon. It was Nell, and Daniel.

'Nell?' Zoe whispered. Nell said nothing but just stared back. Her face had the expression of a trapped, terrified animal. Zoe noticed how weak and thin Daniel looked. She was suddenly overcome with pity for Nell. She's just like all the others who are used by the gangs, she thought, and she wondered, momentarily, what sorts of horrors Nell, Daniel and the others had had to endure in their short lives. Then she stood to one side, leaving a gap, inviting them to escape. Nell didn't move.

'Well, what are you waiting for? Go while you have the chance,' Zoe urged.

Nell looked confused and put her arm around Daniel.

191

Zoe reached out and touched Nell's arm. 'For God's sake, Nell, I'm trying to help you now . . . just . . . *just go*,' she screamed.

Nell glanced nervously at the others and then looked back at Zoe. She opened her mouth as if she were about to say something but turned abruptly and ran for the gap, dragging Daniel by the hand after her. Zoe watched as they disappeared into the crowd.

Within a few minutes the rumpus had died down. The crowd cheered as the first of the battlers emerged from the cwrw-bach. One by one the gang members were led out. Two burly miners escorted Kathleen, who continued to curse and kick. Dic Penderyn followed, his nose bleeding and his eye swollen and half closed.

'Dic?' Zoe whispered.

'Yes,' Peter explained. "I stopped to see what was keeping you and saw you being taken into the cwrw-bach. We ran to The Lamb and brought Dic and his friends . . .'

'That one,' Dic said, pointing at Kathleen, 'was worse than all the men put together.' He grinned at the crowd.

Rhodri and Hywel came out with Tom. 'This lad helped us; he's a Rodney just like us, glad to see the back of the gang,' Hywel said.

'Yes, y . . . yes, we've met. Hello Tom,' Zoe said, distractedly as she looked across to where Dic stood talking to a group of men. Tom didn't appear to notice Zoe's distraction and looked down at his feet and mumbled his hello as shyly as ever.

'Now,' said Dic, 'it's off to the constables and gaol for these, though I don't think I'd better go, as Mr Abbott will be none too pleased to see me.' Despite his injured face Dic was beaming broadly. 'Well I think I've got a quart of ale waiting for me at The Lamb; nothing like a fight to work up a thirst,' he joked. He stopped and spoke quietly to Zoe. 'I'm beginning to get worried about you, cariad,' he said quietly.

'I . . . I . . . don't know what you mean,' she said, feeling flustered.

'You get yourself into almost as many scrapes as I do,' he said.

'Are you all right? After the fire I mean . . . ' she managed to ask.

Dic frowned. 'Angharad's not . . . but yes, I'm fine . . . I'm a tough old miner.' He grinned, winked and added, 'Look after yourself cariad . . . I like a girl with a bit of spirit.'

Zoe's heart pounded and she could feel herself blushing as Dic waved to everyone and walked away.

They made their way back to the tip with their day's takings and also, it had been decided, with Tom. That evening he joined their meal and seemed to go through the same emotions that Zoe had recently gone through on meeting Queen Bee for the first time. Zoe's wounds were expertly treated and dressed by Queen Bee, who used a special ointment made up of herbs, honey and bee's royal jelly.

'It will be your job when you feel a little better,' Queen Bee said to Zoe, 'to look after Tom for a while, until he learns our ways and is able to take his place as a full worker in our colony.'

Chapter 15

Sackings

Tom joined Zoe and the others in their work around town. Their collecting became more for others than for themselves. It was late May and the weather was hot and sticky, adding to the already uncomfortable feeling in the cramped streets and cellars along the riverside of Pontystorehouse. Zoe could see that things in the town were becoming desperate. News came that Mr Crawshay, who had already reduced the wages of many of his workers, had now cut the wages of all his employees and had laid off more than eighty of his skilled workers at Cyfarthfa. The Union was calling for a meeting to ask its members to take strike action as soon as possible. That week some people in Georgetown, Penydarren, Bridge Street and Cross Street had had their few remaining possessions – their kitchen chairs, tables and even beds – taken by the Court of Requests to re-pay their shop debts. It seemed to Zoe that there were more Rodneys and more beggars than ever before.

She, Tom and Catrin worked in one of the two groups, collecting what they could and distributing it to the poor. The Friendly Society was busy, and on a few occasions Zoe saw Dic around the town, collecting, talking, persuading and giving whatever little piece of comfort he could to the less fortunate.

Zoe's group worked in the southern part of the town. With the news of trouble over pay cuts and a possible strike, and with so many people owing money, they found the collecting difficult. After a while Zoe came to expect comments such as, 'sorry, nothing today,' or, 'I'd like to, but you know how it is,' and was quite surprised when they managed to earn a few loaves of bread in return for unloading a delivery cart and stacking sacks of flour at the baker's shop in Cross Street.

The next part of their journey took them along Bridge Street, which backed onto the river. Zoe was struck by the sheer poverty of the place. The buildings, particularly the cellar dwellings, similar to those she'd seen up in Pontystorehouse, were run-down slums. The filth and stink in the street was every bit as bad as in Pontystorehouse. Children sat on the steps of the buildings just staring, and seemed too weary or perhaps simply too weak to play or run around. Zoe was shocked, even after some of the things she'd been through recently, to see young children in this state. They should be playing, or at school even. *School* . . . A sudden and vivid image came to Zoe of roller blades, her own school and her friends, but almost immediately the image started to blur and, frustratingly, her twenty-first century world again seemed to fade into a distant dream. She shuddered as a bony hand gripped her wrist. It was a child younger than herself. The girl – at least Zoe thought it was a girl – was alarmingly thin. The creature's shoulders and arms were little more than skin-covered bones and her large, dark eyes were sunk into deep sockets in a grimy, skeletal face. There were also bald patches where her hair seemed to have fallen out. There were no words, just harsh gasping breaths, and a pitiful pleading look. Zoe's mouth was dry. She stared in horror at the child-beggar.

'This really *is* my world now,' she whispered, handing over her loaf of bread. The child snatched the bread with a ferocity that startled Zoe and then ran down a flight of steps, closely pursued by a band of four or five equally ragged children.

By the time Zoe and her companions had walked back along Bridge Street towards the Iron Bridge and Ynysgau all their collected bread had gone, distributed to beggars who had fought like animals to protect their prize.

It was late afternoon and time to meet up with the others at Castle Square. As they sat on a wall opposite the Castle Inn, Zoe noticed how in this part of town carriages rolled by and pulled up, and elegantly dressed ladies and gentlemen visited the shops and walked along the pavements, mingling with the workers and poorer inhabitants of Merthyr.

'You won't see people like that in Bridge Street,' Zoe remarked to Tom, looking across at a very well-dressed group of men and women who laughed as they walked from the Castle Inn towards a waiting horse-drawn carriage. A young woman held a lace handkerchief to her face, as her gentleman escort helped her into the carriage.

Just then Zoe saw a small figure dart into the crowd outside the Castle. 'John Wylde,' she said, immediately recognizing him. As she watched closely, the boy delicately picked something from the coat pocket of an unsuspecting gentleman who was too preoccupied with his lady-friend to notice. 'Did you see that?' Zoe gasped, getting up off the wall.

Tom pulled her back firmly. 'Yes, I saw it . . . but don't get involved. If you see John Wylde then the Emperor, Shoni Sgubor Fawr is sure to be close by. He's trouble, so just stay out of it,' he advised.

Zoe looked around the group for support but Rhodri nodded his head and said, 'He's right, some things are best left alone.'

As they made their way back to the tip they saw a crowd gathering outside the Unitarian chapel in Goat Street. The people were clustered in large groups and their talk was aggressive: 'It's action we need now, not charity,' one man declared.

'Aye,' another added. 'What can the Friendly Society do? It's the Union we need now. We must stand together and show Crawshay that we mean business.' Their defiant talk continued as they filed into the chapel.

'What's going on?' Zoe whispered.

'Oh, it's the Friendly Society.' Hywel explained. 'The minister, Mr Geraint Jenkins of Aberdare, is going to talk to the ironworkers; give them some re-assurance that the Society will help, I expect.'

'Will Dic be in there do you think?' Zoe asked.

'I don't know,' Hywel said.

'Come on,' Zoe urged, 'let's go in and listen.'

Hywel shrugged his shoulders and led the way through the large wooden door at the back of the chapel. Zoe scanned the rows, hoping to catch a glimpse of Dic. Nearly everywhere downstairs and the galleries upstairs were full. According to Hywel, Mr Jenkins had a bit of a reputation when it came to politics. He had supported Crawshay's campaign for reform and was prominent in the Friendly Society movement.

'The chapels,' Hywel whispered, 'don't like trade unions and are bitterly opposed to the secret oaths taken by union members.'

Zoe only half listened, and was disappointed not to see Dic. She followed Catrin, Tom, Hywel and Peter and managed to squash into a pew. For ten minutes they listened while Zoe, who sat on the end of the row, twisted around, her eyes fixed on the doorway behind. The men raised their voices and thumped their fists into the palms of their hands as they spoke. All the talk was of pay cuts and sackings. As she watched the doorway hopefully, the noise level suddenly dropped. In seconds, the noise faded to murmurs and then to silence. Zoe turned and saw on the platform a young man in a plain, grey suit with a high, white collar and a black bow tie. He stood, staring out over the rows of people. His dark hair was curly and his eyebrows, moustache and side-burns were bushy. He was a small man but Zoe thought he seemed to have a certain power and presence that commanded the respect of everyone there. He stood, silently, and the congregation was also silent. After minutes of studying the rows of faces he spoke, softly at first. His voice was deep and rich, his face stern. As he spoke his eyes appeared to pass over every man, woman and child, at each level of the chapel. Spooky, Zoe thought: it's as if he's talking to every one of us individually.

'Friends,' he said, 'you are suffering. You are to suffer further. Every day you lose your possessions; you lose your power to buy necessary provisions.' He stopped and closed his eyes as if praying. He opened them suddenly and pointed his finger at the congregation, first to the ground floor and then to the upper tier. 'Our Lord Jesus Christ did not feel it necessary to hold on to worldly possessions,' he said slowly. 'You must not be dismayed and you must take heart. You have each other, like the good Lord's disciples. You also have your pride and your dignity.' Mr Jenkins paused and once again scanned the upturned faces before him. Then he looked searchingly at the faces peering down at him from the gallery. There was silence in the building. Suddenly his voice boomed out . . . 'What of these labour unions? What is this I hear about a secret oath? Refusing to accept Mr Crawshay's pay cuts?'

There were murmurs from the rows, yet no one voiced an opinion.

'Might I remind you what the Good Lord said?' Mr Jenkins continued. 'You should help others. The Friendly Society has done what it can. You now need to help each other. If a secret oath is necessary then so be it. If a trade union is needed then let it flourish. If a strike is what it will take to make the Ironmasters see sense . . . then do it, for I say unto you, enough is enough. Working men have been armed with the power to think. We have physical strength and must use it if necessary, but only if absolutely necessary . . . Blessed are the meek for they shall inherit the Earth,' he said quietly, his hands clasped together and his eyes looking towards the ceiling. Suddenly his voice resonated around the building: 'But think, good people; think . . . think of the poor and think of those out of work. It is your duty to help, and now the time has come . . . Justice must be done. Amen.'

There was a tremendous cheer. The sound in the small space was enormous. Mr Jenkins held up his hand for silence. 'Let us pray, and ask God for his understanding and guidance, for we are all in need of it,' he said.

They sang several rousing hymns, and even though Zoe knew few of the words she did her best to join in. The meeting ended and the people left talking excitedly. The mood had changed from anger to defiance and Zoe sensed that a fuse had been lit.

As they walked away from the chapel Catrin noticed Zoe looking around at the faces of the people in the crowd. She linked arms with her and asked, 'Are you looking for someone?'

'No,' Zoe said, sharply, flushing.

Catrin smiled knowingly, leaned closer and said, 'He's probably at home . . . with his wife.'

Things were changing in the town. Apart from the tension over sackings, the summer heat had caused disease to escalate. 'Like an angel of death,' Catrin said, 'bringing Merthyr under the shadow of its ghastly wings.'

The children's work with the poor of Pontystorehouse and Georgetown increased and it was in the cellars near the river that they came across the first case of disease. A young woman and her two children were living in a filthy, vermin-infested cellar room. Zoe had to stoop to enter the cellar. The floor itself was covered with a thin layer of stagnant water, the stench was unbearable, and made her feel ill. The woman and both children were suffering from severe sickness and stomach cramps. Zoe could tell by the way they writhed and groaned that they must be in terrible pain.

'Cholera, they say,' Catrin whispered. 'There have been a few outbreaks in Dowlais, and now it's here in Merthyr.'

They did what they could to help, bringing fruit

and a honey and herb mixture prepared by Queen Bee. Fresh water was difficult to find. They cleaned up the family and their bed as best they could, but despite their help their condition deteriorated. On the third day they learned that the mother and both children had died. Zoe cried all that night, thinking about them. The mood in the hexagonal room back at the colony was sombre and subdued. Rhodri reported that there had been several more outbreaks of cholera, mainly in Pontystorehouse but also in Penydarren and Georgetown. Again the children helped wherever possible, fetching water, washing clothes and bedding, and comforting distressed relatives. A smell of decay and an air of despair seemed to cling to the town.

They were days of glorious sunshine. Zoe got into the habit of going to the garden above the colony before breakfast to enjoy the colours and fragrances of the many wild flowers. The hazy, early-morning sun and the soothing gentle breeze gave her a feeling of well being but she also felt guilty as she thought about what the hot weather would mean for the people of Pontystorehouse and the other poor areas of the town. The cholera outbreak was growing, and Zoe and her friends worked relentlessly, collecting what they could and helping in every way possible while Queen Bee spent her days collecting herbs and honey, and preparing food packages and medicines for the needy.

Zoe found the situation distressing and frustrating: she realised that there were no hospitals and although there were a few doctors they were unlikely to be seen in Pontystorehouse. They were only for the better off. Sufferers had to rely on friends and volunteers like Dic and others from the Friendly Society. The chapel ministers did what they could but many people were without any help whatsoever.

It was early evening and, exhausted from the work and the heat of the day, Zoe trudged wearily with the others back towards the tip. 'There should be more help,' Zoe complained. 'There should be hospitals . . . people shouldn't have to live in these filthy conditions when they're ill. What we really need is . . . ' She stopped in mid-sentence. In the street in front of them people were gathering – angry people by the sound of things – men and women, shouting and cursing. Zoe held on to Catrin's arm as they approached the outer circle. Squeezing past a few people, she could see what was going on: in front of a cottage doorway she spotted an old chest of drawers and a chair. A man came out of the doorway carrying another chair and a cloth bundle. As he stepped out the mob started shouting and jeering. Zoe was pushed as the crowd surged forward.

'Leave them alone, they've done no wrong,' a woman shouted.

'Aye,' a man joined in, 'if you want furniture, take Crawshay's. He's got enough and it's his fault that we're in debt.'

There was a clamour of voices as more joined in, hurling abuse at the man holding the chair. He glared back, and two others joined him as the crowd pushed and jostled them. Another man stepped from the house and held up a large stick in a threatening way. Zoe recognised him: it was James Drew, a special constable. She'd seen him around town on a few occasions and knew that he was particularly friendly with Abbott.

The scene was becoming ugly: people were getting more and more agitated and Zoe began to feel a little nervous. She stuck close to Catrin and Rhodri as the crowd pushed and shoved. Men were cursing and yelling as the bailiffs and constable, all large, burly men, started to load their haul onto a horse-drawn carriage. A man and a thin woman stood in the doorway of the small house – she sobbed loudly, and the man put his arm around her shoulders. Their clothes were threadbare and they both looked pale and ill. Zoe gazed in pity at the distressed couple. The man clenched his fists and spoke for the first time.

'You can take my furniture but you won't destroy me . . . I'm surprised at you James Drew. I thought you were one of us. How low can you get, working for the Court of Requests?' As he spoke his shoulders shook and the tears streamed down his face.

After loading the carriage, the bailiffs backed towards it, keeping their faces to the angry crowd, which pushed against them. Zoe and her friends were caught up in the tide and were shoved closer to the carriage – close enough for Zoe to see how the four men were flushed and perspiring with fear for their own safety. But they managed to scramble aboard and with a crack of a whip the coach inched forward and then picked up speed, as the crowd spilled into the gap it left.

A few people quickly moved towards the couple, who stood clutching each other in the doorway, but all other thoughts disappeared from Zoe's mind as she saw Dic just a few metres away. He was talking to a fair-haired young man and looked sad, she thought, but then as she watched his mood seemed to change to anger. The other man also appeared to be getting angry.

'There's going to be trouble soon,' Catrin

murmured, watching Dic. 'Come on; let's get going.'

Zoe really wanted to go over and speak to Dic, or at least hang about in the hope that he would come and talk to her, but, reluctantly, she followed her companions. As they passed a low, dark alleyway someone grabbed at Zoe's arm. Expecting trouble, she wheeled around to see a familiar face, that this time was full of pleading.

'Nell,' Zoe gasped, her heart beginning to pound as she scanned the surroundings, expecting to see the Bristle Gang ready to pounce out and grab her . . . But there was no gang – only a pile of rags at Nell's feet, a pile of rags with two thin, bony hands. 'Daniel?' she whispered, looking from the bundle to Nell. 'Is he? He's not . . .?'

Nell shook her head. 'No, he's not dead,' she said quickly . . .'but please,' she begged, 'take him . . . he's sick and I can't look after him.' Tom quickly stooped to look at Daniel, and Nell pulled at Zoe's arm again: 'Please,' she begged, 'help him . . . Please?'

'Are you asking all of us to help, or just me?' Zoe asked.

Nell didn't answer the question. Instead she said, 'You're different . . . you're kind . . . You let us get away from the Bristle Gang . . .'

'Nell . . . ' Zoe whispered.

'Don't you see,' Nell managed to say, as her tears fell, 'I am free from them . . . free from all the things they did to me, and all the things they made me do – the robberies, the beatings, and . . . and using me and the other children for their . . . ' she sobbed, and whispered, 'for their pleasure . . . '

Zoe stared at her as the full implication of what she was saying started to sink in. 'Oh Nell, I – I – I never thought . . . I didn't realise . . . How could I have been so stupid?' she murmured. 'I was just thinking of myself.'

'Just take Daniel . . . please, I beg you . . . and I'll always be in your debt,' Nell said quietly. She turned abruptly, and ran down the alley.

'Nell,' Zoe called, 'don't go . . . '

She moved to follow her but Tom pulled her back. 'Let her go,' he said softly, 'just give her time.'

Zoe looked up at him. 'Tom . . . the gang . . . Did they . . . I mean, did they really . . . ?'

'I don't want to talk about it,' he said quickly, 'but you were lucky to get away when you did.' He bent down again and pulled at the rags that were wrapped around Daniel. Zoe shuddered when she saw how thin Daniel had become. He looked really ill – his eyes rolled, he was flushed and very hot, and clearly was unaware of what was going on around him. They agreed that he should be taken back to the colony, and without a word Tom picked him up and carried him.

Later, Zoe watched silently as Queen Bee sponged Daniel with cool water, trying to bring his temperature down. 'He's burning with fever,' she explained, as Daniel groaned, rocking his head from side to side and clutching his stomach. She held a cup of herb and honey-water to his lips. The Queen's large green eyes were filled with sadness as she looked up at the circle of youngsters. 'Cholera,' she whispered. She shook her head, raised a hand to her cheek and pushed back her golden red hair. Zoe noticed a solitary tear roll down her beautiful face.

Chapter 16

Bank Holiday Monday

It was just after eight o'clock in the morning on Bank Holiday Monday, and a little over thirty-six hours since Zoe's disappearance. A large crowd of press reporters, photographers and a local television crew had gathered around the entrance of the police station and jostled Emma and Ian as they got out of the car.

'Detective Sergeant' a reporter called, 'could you tell us how the case is going?'

Emma spoke to the journalist. 'We've been following several leads and have questioned a number of people about . . . '

'Is this an abduction or are we looking at something else?' another reporter interrupted.

'Well, officially,' Emma responded, 'we are still treating it as a missing person case.'

'You say *officially*, Sergeant; does that mean you suspect this is far more serious than simply missing?' the reporter persisted.

'We are following several lines of enquiry and at this stage we cannot rule out any possibilities,' she said.

'Is it true, Sergeant Lewis, that you have a suspect and that your enquiries have, shall we say, been intensely focused on this person?' a television journalist asked.

Emma thought carefully before answering. 'As I have already said, we have been following several lines of enquiry. We are not holding anyone and no charges have been brought against any person.' Emma smiled and added, 'I have nothing more to say at this point, ladies and gentleman, but we will provide a press release as soon as possible. Now, if you'll excuse me . . . '

Emma and Ian moved swiftly towards the police station entrance. Several reporters ran after them, calling out more questions, but two uniformed constables moved forward to block their way. 'That will be all for now, ladies and gentlemen' one of them said firmly.

A man standing away from the main group near the entrance, called out to Emma as the detectives walked up the steps. He called again and beckoned her with his hand. Emma recognised Jack Cooper, a journalist from the local radio station, whom she had known for a few years. She'd been grateful for his help and his extensive knowledge of the local underworld on a number of occasions. In return Jack had been able to secure some good, exclusive stories for his radio station. Emma spoke to one of the uniformed officers and Jack was quickly escorted through the double doors to join the detectives.

Jack grinned and winked at Emma. 'How's tricks, babe?' he asked.

'Never mind that,' she said, looking him up and down, 'you look . . . and smell as if you've been living rough for a month.'

He laughed loudly. His appearance was quite distinctive at the best of times, Emma thought. He stood over six feet five in height, his head was shaved and he had a large skull and crossbones tattoo on the side of his neck. Emma noticed his colossal, dirty, khaki trench coat, which he wore over a threadbare blue rugby shirt and camouflage trousers.

'You know how it is Emma, you have to be there in the thick of it if you want the best scoops and, between you and me, the chiefs at the studio are putting the pressure on for the top tales. Know what I mean?' he said.

'So,' Emma asked, 'what's the word about this case down in the gutter, where you usually hang out?'

'Not much. None of the town's *characters* are involved. Certainly no local form on this one – I thought you could tell me,' he answered, his face now serious.

'All I have is what I've told the others, Jack, which is very little at the moment,' she said.

'What about the old guy you pulled in?' he asked.

'How do you know about that?' she said in alarm. 'No descriptions were given.'

'Come on Emma,' he replied, 'you know what it's like around here: people don't miss a trick and word soon gets around. So . . . is he in the frame?'

Emma shook her head. 'Forensics have been through his things with a fine tooth comb. He's clean, Jack,' she said, 'we have nothing on him, and no one saw him with Zoe, so . . . '

'Ah but,' Jack badgered, 'off the record, what do you think?'

Emma laughed and said, 'Jack Cooper, you're a reporter: you don't know the meaning of *off the record*.'

Jack grinned. 'Okay,' he said, 'but the old guy is still a possibility, right?'

'No, Jack,' Emma said firmly, 'he's not in the frame
. . . Well not yet anyway, but I haven't said that,
understood?'

Jack nodded and Emma went on: 'We had a number
of leads and they seemed strong – still do – but it's all
circumstantial. We have no forensic evidence and no
witnesses, which adds up to
nothing . . . we have nothing to pin on him, Jack.'

'But do you think he's behind this?' Jack asked
quietly. 'Do you think he's abducted her or . . .
whatever?'

Emma shook her head. 'Come on, Jack, you should
know better than that,' she whispered. 'Until there's
some real evidence . . . '

'Yes, but . . . ' Jack insisted.

Ian coughed loudly, looked at Emma and raised his
eyebrows.

'Yes, okay Ian, I'm okay . . . I know what I'm doing,'
she said. 'Look, Jack. You know I shouldn't give you
my opinion, not even off the record . . . Now, I really
must dash: we have to go to Swansea to interview
some of Zoe's school friends.'

'Okay, thanks anyway babe,' Jack said as he turned
and walked through the door.

'I really dislike that man,' Ian fumed.

'Oh, he's harmless enough,' Emma said.

'I don't trust him, and . . . and it's just the way he
looks at you . . . ' Ian added awkwardly.

'Are you jealous?' Emma teased, grinning broadly.
'Come on Tiger, let's go.'

Arrangements had been made for Emma and Ian to
interview Zoe's friends with their parents. Emma
walked around her small office picking up the files she
would need for their visit to Swansea, while Ian read

through the email print-outs that were scattered in an untidy pile on Emma's desk.

'You ready?' she asked.

Ian nodded. 'Are we taking a pool car or yours?' he asked.

Emma picked up her VW car keys, smiled and said, 'What do you think?'

'Hello Mrs Jeffrey. Thank you for seeing us.' Emma held out her police identification as she spoke. "I'm Detective Sergeant Emma Lewis and this is Detective Constable Ian Dixon." This was their third and final scheduled call. They'd found nothing so far and Emma hoped that Sarah Jeffrey, Zoe's best friend, might be able to offer something in the way of a lead. They were shown into the neat front room and Mrs Jeffrey fidgeted with a paper tissue, looking very anxious and upset.

'As you know, Mrs Jeffrey,' Emma said softly, 'Zoe Davies has been missing since early Saturday evening. We were wondering if she's made any form of contact with Sarah, or if you, or anyone you know, has heard anything from her.'

Mrs Jeffrey sniffed, dabbed her eyes with the tissue and shook her head. 'We haven't heard a thing,' she said. 'Poor little girl . . . and what must her mother and father be going through!' She walked to the door and croaked, 'I'll just get Sarah.'

Sarah came and sat down next to her mother. She chewed her thumbnail nervously as she looked at the police officers. She seemed so young, Emma thought, so fragile, so frightened, and it brought home to her Zoe's plight. She stared at Sarah and thought, Zoe's the same age: she's not a photograph, not a statistic, not a case, but a real girl – a vulnerable, frightened child.

Sarah confirmed that there had been no phone calls, no text-messages, no e-mails, in fact no contact at all.

'Did Zoe mention any new or special friends, someone she might have met on the internet perhaps?' Emma asked.

Sarah shook her head.

'It's really important that you tell us anything you know, Sarah. No one will get into trouble for saying. We just want to find Zoe . . . So, did she ever mention anything . . . someone wanting to be her boyfriend, asking her for pictures of herself, anything like that?' Emma probed.

Mrs Jeffrey looked at Emma sharply.

'Please, this is important.' Emma assured her . . . 'So, Sarah?'

'No,' Sarah whispered. 'Honestly, Zoe never mentioned anything like that.'

'Good, I'm glad,' Emma said, 'because you know that can be very dangerous, don't you Sarah?'

Sarah nodded.

'Did Zoe ever mention running away from home . . . or going to visit someone?' Ian asked. Again, Sarah was unable to tell them anything and her mother was becoming quite agitated.

'I'm sorry Mrs Jeffrey,' Emma said. 'I know it's distressing but we do need to ask these questions.'

They declined Mrs Jeffrey's offer of a cup of tea and stood up to leave.

'Oh, such cute puppies,' Emma said, stopping as she saw in the corner of the room a box where six pups clambered over their patient and tolerant mother. 'Can I hold one?' she asked.

Sarah nodded and Emma picked up a small brown,

white-pawed puppy. The pup yawned. Emma stroked its short, soft fur, smiled and handed it back. 'Well thank you for your time Mrs Jeffrey, Sarah . . . And if you do hear anything . . . '

The front door closed as the two detectives strolled down the street to where they had parked Emma's car. Ian looked at a sheet of notepaper. 'Well, that's it for now. We've seen Nicola Stokes and Kelly Jones, and now Sarah . . . '

Emma stopped and looked at Ian. 'They quite obviously knew nothing. They weren't covering anything or anyone – they want Zoe back as much as we do . . . No,' Emma sighed, 'they haven't heard from Zoe, and *that* is really starting to worry me. You know what teenagers are like,' she added. 'They're constantly in touch with each other, texting, phone calls or email.'

'You're right,' Ian said. 'The average teenager transmits more information than MI5!'

Emma stood deep in thought for a few moments. Ian was used to this and walked silently, his hands in his pockets, not wanting to break her concentration.

Emma pulled out her car keys. 'Check all the phone company details again please Ian, and keep checking,' she said. 'I need to know the moment something shows. Come on, let's get back to Merthyr.'

'Yes, I think we'd better go: curtains are starting to twitch,' Ian said. A small group of neighbours stood talking in a huddle on the opposite pavement as the detectives got into the car and drove off up the street.

Emma changed down into second gear as they approached a roundabout, 'Quick Ian, turn the radio up,' she said, 'it's the local news.'

The music faded as the newsreader's voice cut in:

'This is 95.5FM, the Voice of the Valleys, keeping you up to date with news as it happens . . . The hunt steps up as police continue their search for missing teenager, Zoe Davies. We can now go over to our man-on-the-spot, Jack Cooper . . . '

Ian turned the volume up higher as Jack started his report. 'There have been a few dramatic developments since yesterday. So far, the police have refused to confirm local rumours that items of Zoe's clothing have been found. I can tell you, however, that a local man has been helping police with their enquiries. Earlier, a police spokesperson told me that although evidence is circumstantial, they are confident of finding a breakthrough that will lead to charges being pressed . . . '

'What?' Emma yelled, slamming her hand onto the steering wheel. 'The rat! I didn't say that . . . I'll kill him, the two-faced . . . '

Ian frowned. 'It didn't sound good,' he said.

'I'll be for the high jump now,' she moaned.

'But hey, Em, he didn't say that *you'd* said those things,' Ian pointed out.

'Oh come on, Ian,' she fumed, 'it's pretty obvious . . . The Old Man will go spare.'

'Maybe he won't even notice,' Ian said hopefully. 'But, for what it's worth, I agree with you, that man is a rat. I told you so . . . '

*　*　*

The window shattered as the stone hurtled through, sending splinters and jagged shards of glass across the windowsill, carpet and table. Tomos Silford trembled and cowered away into the far corner of the room. An upstairs window smashed and thuds could be heard at the back door. 'What's happening, what's happening?' he whimpered over and over to himself, as the sound of angry voices clamoured around the small cottage. First the police and now this. He didn't understand. He huddled up, his eyes closed, away from the frightening voices. He'd never been able to bear angry voices and had always kept away from other people. Images of his life passed through his mind in sequence, as if offering an opportunity for him to examine his righteousness; a preview of judgement day. He knew he had always led a quiet, decent life . . . I've not done anything wrong, he thought. Why is this happening? From an early age he had developed a love of gardening, and for many years he had worked for the council's Parks and Gardens department. As a young man he had been extremely shy and had found it difficult to mix with people. His job had suited him: most of the work was out in the open, with only plants, animals and the elements for company . . . away from people, from noise . . .

The noise outside the cottage increased. People were shouting abuse, calling him names, threatening him. More objects flew through the now glass-less window frame. He huddled on the floor and covered his head with shaking hands. 'Please, please,' he whimpered over and over again, 'why's this happening? Go away, and leave me alone.'

He wished he were back in happier times with his Emily . . . He'd been a widower for nearly twenty-five years and, since he'd retired he rarely ventured out of his home and garden. He preferred his own company and that of his cats and bees . . . 'The cats . . . the cats,' he whispered, suddenly remembering. He started scrambling to his feet. 'Sam, Holly?' he croaked. A bottle flew through the empty window, and as it shattered against the wall fragments of sharp glass

214

showered down on him. 'Sam, Holly . . . where are you?' he screamed.

When the first patrol car arrived in response to a call about a disturbance at a house near Cyfarthfa Castle, the police officers discovered a large, angry crowd surrounding the property. Men and women were screaming and shouting, and throwing anything they could lay their hands on at the cottage: stones, bottles, pieces of wood. A fence had been trampled to the ground as the crowd spilled over into the garden.

The car edged its way slowly through crowds, its blue lights flashing and its siren wailing. 'We'll need back-up. Get as many units here as possible . . . and quick!' the officer called into his radio.

Within a few minutes police back-up had arrived. The fence had been completely trampled and destroyed and so had most of the garden. One of the wooden garage doors had been wrenched off and the contents of the shelves of the garage were now strewn all over the lawn. As the police moved into the crowd a young man told the officers that he and his friends were searching for the missing girl.

'Aye,' said his friend, 'we knew it was Dai Twp all along!'

A group of men had just succeeded in breaking down the stout back door as police officers moved in, some with riot shields and batons. Another siren sounded as a large white van screeched to a halt alongside the patrol cars and crowd-control vehicles. The mob had grown but the police managed to force the rioters away from the cottage. A senior officer, using a megaphone, issued warnings to the crowd to disperse and, slowly, the sea of angry people was pushed further back, but not before a number had been taken off to the police van.

* * *

'Lewis, you are responsible for an innocent man being hounded, terrified and almost killed,' the Chief Constable told Emma. 'You took your opinions to the press without fully discussing the issue with your superior officers. You should know the golden rule when talking to the press: stick to the facts, and selected ones at that.'

Emma looked across the desk at her senior officers. As soon as she and Ian had arrived back at the station after their visit to Swansea she'd been summoned to the Old Man's office. She knew it was serious with the Chief Constable there. 'I regret what has happened Sir,' she said, looking at the Chief of Police, 'but I thought that we might be able to turn up a few leads by tapping into local knowledge. Jack Cooper, the journalist, has always been reliable and helpful in the past . . . And anyway, I was misquoted,' she said defensively.

'I'm sure your intentions were good, Sergeant Lewis,' the Chief Constable said, 'but you acted impetuously. At best, your actions were naïve; at worst they were reckless and irresponsible.' The Chief Constable was eager to maintain his force's good reputation. The press was going to make a lot of this incident, and so he was going to make sure someone else carried the can for the near riot. 'Nothing has been found locally and the case is not progressing,' he said. 'We need to freshen things up a bit, and so, Lewis, I've decided to take you off the case.'

'But you can't, Sir,' Emma protested.

'I most certainly can and I will,' the Chief Constable

216

said flatly.

'Okay, sir, okay . . . I made a bit of a mistake, and I'm sorry, I'll learn from this . . . Just don't take me off the case, please,' she pleaded.

'Lewis, this is not the only time your judgement has been shown to be wanting,' he said. 'It has also been brought to my attention that you have even been making enquiries about witchcraft. Sergeant, this is a serious investigation. Police work is based on fact, not on whimsical fancies.'

'Sir,' Emma protested, 'that was just an idea put forward by a professional person, a doctor. We have to consider everything, as well you know.'

'I've made up my mind,' he said. 'It's not just these issues, but you also have . . . a bit of a reputation.'

'What do you mean, a bit of a reputation? What are you trying to say, Sir?' Emma demanded.

The Chief Constable became flustered. 'You're known as something of a . . . a troublemaker,' he blurted.

Emma sat and stared at him, her mouth gaping open, momentarily lost for words. 'A troublemaker, Sir?' she finally managed to ask. 'How?'

'Well, young woman, this isn't the first time that your name has been brought to my attention. You're a good detective, I'll grant you that, but . . . but sometimes . . . ' the Chief of Police searched for the appropriate words . . . 'Sometimes you speak without thinking about the consequences.'

'On the contrary, Sir, I speak my mind. Does that make me a troublemaker?' Emma retorted.

The Chief Constable turned abruptly to Inspector Bowen. 'Inspector, would you care to add your opinion?' It was an order rather than a question.

The Inspector moved uncomfortably on his chair and tugged at his collar as he spoke. 'Well Sergeant . . .' he began, and hesitated.

Emma glared at him challengingly. 'Go on Inspector Bowen,' she said, slowly and deliberately.

'Well, there was that incident last year when you spoke out about the allegedly poor condition of the police staff canteen.'

'Oh, I get it now,' Emma said defiantly: 'I speak up for the rights of my colleagues and I'm branded a troublemaker.'

'You are not a shop steward, Lewis,' the Chief Constable informed her. 'You are a Detective Sergeant and you should behave accordingly. Now Sergeant Lewis, you are to have nothing more to do with this case. You can take a couple of day's leave . . . And that is my final word on the matter.'

Chapter 17

Disperse or suffer extreme penalties

For three days and nights Zoe, Tom and Queen Bee tended to Daniel. Zoe and Tom took turns to rest and get a few hours' sleep. Queen Bee, Zoe noticed, took very few breaks from caring for the boy, and when she did she went up to the garden. Daniel's temperature remained high and the bouts of stomach cramps continued. Queen Bee mixed several medicines of honey, royal jelly and herbs. For most of the time he was delirious and things didn't look hopeful. On the third evening, after several doses of Queen Bee's mixtures and bathing to reduce his temperature, Daniel opened his eyes. He seemed better; he even recognised Tom and everyone was relieved, no one more so than Zoe. She felt now that she had a duty to Nell and to Daniel. She felt, also, that there was a bond between them. Daniel, however, was very weak, and Queen Bee advised them that he would still need considerable rest and care.

Meanwhile expeditions into Merthyr continued for most of the group and the news the others brought back to the colony was gloomy. Zoe sat with Queen Bee and Daniel and listened carefully as Rhiannon told them that problems in the town were getting worse. There was more agitation over pay cuts, she reported, more incidents of repossessions from the hated Court of Requests, and an ever-increasing number of cases of cholera.

Zoe got up early and walked through the garden, enjoying the warmth and tranquillity of the morning. There was hardly a breeze to ruffle the masses of wild flowers and as she strolled she listened to the chirping of the birds in the small plantation of young alder trees. Directly ahead she could see the green dress and the fiery red hair of Queen Bee as she sat on the grass of the hexagon, inside the large stone circle that was marked with the points of the compass and was the centre of the garden.

Zoe hesitated, not knowing whether to approach or not, but Queen Bee looked up and smiled. 'Bore da, good morning,' she said, warmly.

Zoe beamed. She loved the way Queen Bee spoke. 'Bore da,' she responded. She also loved the way she looked – the flowers in her hair, the long green dress with embroidered red patterns on the sleeves, and the silver torque bracelet – very retro, she thought, like the hippy girls in my dad's DVD of the Woodstock music festival. She realised suddenly that she was thinking about her other world. Over the last week or so her memories had got worse. Whenever she thought about her family, her home, her friends and her school, the images rapidly faded and she found it very difficult to hang on to anything. She tried desperately to focus on what she'd just thought, but once again the details seemed to evade her . . . and the rich fragrance of the garden's flowers around her were real . . .

There was to be a meeting for the workers of Merthyr's ironworks and mines up at Waun Common near

Dowlais and some of the older members of the colony decided to go along to find out what was going on.

Zoe was excited as they set off for Dowlais. On the way they met with large crowds of people coming from every side-street – like tributaries joining a main river, she thought – and all heading in the same direction. Everyone was talking about unions, pay cuts, Crawshay, and the Court of Requests. As they approached the large, open common the groups of people merged into a single, wide column, moving with determination and purpose in the same direction, like an army on the march.

From the vantage point of a raised grassy mound Zoe and her companions could see thousands of people. 'This is just like a music festival,' Zoe said suddenly. 'It's like The Millennium Stadium or . . . or Glastonbury,' she blurted. Tom looked at her in bewilderment but Catrin had long since grown used to her strange talk. Zoe tried desperately to fix the images in her mind, but, again they seemed to fade, leaving her confused and disorientated. She shook her head and looked out at the scene in front of her. Some people were climbing up wooden steps onto a large farm cart, and she recognized a young fair-haired man as the person she had seen talking to Dic just a few days before.

'There's Dic!' Will Canal shouted, pointing to a spot near the steps, and Zoe's heart slowed and suddenly speeded up as she saw him too.

Soon, a middle-aged man walked forward and held up his hand for silence. The buzz of excitement, the shouts and the chatter died away until Zoe could hear only the gentle swish of the evening breeze in the gorse and grass. Her eyes were still on Dic who stood on the steps at the side of the cart. She heard a deep voice boom out and, reluctantly she looked away from Dic towards the centre of the platform.

'Brothers, sisters, fellow labourers,' the man said, 'welcome to this meeting, which has been called to discuss the plans that need to be made because of the intolerable situation in the ironworks of this town.'

A guest speaker from Monmouthshire was introduced. 'You must take the Union oath,' he urged. 'You must refuse, as one, to accept the masters' conditions . . . You must bring their works to a standstill . . .You must cut *their* livelihood . . . '

The crowd roared its approval.

The next person to step forward, Zoe noticed with interest, was the fair-haired young man. There was a confident, almost arrogant, air about him. He started to speak and the crowd fell silent as he also called for action to be taken against the masters. 'We must strike now,' he implored. His speech was full of passion, his voice ranging from a near whisper to a shout. The crowd loved him, cheering and clapping, hanging on his every word.

'Who is that?' Zoe asked.

'Lewsyn-yr-Heliwr – Lewis the Huntsman, or Lewis Lewis by his proper name,' Catrin answered. 'He's a haulier at Cyfarthfa, strong for the Union mind you.'

'I saw him talking to Dic the other day,' Zoe said.

'Yes,' Catrin replied, 'they know each other well,'

Zoe looked to the platform again. Lewsyn-yr-Heliwr was talking about the Court of Requests, and the crowd became noticeably agitated by his words: 'The hated Court must be abolished,' he demanded. 'It must be destroyed, never to darken our fair town

222

again.' The people were with him, roaring their agreement, shaking their fists.

As Zoe scanned the crowd she noticed a familiar figure standing near the stage. It was Abbott, the barber and special constable. He was speaking to another man and his face was stern. As she watched, the other man turned away and pushed through the crowd, moving away from the speaker's platform. Zoe watched until he disappeared from sight. What was that about? she wondered.

It was dark by the time the meeting ended. There had been many speakers and they had all given the same message: resist the Ironmasters, stick together, reject pay cuts and insist on better conditions . . . and, of course, demand the abolition of the Court of Requests.

Catrin linked arms with her as they moved off the grassy bank and joined the crowds heading back towards Merthyr. She noticed that most people were silent as they walked. Enough had been said at the meeting, she supposed, but the expressions on people's faces told her that a confrontation, and a big one at that, was on its way.

The next day the conversation was naturally about the previous evening's events. As Zoe and her companions came out of a baker's shop, a boy ran excitedly through the street calling to everyone around: 'They're at Lewis the Huntsman's; they're at Lewsyn's.'

The boy ran into Zoe and she held him at arm's length. 'What did you say?' she asked.

'They're at Lewsyn's,' he repeated, 'and they're taking things.'

'Who are?' she asked again. 'What are you talking about?'

'The bailiffs and the men from the Court of Requests . . . they're taking Lewsyn's furniture,' the boy panted. 'They're in Lewsyn's house, come on.'

By the time they reached the home of Lewsyn-yr-Heliwr a large crowd of people had gathered and were pushing towards the house. Some were chanting angrily and Zoe could feel the tension.

'Give me a lift,' she said to Tom, and with Rhiannon's help she climbed up on to his shoulders and looked across the crowded street. A few items of furniture were out on the road, but the crowd was closing in tightly around them.

'What's going on?' Rhiannon asked.

Zoe gave a running commentary to her friends below. There were a few bailiffs, she explained, and several special constables with linked arms, forming a ring around the doorway. People at the front of the crowd were pushing and swearing at the constables; James Drew and James Abbott were amongst the officials. 'Hey, there's Lewsyn,' she said. Lewsyn stood on the doorstep, prodding his finger into the chest of a man, who was, as Zoe was later to find out, Mr Bruce, the Chief Magistrate of the town.

They could all hear Lewsyn's forceful voice. 'If you take my possessions away,' he yelled defiantly, 'I will fight . . . and so will my friends.' The crowd roared in agreement. 'I am not a weak old man; I am not a widow. You've met your match, Bruce,' he said, glaring at the magistrate, their faces only inches apart.

Mr Bruce backed away. 'Don't be a fool Lewis,' he urged. 'If you do fight, you'll go to prison for resisting the law.'

'You okay, Tom?' Zoe asked.

'Don't be too long,' he replied, 'my shoulders are hurting.'

'Well you're lucky I'm just a size ten,' she said. Suddenly, alarmingly, her head was filled with the sound of howling wind, and she saw in her mind's eye images of people, places and things . . . everyday things: clothes, shops, computer screens . . . The sound stopped just as suddenly, and she shook her head. 'What did I just say?' she whispered. My other world, she thought. She felt dizzy and lurched forward. Rhiannon and Rhodri grabbed her and helped her down. Her legs were shaky and she felt disorientated.

Catrin looked very concerned. 'Are you not well?' she asked.

Zoe took a deep breath. "I'm fine, really," she said quietly. 'I don't know; something came over me suddenly.'

The noise level rose. People were shouting and yelling, and the constables were having difficulty holding them back. The argument continued between Lewsyn and Bruce, and in the end a deal was struck. Bruce agreed to leave the furniture but to take away one trunk to cover Lewis' debts.

The constables, bailiffs and magistrate made their way nervously to two carriages that were waiting nearby, and they were jostled and shoved as they pushed slowly through the crowd. Zoe watched as people spat, hissed and struck out at the retreating officers. They climbed aboard the carriages, with the crowd close behind them. Lewsyn raised a fist and shouted, 'You've not heard the last of me Bruce, and you can tell that to Joseph Coffin himself.'

Rhodri turned to the group. 'Now it's beginning.

Trouble has been predicted for a long time, but the people have never resisted the bailiffs in this way before,' he said.

Collecting became difficult for the children. They were dismayed to find that many shopkeepers had closed and boarded up their shops. On the Wednesday evening news reached them that Lewsyn-yr-Heliwr and a group of Cyfarthfa workers had marched to the nearby town of Aberdare, and, with the support of Aberdare ironworkers, had attacked the premises of a shopkeeper there. Zoe sat with Catrin, Tom and Daniel, who was over the worst of his illness and was now able to sit up. They listened in silence as Rhodri explained that the shopkeeper at Aberdare had received Lewsyn's trunk the day before for a debt owing to him. The mob, led by Lewsyn himself, Rhodri said, had recovered the trunk and had then demanded bread and cheese for everyone. The terrified shopkeeper had been forced to distribute his entire food stock before the mob had left him alone. Rhodri hesitated and then went on.

'Lewsyn and the mob are on their way back to Merthyr and they're looking for trouble,' he said. 'I've also heard that hundreds, maybe thousands of workers from the eastern valleys are on their way, and that many men from Cyfarthfa are waiting for Lewsyn's return and are pledging their support for further action.'

Zoe sat up straight as Queen Bee said, 'What about Dic Penderyn? What does he have to say about this?'

'As far as I know, Dic is not with Lewsyn, and I've not seen or heard anything of him for a few days . . . so I don't know,' Rhodri replied, 'but he won't be happy

226

about all this.'

It was Thursday, and the second day of June. Zoe and her companions were in Georgetown distributing the small amounts of food that they were able to spare, when trouble broke out. It was late afternoon and a stiflingly hot day. Peter brought the message that a very large crowd of workers, led by Lewsyn, had gathered outside the house of Thomas Lewis, the moneylender. This man, Catrin explained to Zoe, had been responsible for a great deal of the action from the Court of Requests, because of money owed to him. Zoe ran with the others across Jackson's Bridge to the area where the moneylender lived. There was a sound of breaking glass, and the crowd was chanting, shouting and pushing forward, demanding that confiscated goods be returned to their rightful owners.

Zoe turned sharply as the clatter of horses' hooves and the rumble of wheels echoed around the street. A carriage made its way steadily through the crowd. She didn't know whether to be alarmed or relieved to see several special constables walking behind it. She could see the face of Mr Bruce, the magistrate peering through the window. As the carriage came to a halt Mr Bruce climbed out, clambered up onto the driver's seat and held his hands high. Zoe strained to hear as he tried to raise his voice above the din of the angry crowd.

'We only want Thomas Lewis,' an old woman called. "Teach him to steal from widows."

The crowd chorused their approval. Zoe glanced around and gulped as she spotted the unmistakable figure of Pontystorehouse's underworld Emperor, Shoni Sgubor Fawr, and at his side as always, the young pickpocket John Wylde.

Mr Bruce waved his arms and again appealed for calm. 'Go back to your homes,' he implored. 'Take no further part in this stupidity.'

The crowd, led by Shoni, roared back defiantly.

'Then I have no alternative,' Mr Bruce shouted, 'but to read the Riot Act.' He started to read the official document, projecting his voice as best he could . . . 'In the name of the King . . . ' The crowd was ordered to disperse within the hour or 'suffer extreme penalties'.

Zoe grabbed Catrin as they were shoved forward, carried along with the surging crowd. She ducked instinctively as stones were hurled at the carriage and at Mr Bruce himself. Hastily, the coach driver sprang into action and, pushing Mr Bruce down onto the seat, coaxed the frightened horses to move forward. The carriage picked up speed and escaped from the street. Zoe and the others moved away as fights began to break out in the road between Shoni's thugs and the constables, who, realising that they were greatly outnumbered and fearing for their lives, soon turned and fled.

Zoe watched from a distance. The mob charged at the door of the moneylender's house. It splintered and disintegrated, and the rioters poured inside. Within moments, furniture, clocks, clothes and all sorts of objects were being thrown from the windows onto the street. John Wylde emerged from the doorway, grinning broadly as he stuffed several pieces of jewellery into his pockets.

Then Lewsyn came out of the house and stood on the front steps, waving his arms. 'Don't waste anymore time here lads,' he called. 'On to the Court itself. We'll visit Joseph Coffin!'

They were caught up in a stampede and swept along as the crowd rushed down the narrow street, shouting and yelling, leaving smashed furniture, glass, wood and ripped clothes strewn everywhere. Within minutes they arrived at the grey stone-fronted home of Joseph Coffin, President to the Court of Requests.

Windows were smashed and a door was battered down, and the crowd surged inside. Books and papers were thrown from the upstairs windows, much to the delight of the mob in the street. Beds, chairs and other articles were dragged from the house and out into the road. A bonfire had already been started, with the books and documents from the Court supplying the fuel. From inside the house Zoe could hear the muffled noises of shouting, crashing and hammering; it sounded as if the interior was being completely wrecked. Soon after Zoe saw smoke coming from an upstairs window. Within a few seconds flames were licking their way along a window ledge.

As the house of Joseph Coffin and the home of the Court of Requests burned and crackled, word spread that Coffin and his family had escaped earlier, before they'd arrived.

'This is only the start,' Lewsyn shouted. 'They wanted trouble, now they've got it. The magistrates and Ironmasters are talking. They've made their base at the Castle Inn and . . . I've heard that news has reached Brecon Barracks. The King's soldiers are on their way here at this very moment.'

'Look, there's Dic,' Hywel said, pointing.

Dic was standing in front of Lewsyn, talking to him heatedly. Lewsyn was red in the face, his expression angry. Dic shook his head, in exasperation Zoe thought, and as she watched he turned and left, pushing his way through the crowd. Please don't go, she thought, we need you here . . . I'm frightened . . . *I* need you here. She stared into the crowd as he disappeared from sight.

The Court House burned and Shoni Sgubor Fawr, John Wylde and their cronies stood in front of it, laughing, uninterested in politics and strikes, but delighted with the prospect of further violence and looting.

Chapter 18

The Castle Inn

'Come on,' Rhodri called. 'Let's go after Dic'
Hurriedly, Zoe and the children threaded their way
through the crowd, moving in the direction that Dic
had taken. They didn't have to go far. He hadn't left
the street but sat on the outskirts of the crowd. Behind
them the burning house crackled and spat, the acrid
smoke drifting across the road. Dic sat against a wall
with his head bowed and his face towards the ground.
This was an attitude of despair that Zoe found difficult
to see in the usually cheerful miner.

'Dic?"'she said quietly as they approached.

He looked up and nodded.

'What's going to happen now?' she asked.

He opened his mouth as if to speak, then turned his
face to one side, shaking his head . . . 'There are enough
reasonable people here . . . ' he began. 'We must talk
now. We've given the magistrates and masters a fright,
but now we must talk.'

'But the soldiers are coming,' Rhodri pointed out.

'Aye and the hot heads here will turn this into a
bloodbath,' Dic said, bitterly. He stood up, his face
searching all of theirs in turn. 'We must stop this going
any further,' he said. 'There are reasonable people here.
You must stay too. We must make the idiots see reason.

We can't win against muskets and bayonets.'

'Dic's right,' Rhiannon murmured.

Dic stood up and paced back and forth. 'We must get the majority of the crowd to see sense,' he repeated. 'We must get them to talk to Crawshay, Hill, Guest . . . and the Magistrates.'

Darkness fell and the children stayed near the burning house with the crowd, which had not dispersed, although it was now fairly quiet. Sean and Liam were sent back to Queen Bee with news. Everyone seemed to be waiting, and the quiet seemed ominous after all the noise.

Dic moved around from one group to another, talking to people, appealing to them, trying his best to persuade them to consider their actions and the consequences. Zoe watched his every move. Lewsyn approached him and the two men talked quietly. At one point Dic put his hands on Lewsyn's shoulders, his face full of pleading, and they continued to speak for a long time.

Zoe was exhausted, and with her back to a wall she dozed off, uneasily – exhausted by the fear and events of the day. The crowd, now calm, sat and waited or lay and slept under the stars of the warm June night.

Feeling cold and stiff, Zoe was woken by shouts and the sound of tramping boots. One by one, people in the crowd rose to their feet. Zoe stood and saw in the murky light of dawn red uniformed soldiers marching down the street. It was a magnificent *and* frightening sight to her.

Rhodri groaned when he saw them. 'Redcoats,' he said. This was a company of highly experienced professional soldiers from the Brecon barracks, he explained. 'It wouldn't be wise to try to fight with these people.'

Zoe chewed her lip nervously as she watched the regiment of soldiers, dressed in red tunics and kilts, carrying guns and bayonets, march through the street. A soldier, who Zoe presumed to be an officer, marched at the front and to the left of the advancing column with his sword held against his shoulder, as a sergeant bellowed out orders. The crowd, wisely, stood aside as the soldiers marched down the middle of the street.

As they passed some women taunted them: 'Where are your trews?' they sneered. 'Go and put them back on.' Several people laughed and others made abusive comments, yet no one openly challenged the Redcoats.

Zoe stood back as Will darted into the circle of friends. He had been sent to find information and now he crouched with his hands on his knees, panting as he gave his news. 'They've sent to the ironworks to tell everyone about the soldiers,' he gasped, breathlessly, 'and that reinforcements of workers are needed!'

'Come on,' Rhodri said, 'let's find Dic.'

They pushed through the crowd and after a few minutes they spotted Lewsyn. 'Get as many as possible to the Castle Inn,' Zoe heard him say to a messenger.

A second later Dic came up to Lewsyn and pleaded with him. 'see sense, man,' he said. 'You saw what those soldiers were carrying,' but Lewsyn pushed Dic away and walked off.

Zoe and her companions moved along with the crowd, following after the soldiers. She spotted Nell, standing silently, watching her.

'Nell,' she called . . . 'Come here.' Nell fidgeted nervously and made to move off as Zoe approached. 'Nell, come on . . . it's . . . it's about Daniel.'

'Leave this to me,' Tom said softly, and approached the sad, hunched figure. They spoke for a few moments, Nell looking up, glancing over Tom's shoulder at Zoe. She seemed so vulnerable and in need of a friend, Zoe thought, so she smiled at Nell. She couldn't help feeling sorry for her. As Zoe watched, she thought she saw a faint trace of a smile on Nell's face. Abruptly, Nell turned and disappeared into the moving crowd.

'What did she say?' Zoe asked as Tom rejoined them.

Tom said that he'd told Nell about Daniel's improvement.

'Yes, but what did *she* say?' Zoe asked impatiently.

'Oh, very little, but that's Nell for you. She just asked if Daniel was going to live. I told her that I thought he would . . . then she left.'

'But I thought I saw her smile at me,' Zoe said.

Tom raised his eyebrows. 'Well she does seem different . . . and I know she's very grateful to you,' he said.

'Why, what did she say?' Zoe nagged.

'Nothing,' Tom replied, 'but I saw the way she was looking . . . I know Nell . . . I just know, that's all,' he added softly.

They reached the broad street outside the Inn. This was like the Waun Common meeting all over again, Zoe thought: there were thousands packed in and more were arriving. She caught sight of Dic and together they pushed their way through to where he stood.

'The Ironmasters and the Magistrates are here,' Dic said abruptly. 'Come on let's get nearer to the front. If there's any talking to be done I don't want Lewsyn to be our only spokesman. I want to have my say.'

Zoe began to feel uneasy. The crowd pushed from behind, and facing them, with their backs to The Castle Inn, was a row of red-coated soldiers. Behind them were more soldiers – 'From the Glamorgan Militia,' Hywel said – and many special constables. The soldiers stood, unblinking, holding guns with sharp, pointed bayonets. Above them, every window was open and manned by several soldiers, their guns levelled, pointing at the crowd.

Eventually Mr Bruce, the Magistrate, appeared on the raised steps in front of the building and held his hand up. He ordered the crowd to leave but was greeted with jeers and shouts of abuse. He turned to an official, who handed him a piece of paper, then turned back to the crowd. 'I have no alternative,' he said, 'but to read to you the Riot Act . . . '

Again, as on the evening before, he declared, in the name of the King, that within one hour the crowd should disperse, or else . . . Suffer severe consequences. Mr Bruce gestured to an Army officer. 'Major Falls does not want trouble,' he said, 'but he and his men have their orders and will do their duty . . . '

The military commander gave a swift order and Zoe clearly heard the sound of sharp metallic clicks, as the hammers of the musket guns were pulled back and primed, ready to fire.

At that moment, an elegant gentleman emerged from the doorway. 'It's Anthony Hill, from the Plymouth works,' the murmur went through the crowd.

'People of Merthyr,' Hill said, 'we are prepared to listen to any reasonable demands. We want no further trouble, nor do we want unnecessary violence. I ask you to send a delegation from your ranks to meet with us, and to discuss the situation.'

There was a buzz in the crowd and Zoe saw that Lewsyn-yr-Heliwr had immediately stepped forward, calling to two other men, both of whom she had seen on the platform on the night of the Waun Common meeting. A few more men were called by Lewsyn to join the delegation. As they walked towards the steps, Dic quickly pushed forward and stood in Lewsyn's path. There was a moment of silent eye-to-eye contact, before Zoe clearly heard Dic say . . . 'If there's to be any talking, I think I should be in on it. We need to offer options.'

Lewsyn looked to the others and then nodded to Dic. The group of men approached the doorway, which was guarded by Special constables. Zoe tensed as the delegation entered the crowded passageway of the Castle Inn, where Dic came face to face with James Abbott. The Constable made a move towards the party then sneered and stood aside as the men disappeared inside.

Everyone in the crowd was becoming restless and irritable. The day was getting hot and sticky and, like everyone else, Zoe was finding the heat difficult to tolerate. The soldiers were becoming agitated as people jostled and shoved against them.

After a long and uncomfortable wait three members of the delegation appeared in the doorway, and then Lewsyn emerged, followed by the High Sheriff of Glamorgan. Zoe couldn't see Dic or any of the other delegates. The doorway at the top of the steps was crowded with officials, constables and soldiers. Lewsyn looked furious. He stepped forward and shouted, 'They will not agree to our demands now.

They want us to go away and talk later, when the situation is calmer.'

A man in the crowd shouted: 'I'll leave when my family's got enough bread to eat.'

Others joined in and the crowd started to chant, 'Caws gyda bara!' – 'Bread and cheese!'

A young man pushed through the crowd and leapt towards the steps waving a large, ragged red flag.

Several people at the doorway were shouting for calm. Josiah John Guest, owner of Dowlais works, appealed to the crowd, which grew angrier.

'Where's Dic?' Zoe asked. 'Why isn't he with Lewsyn? What's happened?' Her hands shook and her mouth was dry, and she suddenly needed the toilet.

Mr Bruce called out to the crowd that the hour since his reading of the Riot Act had elapsed and that they should now disperse. Angry people whistled, screamed and yelled as the Magistrate struggled to make his announcement heard.

Lewsyn was hoisted onto the shoulders of a man near the front. He raised his arms and shouted, in his powerful voice, to the pushing and volatile crowd: 'We wanted bread but the masters have brought soldiers against us. They are for *their* protection. But they are not protection enough! People, if you are of the same mind as me, fall on them, take their muskets away. Off with their guns. *Remember the Bastille!*'

The street outside the Castle Inn erupted into an explosion of violence, and Zoe was pushed forward several feet and almost lost her balance. She ducked, instinctively covering her head with her arms as stones, sticks, bottles and anything movable was thrown. The crowd surged forward in waves, rushing at the front rank of soldiers. The flying debris smashed windows of the Castle Inn and the adjoining buildings. Men in the crowd were lashing about wildly with wooden clubs. Zoe screamed as she was pushed this way and that, and was separated from her friends. All around her people were fighting; some were falling under foot.

A man hidden in the crowd urged the workers to get behind the soldiers. 'Take the wall and then take the Inn,' the voice yelled. 'Get behind them and they will break. Seize their arms!'

A group of soldiers, with bayonets pointing forward, rushed suddenly towards Zoe and she screamed. The crowd dispersed, running in all directions. At a command the soldiers stopped and knelt, and Zoe was left standing alone in the open space. She saw the military officer raise his arm. The guns of the soldiers on the steps, together with those of many other soldiers in the windows above, were pointing in her direction.

'At the ready . . . ' a voice commanded . . . 'Take aim . . . Fire!'

Zoe felt the heavy blow to her head, shoulders and chest at the same moment as she heard the explosion of gunfire. She staggered and fell backwards onto the road and it took a moment for her to realise that it was not gunfire but a human being who had knocked her down, just in time. She looked up in shock into the bulging eyes of Nell, only inches from her face. Nell had saved her from being shot, but now blood was trickling from Nell's mouth; she was shuddering violently, her grip on Zoe slackening. Her breathing was heavy and irregular. She raised her hand so that Zoe could see, gripped in her fingers, a small silver object. 'Your magic light,' Nell croaked. 'Tell Daniel . . .

please . . . tell my brother,' she said, but contorted in pain, she rolled from Zoe onto the blood-soaked cobbles.

Zoe stared in shock at Nell's broken and bloodstained body beside her. Without thinking she grabbed her mobile phone and scrambled up. The air was full of smoke and an odd sulphuric smell. Workers armed with wooden clubs and shovels were in a ferocious hand-to-hand fight with a group of soldiers. A few of the rioters now held guns that they had taken from the Redcoats. Zoe stood, bewildered, and watched as militiamen and special constables helped two disarmed soldiers up the steps; one of them had clearly been wounded and looked to Zoe to be in terrible distress. The military commander was hauled from the crowd and dragged up the steps away from the rioters; blood was streaming down his face and neck. A young officer quickly took command and another volley of gunfire rained down on the crowd outside the Inn. Zoe heard the crash, and saw the flash from the guns and the billowing white smoke . . . but everything seemed to be in slow motion and far away, and the sounds around her became muffled as if she were listening to them from under water. Suddenly her ears popped and again the noise was deafening as people screamed and shrieked and ran in all directions. Again, Zoe stood alone, exposed to great danger in the space they'd left. Blinking in horrified disbelief, she looked from one to another of the bodies that lay on the ground covered with blood, some with gaping wounds, their lifeless eyes staring.

This is a nightmare, she thought, it can't be real, it *isn't* real. She looked up at the rows of guns aimed in her direction. Directly in front of her soldiers were moving forward in formation, their bayonets pointing menacingly. They stopped and knelt as, behind and above them, she heard again the clicks of guns being primed in readiness to fire. Dimly she became aware of someone screaming her name, and saw Dic running from an alleyway at the side of the Inn and waving his hat frantically.

'Zoe, get down, get down,' he shouted.

Unable to react, she felt the impact as he dived at her and pushed her to the ground again. There was another explosion and billowing smoke. Coughing and breathless Zoe saw people falling behind her, struck down by the terrible gunfire. Dic was quickly on his feet, crouching over her, and she gasped for breath as he hauled her up and pulled her forward, dragging her along.

'Come on,' he shouted, 'before they reload.'

They ran as best that they could, tripping and stumbling over bodies as they picked their way through the chaos. In the smoke and confusion it was difficult to see where they were going, but it also obscured the horrible details of what was happening. There were bodies everywhere, some wounded and groaning with pain, and others obviously dead. The cobble stones were wet and slippery with blood. People, dazed and hysterical, were wandering around looking for loved ones. Many, like Zoe, were in a state of shock, not knowing what they were doing. She stopped and looked at a body near her and felt suddenly very sick.

'Come on, girl; don't stop for pity's sake. Keep going,' Dic pleaded.

They stumbled on and were quickly out of the square, running, pushing and shoving with many others. The streets were clogged as people fled from the terrible carnage: they were quarreling and fighting and falling in their panic to get away.

At last she and Dic stopped and leant against a wall.

'You get back to the tip. Hide, keep out of sight; the soldiers will be out looking now,' Dic said, between heavy, rattling gasps for breath. 'The hot-heads have muskets and many more soldiers will come and look for anyone involved.' Sweat ran down his red face, and he crouched, almost doubled with pain, trying to catch his breath. Dic was right; Zoe could hear the crack of gunfire and could see small drifts of smoke from the top of Morlais tip where the rebels were now firing on the soldiers and militia below.

'Go on, be off with you,' Dic gasped as he pushed himself from the wall and ran off.

'Dic,' Zoe cried, 'don't go . . . don't leave me . . . ' She watched despairingly as he disappeared into a crowd of people heading out of Merthyr. 'Please,' she whispered, as the tears rolled down her face, 'take me with you . . . cariad.'

She turned and walked slowly up Georgetown Hill towards the tip. She was crying pitifully as she thought of Dic Penderyn and then she stopped abruptly as she thought about the other members of the colony. The last time she remembered seeing them was when Lewsyn had emerged from the Inn and had urged the crowd to take the muskets from the soldiers. 'Where are they?' she wondered. 'Please let them be safe.' She recalled, again, the gunfire, the smoke, people falling, the blood . . . and Nell. 'Poor, poor Nell,' she sobbed suddenly, 'she saved my life . . . she did it on purpose.' She remembered Nell holding out the mobile phone . . . . 'Your Magic light.' It was still in her hand. She stared at it. She knew it belonged to her, but somehow she felt confused at the sight of it. It seemed so strange, so alien; the feeling frightened her. She pulled her skirt up to put the phone in the pocket of her jeans, and she saw that the wool of her skirt was saturated with blood . . . Nell's blood. 'No, no, no . . . *please no,*' she screamed, and she ran up the steep hill, tears streaming down her face, and Nell's blood on her hands and clothes.

Chapter 19

The capture

The others arrived at the colony shortly after Zoe. Soon they were all accounted for except Rhodri. He had been separated from them during the pandemonium outside the Castle.

All that evening Zoe sat in the middle of the hexagonal room with a few of the youngsters around her as they waited and hoped for the Rhodri's safe return. Queen Bee said nothing but paced up and down, back and forth. No one spoke; the only sound came from the soft sobs of Zoe, who was still in shock after her ordeal. Tom and Catrin sat close by, offering her comfort.

Rhiannon had taken Mary and Martha to bed. Earlier, the twins had stood wide eyed as the children had returned one by one, bruised, cut, bleeding and blood stained. Hywel had a nasty gash on his forearm, which had been dressed by Queen Bee. Peter was bruised and cut on his head from being struck by a stone. Zoe had been mostly unhurt, but when she staggered into the colony with her skirt and bodice covered in blood, she had caused quite a stir.

Zoe spent a very disturbed night, drifting in and out of sleep. When she did manage to sleep her dreams were vivid: of blazing torches all around the hills of

Merthyr, adding to the eeriness of a strangely silent town. Then, out of silence she would hear the sound of tramping feet getting louder and louder as thousands of armed men marched behind a ragged flag soaked and dripping with blood. Time and time again she would sit upright in her bed screaming, trying to wipe imaginary blood from her arms and hands.

The following morning, Saturday, there was still no sign of Rhodri. They began to fear the worst. By midday, Hywel, Rhiannon and Will were sent out to look for him, or at least to find out if anyone knew of his whereabouts. After a few hours they returned, still without Rhodri. No one, it seemed, had seen him or heard anything of him. Their mission had been difficult, they reported. The town was effectively in a state of war. The workers had re-grouped in their thousands on the outskirts of Merthyr. They were seizing weapons and arming in any way they could, Hywel said, and the troops and magistrates were expecting another onslaught and had moved their base from The Castle to a safer location in Penydarren House. Hywel paused. He shuffled uncomfortably and there was an uneasy silence. Then, looking directly at Queen Bee he said: 'Many were killed yesterday . . . Outside the Castle. Many more were wounded, they say, soldiers included. The army and magistrates won't let anyone take the bodies away. They wanted to find out who was involved . . . '

Queen Bee turned her back. After a long silence she spoke quietly. 'We must not give up hope . . . not until we know for sure.'

On the following day, Sunday, a few of the children were sent out again to see what they could find, but returned hours later with nothing – the story was much the same as the day before, and it remained that way most of the week. Their work had come to a halt. Daniel was much better but still very weak, and the time was not right, Queen Bee decided, for him to be told about his sister, Nell.

After several days they were shocked to hear a sudden noise from the tunnel leading into the colony. There, to everyone's amazement, stood Rhodri, a filthy, bloodstained bandage around his head, his clothes dirty and ragged.

'Rhodri!' Rhiannon shouted as she raced across the room and flung her arms around him. They all gathered round the weary figure, firing one question after another at him. After having had his wounds cleaned and dressed, Rhodri told his story: Like many others he had fled from the guns and had been caught up in a group of workers who had just run, as far and as fast as possible, not knowing what dangers might await them if they returned to Merthyr. On the Saturday, the mood had become more confident and defiant. They'd found or stolen guns, swords, pitchforks and knives. The men began to prepare a counter-attack on the soldiers. The same day, they attacked a troop of Yeomanry who were on their way from Swansea to reinforce the soldiers in Merthyr. The workers outnumbered the soldiers, and they took their guns, sabres and ammunition. Now heavily armed, the men marched to the outskirts of the town, where they met with another large and armed group preparing for a further attack.

Rhodri had joined many others on Waun Common, where Merthyr's workers re-grouped and were armed and formed into military battalions. He was given a musket, powder and shot and had been trained in how to use them. Shenko, the gaffer from the Cyfarthfa mines, was the leader of Rhodri's battalion. The rebels prepared for battle, and it had looked as if there would be a major clash, as Redcoats were arriving from several big towns and cities across Britain to deal with the incident. The Government was calling the events in Merthyr a riot and a disturbance, but it deployed troops in preparation for war.

A number of moderate men, though Dic was not amongst them, had talked with the masters and had eventually persuaded the rioters not to attack Penydarren. A delegation of workers had been asked to go to Penydarren House and they had returned to the main body of rebels with Crawshay's offer to restore the level of wages. This had divided the workers. Some wanted to accept the offer but others demanded pay increases and reform. Some workers left the ranks and headed for home satisfied with the offer and clearly worried by the threat of more soldiers arriving. Sensing the divide and fearing the loss of momentum, Lewsyn and Shenko urged the armed battalions to march from Dowlais to Penydarren.

'We marched in columns, four abreast,' Rhodri whispered, staring ahead as he relived the moment. 'Down the hill we went on the way to Penydarren. Then we saw it – a solid wall of red! The 93rd Highlanders were formed in two lines across the road; the front line was kneeling; their muskets pointing at us, the ones at the back with bayonets at the ready. We stopped and faced the soldiers. Then we saw more soldiers in doorways, windows and behind fences of the buildings on both sides. Their leader introduced himself as Captain Morgan and he talked to our leaders. He spoke in a loud voice so most of us could hear what he said. He told us that he was a reasonable man and that he had no personal quarrel with us but that he would do his duty. He told us to disperse and go to our families in peace and good health. There were murmurs among the men. Shenko and Lewsyn turned and said we should rush them. We outnumbered them and we *could* take them, Lewsyn told us. Captain Morgan stayed calm, but then he nodded to his officers. We thought we might have taken them, but we also knew it would be just like last week at the Castle Inn. Lewsyn protested but men started drifting away. I joined them and I dropped my musket onto the road as I walked.'

On the same day, Rhodri reported, many thousands of armed men had marched from the eastern valleys to support them. They were met by a large number of troops on the road, and there was almost another slaughter. 'Luckily though,' Rhodri said, 'it didn't come to firing. When they saw the soldiers, many men threw down their weapons and went home. I should warn you though, that the soldiers are out in the town now. They are going to people's homes, looking for everyone who was involved in the past few days.'

Rhodri was right. Over the next few days Zoe and her companions heard in bits and pieces how the Magistrates' henchmen and soldiers had raided many homes in search of the riot's ringleaders. Many had been arrested and taken off to gaol. These included Lewsyn-yr-Heliwr, who was found hiding in woods at Hirwaun.

It was with disbelief and dismay that the children learned from Solly Pysgoden the fishmonger that Dic had also been arrested. Zoe was distraught. 'We must do something,' she kept insisting, and when Queen Bee told her, firmly, that there was nothing they could do for the time being, she cried in anger and frustration.

Dic and Lewsyn had been brought to Merthyr under heavy armed-guard and questioned thoroughly.

That evening as they went to their beds Zoe whispered to Catrin, 'I can't sit here in the colony and do *nothing*, Catrin; I must try to help.'

Catrin looked puzzled. 'What are you talking about?' she asked.

'Dic,' Zoe explained in exasperation. 'I must try to help him . . . I must at least try to go to him . . . to be there for him.'

Catrin gasped. 'Don't be twp! The soldiers will arrest you . . . or shoot you,' she said. 'Don't you understand how serious this is?'

Zoe put her head in her hands. 'I have to do something,' she cried, 'It's just that I . . . he's . . . ' She thought of how he'd saved her life . . . and then, after, of Nell . . . and she began to cry.

Catrin put her arm around her and helped her to her bed. 'Shush, shush, try to sleep,' she whispered soothingly.

Those days after the terrible events outside The Castle Inn seemed unreal to Zoe. She would sit in the garden, under the hot summer sun, staring at the honeysuckle and yellow iris, foxgloves and trailing roses, listening to the gentle breeze in the hawthorn bushes and the buzz of the bees, flitting from flower to flower. She would stare, not seeing the tranquillity of the garden and Queen Bee's stone circle but Dic's face, or the grey walls of the Inn, the gunpowder smoke and the red uniforms of the soldiers. Sleep was no better and every night she would be tormented by the same terrible nightmare. She would wake, soaked in sweat, brushing frantically at her hands like Lady Macbeth, calling out, 'Nell, Nell.' She would drift back into a doze only to leap from her bed in terror as she'd dream of the row of guns aimed at her.

Gradually, the town returned to normal, but things would never be quite the same in Merthyr. The Honeycomb Children resumed their duties in the colony and their collecting in the familiar streets, though Zoe could not bring herself to go anywhere near The Castle Inn, even preferring Pontystorehouse to that place. She, like the others, was dismayed to learn that there was widespread cholera, mainly in Pontystorehouse's cellars and riverside areas. The children did what they could to help, wherever possible.

Solly Pysgoden told them that those arrested for their part in the riots had been transferred to Cardiff gaol to prevent further trouble in Merthyr. It was also to keep fellow workers from trying to help them escape. It was at Cardiff that the prisoners, Dic and Lewsyn included, were to be kept until their trial.

The date of the trial was to be July 13th and when it was announced it caused a great deal of discussion and tension in the town. There were rumours that the authorities were going to make an example of the rioters, and were going to take severe action to ensure that nothing like it would happen again.

In the colony, Daniel had been making a rapid recovery but Zoe was suffering. The shocking events had left their mark on her. Daniel had been told about his sister Nell, and how she had saved Zoe's life. After his initial grief, he became even more attached to Zoe, helping her, comforting her, reassuring her, but still her nightmares continued, and she was unable to explain to him, or to anyone else for that matter, the pain she felt for Dic Penderyn. Whenever she thought of him awaiting trial a terrible sense of anxiety and foreboding and helplessness gripped her.

Queen Bee also seemed distressed. Then, one evening a few days before the trial was due to begin, she announced to the children that she intended to go to Cardiff for the trial. No one spoke; they just stared at her. She looked around the room. "You can come too, if you wish," she said quietly.

Later that evening the youngsters were in their beds and Zoe, unable to sleep, got up and walked to the main room. She stopped when she saw that Queen Bee was sitting alone, staring ahead as if in a trance and crying softly, almost silently. She could see the wetness of the tears on Queen Bee's face shining in the candlelight.

'Would you like some company?' Zoe whispered. For a moment there was no response and she wondered if Queen Bee had heard her, or if she had even noticed that she was there.

Then Queen Bee turned to her and smiled sadly. 'I saw this happen you know,' she said. There was a weary sadness in her voice. 'And I know that you understand what I mean."

Zoe frowned. 'What did you see happen? What do you mean?' she asked.

Queen Bee sighed and looked away. 'Everything! I saw all the events of the last week happen.'

'How? Where? What do you mean?' Zoe asked. 'And what did you mean by saying that *you know that I understand*?'

Queen Bee seemed to be choosing her words carefully. 'Well, I know that you see things clearly in your dreams, more clearly than most people. We've talked about it, remember? I have watched you during the day and I have heard you during the night. Your dreams and visions are very clear. It is as if you are a real part of things that happen in the dreams. Am I right?'

'Well . . . yes and no . . . Although I see things clearly in dreams and visions I'm finding it harder and harder to remember things about my home and my real life. But, anyway, what exactly do you know about my dreams? I know I've said things to you . . . but surely . . . you can't tell from just listening to me when I'm asleep, can you? Hey . . . ' Zoe's eyes were wide, 'can you read my mind? Because I've often felt that you can . . . '

Queen Bee laughed softly and turned the Celtic knotwork bracelet on her wrist, an action that didn't go unnoticed by Zoe. 'It's because I, too, feel that sometimes I live within my dreams,' Queen Bee said. 'Sometimes I see things happen, things that I can't explain and it's as if I'm really there. I can see and hear things clearly; I can smell things and I feel joy, sorrow and fear as if it were a real situation.'

'That's what I feel at times too,' Zoe murmured thoughtfully. 'Catrin has told me that sometime you have nightmares,' she added.

'Oh yes, over and over again. Just like you,' Queen Bee replied. She stared at the candle 'It would appear that we are alike in many ways Zoe.'

Zoe nodded. 'Catrin said that you are a *Child of the Heavens and the Earth, and of the past and the future.* What did she mean by that? I know it's a ridiculous question but can you really see the past and the future? Or . . .' Zoe paused for a moment but there was no turning back now . . . 'Have you lived in different times?'

'Ah,' Queen Bee said softly, 'Mair Gwenyn.' She responded to Zoe's question with a question of her own. 'Where, exactly, have you come from Zoe? I could ask you the same thing. If you've not come from Annwn then where are you from?'

'I used to think I knew where I came from,' Zoe answered, 'but I'm not so sure now, it all seems so hazy and distant . . . and I don't understand why I'm here or how I got here. I . . . I'd always hoped you could explain things to me. After all, you have special powers.'

Queen Bee reached out and took Zoe's hand. 'When we first met I knew you were different to the other Rodneys of Merthyr.'

'Exactly,' Zoe said, trying to find words that would make sense. 'I'm not from Merthyr . . . and I'm not from Otherworld or Annwn, or whatever you want to call it either. I . . . I . . . I'm not from this time. Oh I know this might sound daft, and that's why I asked if you have lived in different times, but . . . look!' She hitched up the new skirt that had been given to her after the riots, and pulled her mobile phone from the pocket of her jeans. The battery was completely dead but she flipped the phone open and held it out to Queen Bee. 'This is something we use in my other time. I know it's mine, it feels and looks so familiar . . . but I can't remember what it's for,' she whispered. She looked at Queen Bee and said, 'But the point is that this surely

252

proves . . . ' she stopped and sighed. 'Oh, I don't know what it proves,' she said despairingly . . . 'I just wish I knew how I got here and what's going to happen to me now.'

Queen Bee glanced at the phone but showed no signs of surprise or curiosity. 'I think I have glimpsed your world; well some of it, at least. I thought it was Otherworld but you have put doubts in my mind, and I'm afraid I can't explain how you got here. I don't know or understand everything. It is true that I have special powers, but I suspect Zoe, that you also have powers!'

'It's very confusing,' Zoe said.

'Yes, that is how I often feel – confused. Having special powers or abilities can also bring a great weight of responsibility. To see so much can be very frightening at times.'

'You said that you've seen my world, and I think my world is the future. *Can* you see the future?' Zoe persisted.

Queen Bee raised her eyebrows. 'I see many, many visions, sometimes very clearly, but until those things happen in the real world I can't really be sure that they are pictures of things to come.'

'And do you know if I will I ever get back to my world?' Zoe asked, her voice shaking.

Queen Bee sighed and squeezed Zoe's hand.

On the night before the trial began, Zoe and the children of the colony set off on their long journey. For the first time, every member was present, including Queen Bee, Mary and Martha. They walked across Jackson's Bridge towards the Pontystorehouse wharf, where Will Canal had arranged for them to travel by barge down to Cardiff. The slow journey took them southwards and east passing through many lock gates.

Zoe sat among her friends on the deck, under the cloudless, star-lit sky. Some of the youngsters dozed but Zoe stayed awake and stared blankly at the canal paths, the stacking yards and the warehouses along the route. Her mind was filled with the trial, and the thought that very soon she would see Dic. She wondered what would happen on the following day. Why had he been arrested, she wondered; what was he supposed to have done? The trial would show his innocence anyway, she reasoned. He had done no wrong. After all, it had been Dic who had tried to prevent further trouble. And what about Lewsyn, she asked herself. He was the true ringleader. How would the authorities treat him? He must have been questioned, and there must be other witnesses. Surely he was the one who was guilty if anyone was.

Chapter 20

The trial

Zoe opened her eyes and realised that she must have been asleep. It was early morning and the sound of seagulls, the smell of salt and tar and the general hustle-bustle of Cardiff docks greeted her as the barge pulled in at a busy wharf. She stepped off the boat with Catrin and joined the group as Will quickly led them away from the docks and across town to the Courthouse. They were among the first to enter the public gallery but many more were to follow; to watch and listen to the extraordinary cases of the Rebels of Merthyr. Even though the trial had not yet started, Zoe's eyes were fixed on the witness stand as she waited desperately to see Dic. She half listened to the many conversations going on around her in Welsh and in English. There was a great deal of speculation: Had this simply been a riot for better conditions? Or, as some believed, had it been an attempt to bring about a revolution, like the one started at the Bastille in Paris over forty years before? 'After all,' someone said, 'a red flag was raised and armed workers laid siege to the town for days, attacking the soldiers of the King.'

'Bridie's not here,' Rhiannon said softly to Queen Bee, and Zoe turned and looked around the room rapidly at the mention of Dic's wife.

At last the trial started. Zoe fidgeted impatiently as the first three cases dealt with the attacks on the property of Thomas Lewis the moneylender, and the house of the President of the Court of Requests. Four defendants were found guilty and sentenced to transportation – to a convict colony, Queen Bee explained, but Zoe knew exactly what transportation meant.

At last the fourth case was announced. The packed crowd murmured, and Zoe gripped a brass rail in front of her as the defendants were led through the door. Her mouth was dry and she leaned forward, her knuckles white on the rail. Lewsyn and Dic stood facing the packed courtroom as the charges were read. 'Lewis Lewis, known commonly as Lewsyn yr Heliwr, you are charged with the offence of causing riot on June 3rd 1831 at the Parish of Merthyr.' The clerk of the court paused for a moment before continuing. 'Richard Lewis, known commonly as Dic Penderyn, you are accused of seizing a bayoneted musket from a soldier Donald Black, and attacking the said Donald Black with it, causing a wound to the hip. Richard Lewis, Dic Penderyn, you are charged with intent to murder a soldier of the King.'

There were gasps from the people in the room at the seriousness of the charges.

'This is stupid,' Zoe whispered as Dic shook his head and laughed in disbelief. Lewsyn stood impassive, at his side.

Donald Black, a soldier of the Highlanders on duty that day outside The Castle Inn, was called to give evidence. He stood in the witness box, impressive in his military uniform. All eyes were fixed on him. The courtroom was hushed and members of the jury sat forward, listening intently as Black was asked to give his account of the events.

'I was outside The Castle Inn at Merthyr on the day of 3rd June 1831,' he said in a clear voice. 'The mob made a rush at us and I was wounded. My musket was seized and pulled from me, and it was then that I was wounded in my right hip.' Black was leaning on a stick. He pointed to where he had been injured.

'And is the man who stabbed you in this courtroom today?' the prosecuting lawyer asked.

Zoe held her breath.

'I don't know the man who wounded me,' Black replied. 'I saw both the prisoners, here today, in the crowd. I did not see them laying hands on anyone. I only saw Dic Penderyn take off his hat and wave and shout to the crowd, but I did not see him attack anyone.'

'Yes,' Zoe said loudly, and the Judge looked sharply in her direction.

The man defending Dic questioned Black. 'Did you actually see the prisoner, Dic Penderyn, take your bayonet and attack you, causing injury?'

Hesitation showed clearly on the hitherto expressionless face of the soldier. His dark eyes flashed quickly around the hushed courtroom; his free hand brushed nervously at his bushy beard.

'Go on, tell him, tell him,' Zoe muttered

Black cleared his throat and said slowly, 'No, Sir, I did not see who attacked me.'

Zoe closed her eyes as a wave of relief swept over her. 'Thank you, thank you,' she whispered as the noise level rose through the court, particularly in the public gallery. The judge struck his hammer several times and called for silence.

Two more witnesses were called for the prosecution, but they too were unable to say that they had seen Donald Black attacked. They were certainly in no position to give direct evidence against Dic. Both declared that they had seen Lewsyn and Dic at the scene, and both gave evidence against Lewis Lewis as far as causing riot was concerned, but nothing further was established.

Zoe turned to Catrin, gave a thumbs-up sign and smiled at Catrin's look of puzzlement. She noticed Queen Bee staring across the courtroom, and following her gaze, saw at the opposite end of the room, leaning forward and staring back a well-dressed, wealthy-looking middle-aged man.

'Who's that?' she whispered to Queen Bee, but even as she asked she felt she knew the answer.

'That's William Crawshay,' Queen Bee answered softly.

So that's the great man himself, Zoe thought. He certainly doesn't look like the monster I'd once imagined him to be. 'Hey, why is he staring at you?'

Queen Bee shrugged but said nothing.

The air in the courtroom was still and the temperature hot. Dic sagged a little; weary from standing, and suffering, no doubt, from the strain. Zoe wished she could go to him, to say a few words of encouragement, to offer him a drink, to help him. She knew that that would be impossible, so she tried to catch his attention. She just wanted him to know that she was there.

The next witness stepped onto the stand. Zoe's heart sank. She looked at Dic. He, too, looked dismayed, his face pained. It was the barber and special constable, Abbott. As he gave his evidence he looked very satisfied. He kept glancing in the direction of the prisoners and seemed to be enjoying Dic's discomfort.

'I was stationed in the passage of the Inn . . . ' Abbot began. 'I saw a soldier coming up the steps and saw him struggle with two or three men to keep his musket, which he lost. Dic Penderyn was one of the men. He charged the soldier with a musket and bayonet and stabbed him at the top of his leg. I saw a large hole, bleeding like a pig. I have not the slightest doubt of the person I saw. He is standing there now.' Abbott pointed at Dic. There were gasps from all around the courtroom. Dic staggered and stumbled a little where he stood. Abbott grinned as the judge called for order.

The next witness to be called was another constable, James Drew. He quickly gave his evidence: 'I was at the Inn on June 3rd. I saw both prisoners. I saw Dic Penderyn wrestling with a soldier . . . and then he pushed a bayonet into his thigh.'

Dic was shaking his head; the courtroom was in uproar.

'No, no, no,' Zoe yelled, 'he was with *me*.'

Order was restored and after a brief discussion between the judge and the lawyers the case for Dic's defence began. A few witnesses came forward declaring that throughout the riot Dic had remained in the alley at the side of the Inn. One man stated that he had seen Dic run from the passage into the crowd, away from the soldiers and soon disappear from sight. Zoe nodded eagerly and looked, searchingly at the faces of the members of the jury, hoping that they, too, would see this as the truth.

The next defence witness was a special constable,

Thomas Darker.

'Oh no,' Zoe groaned, 'not another special constable.'

'I saw Richard Lewis in front of the Castle Inn with his hat off,' he said. 'He waved his hat and he shouted but I did not see anything else.'

This is promising, Zoe thought, feeling a little more hopeful. She looked over to Queen Bee and was alarmed to see that she was very pale and her eyes were closed. Zoe quickly swapped places with Catrin and shook Queen Bee's arm. 'What's the matter?' she whispered.

Queen Bee opened her eyes, stared at Zoe and shrugged her shoulders.

'Come on. What is it?' Zoe insisted.

'Oh, I think you know,' Queen Bee said, closing her eyes again.

Zoe was baffled, but her attention was drawn back to the proceedings as Thomas Darker was questioned by the prosecution.

'Richard Lewis was standing near the door of the Inn with his hat up,' Darker said. 'Something was said from the window of the Inn just before he waved his hat, but what was said I did not hear . . . '

'That's right, that's it,' Zoe shouted, 'The soldiers were in the windows . . . the officers must have been giving orders to fire. Dic heard it and waved his hat

'Silence,' the judge called, banging his hammer, 'I will not tolerate such outbursts . . . '

Zoe whispered, 'But he was trying to save my life.' Dic was looking in her direction, and for a few seconds their eyes met. During those few seconds it occurred to her that Thomas Darker had consistently referred to Dic as Richard Lewis, yet, she thought, everyone knew him as Dic Penderyn. Something stirred in her mind. He *is* well known . . . he is famous for something, but what is it? I should know, she thought, as a feeling of unease grew and nagged at her.

At last Dic was called to give evidence. He looked tired and thin, exhausted, Zoe supposed, by his stay in prison and by the ordeal of the case against him. He looked towards the public gallery, and Zoe noticed that Queen Bee was now leaning forward with her hands on the brass rail. She appeared to be chanting something under her breath, over and over again.

The defence lawyer asked Dic to give his account of the incident.

'I declare my innocence of the charge brought against me,' Dic said wearily. 'I was standing in the passageway at the front and to the side of The Castle Inn. I heard an order given to the soldiers to load and prime and seeing a friend, a child, in the crowd, I waved my hat and told her to get down. Then I heard gunfire and I ran to try to help her. That is when another volley of gunfire occurred and we ran from the scene of fighting towards the river and into Georgetown.'

Zoe stared at Dic as vague memories started to form – something about him was starting to register in her mind. It was like having a word on the tip of her tongue.

Dic was questioned by the prosecution.

'You have heard the clear evidence of the witnesses; witnesses who are reliable men – special constables. They say that they *clearly* saw you stabbing the soldier, Donald Black. How do you answer that?'

Dic looked taken aback and seemed to struggle to find an explanation. Just as Zoe thought he was not going to be able to answer he started, falteringly, 'Earlier this year . . . on the evening of the Reform meeting,' he said, 'I . . . I had been involved in a scuffle with Mr Abbott. A few days later we were involved in another fight in which I knocked him down . . . '

There were gasps and whispers from all around the courtroom, and Zoe saw William Crawshay lean forward and whisper something to a court official. The judge called for order again and Dic glanced around nervously. He looked so alone and so vulnerable, Zoe thought, and she wanted to rush across to the stand and answer the questions for him. At the same time something in her mind . . . something about Dic was making her uncomfortable. Something . . .

Dic spoke again. 'After the fight,' he said hoarsely, 'Abbott said that he would get even with me the first chance he had.'

'You were fighting,' the prosecution lawyer boomed, 'and you knocked the constable down? From your own lips you have stated, and we have clearly heard, that you are a violent man, Lewis. I rest my case, my Lord.'

With the evidence over, Dic left the witness box and was led back to the dock. The judge summed up the evidence: 'There are several inconsistencies,' he pointed out. 'Much has been said, and debated, about the whereabouts of Richard Lewis during and after the riot. This, however, should not be the focus when considering guilt or innocence of the allegations made. Members of the jury, you must consider the evidence given by reliable witnesses with regard to the specific charge of wounding with intent to murder . . . '

Zoe felt suddenly faint. She went hot and cold, and found it difficult to breathe.

The judge gave his final directions and the jury retired to consider its verdict. Everyone in the courtroom appeared tense and fidgety. Zoe slumped forward slightly as she felt giddy. Everything went black as the sound of roaring wind started to build in her head. The noise increased to a painful level, making her want to scream . . . then, suddenly there was silence, and the sensation of floating, and her father's voice, as they were driving, when she was little, in Merthyr. 'The story of a hero,' he said. 'Merthyr's second martyr . . . '

'Zoe, Zoe . . . ' Catrin's voice echoed in her head, getting louder and clearer. Zoe opened her eyes. Catrin and Rhiannon held her arms. 'You were unwell again,' Catrin said, fussing and wiping Zoe's sweating face with a corner of her shawl, 'but you're safe now . . . '

'Oh . . . my . . . God . . . ' Zoe said, staring ahead and ignoring Catrin. 'I know what's going to happen.' She put her hands to her mouth and turned to Queen Bee who sat silently at her side. 'I know what's going to happen,' she repeated. 'My father . . . I remember now. My father told me. I remember who he is now . . . and I know what's going to . . . happen.' She looked at Queen Bee who stared back sadly. 'You know too, don't you?" she whispered. Queen Bee closed her eyes and said nothing. Zoe leapt from her seat, her eyes wild as she grabbed Queen Bee's shoulders. Rhodri, Rhiannon and Catrin tried to pull her back but she struggled against them and pleaded with Queen Bee, 'We can do something . . . There's still time, we can change things . . . '

'What do you think you are doing?' Rhodri snarled, pulling at Zoe's arm.

'Stop!' Queen Bee snapped. She held up her hand

and looked around the group of youngsters. 'Zoe is upset,' she said softly. She stood and placed her hand gently on Zoe's shoulder. 'What must be, will be.'

Zoe sat in silence, staring blankly at the empty dock. She felt drained and her head ached. Her father's voice, what he'd said and what she remembered began to dissolve in her mind. She tried, desperately, to recall the details but couldn't remember what for a moment had been so clear. After a while she was too exhausted even to try. The premonition, however, remained with her: it hung on her as a terrible burden of foreboding and dread.

After a long, hot wait, the jury returned and the prisoners were led back to the dock.

'Have you reached a verdict upon which you are all agreed?' the clerk of the court asked.

'We have,' the foreman declared.

'Do you find the defendant Lewis Lewis, known as Lewsyn-yr-Heliwr, guilty or not guilty of causing a riot?' the clerk asked.

'Guilty,' the foreman declared without hesitation.

Murmurs rippled through the packed courtroom. One man in the public gallery stood and shouted, 'Disgrace.'

The judge banged his hammer furiously and glared at the man. Zoe turned to look, with everyone else, as the door to the public gallery opened and a number of court officials, special constables and four red-coated soldiers filed in and stood along an aisle. Order was restored and the clerk of the court continued: 'Do you find the defendant Richard Lewis, known as Dic Penderyn, guilty or not guilty of wounding with intent to murder.'

This time, the foreman hesitated and glanced

nervously at his fellow jurors.

Zoe tensed and gripped Queen Bee's hand in both of hers.

The foreman coughed, looked directly at the clerk and said, 'Guilty.'

The room was in uproar. Men and women shouted, whistled, and stamped their feet. Zoe stood and leaned forward against the rail, her tears splashing down. Dic stood motionless, his head bowed. The constables and soldiers moved further into the public gallery, and Zoe saw that several more soldiers had taken up positions in front of the dock. After a considerable time the clerk to the court ordered everyone to stand. The Judge, who had left the room during the angry scene following the verdict, returned and nodded to the clerk. Everyone sat and the Judge looked across at Dic and Lewsyn. 'Lewis Lewis, Richard Lewis,' he announced, 'you have been found guilty of most serious crimes; inciting riotous assembly and attempted murder against a king's soldier . . . As far as the sentence is concerned . . . I have little choice.'

Zoe looked into Queen Bee's eyes. 'You've seen *this* too, haven't you?' she murmured. The Queen nodded slowly . . .

The Judge reached forward, picked up a black cap and placed it on his head. Looking directly at the two prisoners, he declared solemnly, 'The sentence of this court upon you is . . . that you shall be taken from here to a prison and from there to a place of execution, and there you will be hanged by the neck until dead. May God have mercy on your souls.'

Chapter 21

In the midst of life we are in death

Over the next few weeks Zoe and the other children learned that many efforts were being made to change the sentences of death that hung over Dic and Lewsyn. Solly Pysgoden kept Rhodri informed. Even the Neath Ironmaster, Joseph Tregelles-Price, collected evidence on behalf of both men. He raised petitions, which were sent, together with the evidence, to Judge Bosanquet and the Home Secretary Lord Melbourne. A delay was ordered on the execution, and on 30th July, despite his obvious involvement in starting the riot, Lewsyn-yr-Heliwr's sentence was changed to transportation to a convict colony in Australia.

Just over a week later Rhodri returned to the colony from town. He was distressed and could hardly speak. Eventually he managed to tell everyone that rumours had finally been confirmed that the Judge of the trial had received a letter from the Home Secretary instructing him that the death sentence imposed upon Dic Penderyn was to stand and should be delayed no further.

The news had a devastating effect on the children of the colony and on the people of Merthyr generally. In the streets of Georgetown, in the taverns of Morlais and in the cwrw-bachs of Pontystorehouse the name on everyone's lips was that of Dic Penderyn.

It was the beginning of August, and in the days after the Lughnasadh harvest festival, which they celebrated, Queen Bee spent many hours alone, not speaking and not joining the others for meals. The grief Zoe felt for Dic was immense and like nothing she'd experienced before. She was tortured by thoughts of what was to happen to him, and to make matters worse her nightmares continued . . . The black void, the click of metal gun hammers, the crash of musket fire, the smoke, the blood . . . and the sobbing child.

On the morning before the day of execution, Zoe awoke from a very troubled and restless night. She had a severe headache and she felt uncomfortably hot. Later that morning, whilst sitting in the garden, she suddenly felt extremely sick. Catrin looked very concerned and took her back to her bed. For a few moments Catrin whispered to Queen Bee who kept glancing in Zoe's direction.

Zoe felt wretched; her head ached and so did her stomach. Feelings of sickness kept washing over her. Queen Bee brought her a herbal medicine mixture and bathed her face with a cloth soaked in cold water. As her temperature climbed the feeling of dread over the execution grew. That evening they were again to make the journey by barge to Cardiff; the next day was the dreaded day. Despite her illness Zoe begged to go. Queen Bee tried to dissuade her but Zoe was determined to make the journey. Too weary and upset herself to persist with her protest she gave in to Zoe's wishes.

The journey was very uncomfortable for Zoe. Despite her high temperature, she shivered and was cold. She pulled her shawl tightly around her.

As the barge proceeded slowly down the waterways towards Cardiff docks Zoe felt dreadful. The stomach pains were getting worse and on a few occasions she had to lean over the side of the barge to be sick. Queen Bee brought her a thick blanket and draped it over her head and around shoulders to keep out the cold night air, but still she shivered violently and her teeth chattered as she rested her head on the barge's wooden side rail.

Shortly before dawn it started to rain. By daybreak persistent drizzle soaked the faces and clothes of Zoe and her friends. Cardiff was shrouded in a thick, grey mist – befitting the occasion of an execution, Zoe thought miserably, and the buildings, warehouses, gantries and boats along the canal route appeared to her as ghostly, formless shapes.

The barge was guided towards a wooden jetty and was pulled in by a gang of bargemen. Silently, the youngsters disembarked, Zoe was helped out by Hywel, Tom and a barge hand. Queen Bee remained seated, staring ahead, her cloak-shawl covering her golden-red hair. Catrin stepped back aboard and knelt before Queen Bee. Zoe and the others looked on as Catrin bowed her head. No words were spoken and after a few moments Queen Bee took Catrin's hand and both girls stepped off the barge to join the waiting party

Will Canal led the way through the clinging mist and narrow alleyways that separated the tall dockland warehouses, and as they made their way towards St Mary's Street the crowds started to thicken. Soon they were within sight of the prison. They turned a corner and entered the broad space of St Mary's Square, to be greeted by the gruesome sight of the gallows platform

Zoe had to stop and lean on Tom when she saw it. Despite her terrible sense of premonition and her vague memory of knowing about this awful event, she still hoped that there would be some last minute reprieve and that the execution would not actually take place. Things might change, she thought. All it will mean is that books will say different things in the future . . . give a different ending and no one in the future will be any the wiser . . . She knew, however, that the hope was unrealistic, and her heart sank as she saw that the base of the wooden gallows was guarded by a double line of red-coated soldiers with muskets and bayonets at the ready – well prepared for the possibility of trouble, or a rescue attempt.

Weak and sick, Zoe had difficulty standing. Tom and Rhodri supported her. The blanket was still wrapped around her. Queen Bee stood silently, her head covered with a dark shawl, staring at the gallows with its rope and noose swaying gently in the soft, early morning drizzle.

The bell in the prison chapel struck a deep note followed, slowly, by seven more chimes. The large crowd stood still and silent. Zoe looked around and saw many faces that she knew. There were miners and ironworkers from Cyfarthfa and Ynysfach, Solly Pysgoden, and even Shenko, the Gaffer from the Cyfarthfa quarry. They all stood quietly, faces upturned toward the platform.

A small wooden door opened just to the right of the large main gates of the prison. Soon, a small group of people, escorted by Redcoats, started to move towards the wooden platform. The soldiers marched ahead of the main group to the slow steady beat of a drum, clearing a path through the crowd. In a few minutes the sad procession had reached the wooden steps. Dic walked between two prison guards, his hands tied behind his back. He spoke to both guards as they walked but Zoe couldn't hear his words. She stared at his face. "Please," she whispered, "someone do something . . . "

Slowly Dic climbed the steep wooden steps followed by his guards and Geraint Jenkins, the minister of the Unitarian chapel in Merthyr. The masked executioner stood, waiting on the platform above, arms folded, not looking at Dic but staring towards the sky.

As he reached the top of the steps, Dic turned to the crowd and called in a clear voice, 'O Arglwydd, dyma gamwedd . . . I am going to suffer unjustly. God, who knows all, knows it is so.'

Zoe was doubled over with pain, and fell to her knees. 'No, no,' she cried, 'He saved me. He saved my life. I must do something; I must . . . Dic . . . Dic!'

The noose was placed over Dic's head. Mr Jenkins read from the Bible, his hands shaking, his face white as he spoke the words quickly.

'Please,' Zoe said weakly, *'Someone do something . . . stop this . . . now.'* She opened her mouth to scream but no sound came out. Tom gripped her hand tightly. Catrin sobbed. Rhiannon buried her face in her hands.

The Minister stood back and the executioner pulled a lever . . .

The crowd groaned as Dic's body fell, jerked violently then hung and swayed in the breeze.

Zoe clenched her eyes tight shut; Nausea swept over her again and she lurched forward to be sick on the cobblestones. Queen Bee stood, alone; staring at Dic's limp, hanging body and the tears streamed down her face. At that moment the sky turned even darker, the drizzle turned to heavy rain and a flash of sheet lightning preceded the deep rumbling thunder, which rolled and crashed overhead.

Zoe was helped up by Catrin and Rhodri. Queen Bee silently gathered her group together. They held onto each other, some weeping, others in a mute state of shock. The grief-stricken youngsters turned and trudged slowly through the rain puddles and made their way out of the square. A company of soldiers had formed a broad line and slowly moved forward, shepherding people away from the wooden platform, but Zoe saw, through the crowd, a huddle of people still facing the gallows. At the centre of the small, sad group stood young Bridie Lewis. Her head was uncovered and her hair and face were soaked by the torrential rain as she sobbed pitifully. Her neighbour, Angharad, held Dic and Bridie's baby in a shawl, rocking him gently while other friends, neighbours and ironworkers stood around helplessly.

Queen Bee walked across to where Bridie stood and put her arms around her. Zoe watched as they stood silently for a few moments. Then Queen Bee reached out, stroked the baby's head and said a few words to the distraught young widow. Bridie nodded slowly, gripped Queen Bee's hand and rested her head on her shoulder. At that moment three soldiers, their muskets held diagonally across their chests, ordered the group to move on. Queen Bee turned and fixed the Redcoats with a piercing stare. Not a word was said but the soldiers backed away and moved off in another direction.

*　*　*

Emma looked out of her kitchen window; the sky was an overcast, lead-coloured grey. The rain drummed against the windowpane. It was dark in the kitchen even though it was not yet five o'clock. She stood in the gloom and stared out at the storm. 'May,' she muttered bitterly. She was angry – upset at the way she'd been treated by her senior police officers. "I don't want a few days' leave; I don't want to be off the case," she said angrily, kicking the washing basket. She sighed, and as she went back to removing laundry from the washing machine she heard the front doorbell ring. She tutted irritably as the ringing persisted and she walked towards the front door. She just wanted to be left alone.

'I thought *you* might want some company,' Ian said from under a black umbrella, the rain lashing against him as he smiled and held out a bottle of wine. Emma said nothing but left the door open and walked back into the house with Ian following.

Without warning she turned and snapped at him sharply, 'I thought you would have supported me.'

'Hey, I'm your friend, remember,' Ian said, looking startled.

'You could have spoken up, Ian; you know how much I care about this case,' she persisted.

'I'm just a lowly detective constable. I do as I'm told and anyway, you're off duty now, I'm here as a friend,' he protested.

'Oh go on, rub it in, *you're off duty*,' she mimicked cruelly.

'Please Emma . . . ' He looked hurt.

'Well I suppose you'd better sit down then,' she said, less irritably.

The two young detectives could not talk about

anything but the case. Ian told Emma that there was still no sign of a breakthrough. There was no evidence to support a murder enquiry, and there was no evidence of abduction, even though that was what Inspector Bowen believed they were dealing with. He mentioned that the Old Man was considering bringing in specialist help – people with expertise in child abduction cases and criminal psychology. Merthyr could soon have the benefit of expert help from some of Britain's biggest cities, he told her, while National police forces, especially the Metropolitan police would continue to make enquiries and look for Zoe.

'Anything more from forensics on the sweatshirt?' Emma asked.

'Nothing at all,' Ian replied, 'and certainly nothing to implicate our Mr Silford.'

'How are Bethan and David?' she asked.

'Don't know really. I haven't seen them since we were there last. They're still at his grandmother's place; I expect they won't leave until something definite turns up,' he said.

'Poor things,' Emma whispered. 'It's only been two days but it feels like a lifetime, I dread to think how they feel . . . Perhaps I should pop along there and . . . '

'No Emma, you'll only get into further trouble.' Ian warned.

'Trouble . . . *trouble*? Why does everyone keep saying I'm in trouble? I feel I'm on trial; I've done nothing wrong. This is an injustice, can't you see that?' Emma's voice had risen and she was shouting now. 'For goodness' sake, I want to *help*. Do something Ian. Speak to Inspector Bowen; get me back on the case.'

'I can't Emma . . . I wish I could,' he said apologetically.

'Then go away. Go on . . . *get out; you're no friend of mine*,' she yelled.

After a few moments of awkward silence Ian got up and walked slowly to the door. He stopped and turned back to Emma.

'I mean it Ian, *just go*,' she sobbed.

He shrugged and walked out.

After a few seconds Emma stood up, rushed down the hallway and fumbled with the lock on the front door, 'Ian,' she called, 'I didn't mean . . . ' but she was too late and could only watch as his car pulled away from the kerb and drove off into the rain.

She was furious with herself for her outburst; she knew it wasn't his fault . . . He really is a good and true friend, she thought miserably. She closed the front door – the storm was getting worse – and walked slowly to her living room window. Her mind was in turmoil; she couldn't stop thinking about how badly she'd been treated, and about how badly she'd just treated Ian. Details of the case kept whirling around her head and she couldn't stop wondering about Zoe. The heavy rain showed no signs of easing and the sky was almost black even though it was still early. This is eerie, Emma thought, and she shivered as thunder rumbled in the distance. 'Typical bank holiday weather,' she thought sardonically.

*   *   *

Zoe's condition had deteriorated. She was suffering from intestinal cramps, high temperature, diarrhoea and nausea. Queen Bee and Catrin helped her as they joined the many mourners on the funeral procession. Rhodri had been able to get them onto a horse-drawn cart that was owned and driven by Solly Pysgoden

They followed the coffin across the Vale of Glamorgan to Aberafon, Dic's home parish and soon to be his last resting-place.

They stood with crowds of people in the mud of St Mary's churchyard as the incessant rain drove against them and soaked into their clothing. Zoe felt numb and detached, as if she were watching a film. After the burial service ended, the mourners started to move away, and Zoe joined the others at the graveside. Queen Bee held Bridie's hand and they both sang something quietly, but Zoe couldn't make out what they were singing. Rhiannon passed a small bowl around the group and, following Queen Bee's example, everyone took some flower petals from the bowl, sprinkled them into the grave and said, 'Blessed be.'

Zoe reached for the bowl but couldn't bring herself to look into the grave as the numbness suddenly retracted and was replaced by her overwhelming grief. She reeled forward, crying bitterly as her legs gave way under her. Queen Bee and Hywel managed to stop her falling, and Bridie reached out and touched Zoe's face. 'Be strong, cariad,' she whispered.

Zoe looked into Bridie's eyes. How could I have been so self-centred, she thought, and what must she be going through? 'What will you do now?' she asked quietly, her voice shaking.

'I'll go back to my family; there's nothing left for me in Merthyr,' Bridie said, sadly. She turned and bowed her head slightly to Queen Bee. Zoe stood silently with the others in the pouring rain, and watched as the broken young widow, clutching her crying baby tightly, walked alone from the churchyard on the road towards Swansea and Greenhill.

It was late by the time they returned to Merthyr. The weather had worsened; rain and wind battered the weary travellers. Thunder crashed and occasionally lightning illuminated the foaming water that gushed like a river down Georgetown Hill as they trudged towards the tip. By the time they reached the colony Zoe felt extremely ill. Catrin helped her remove her thick woollen skirt and bodice, and draped a dry shawl loosely over her shoulders, covering her jeans and vest. She was in severe pain and was beginning to slip in and out of consciousness. Queen Bee mixed up a number of strong honey-based medicines and gave them to Zoe.

All the children sat near her bed, Daniel close by and Catrin holding Zoe's hand. Zoe was hot and dizzy; she tried to sit up but the pain was too great. She tried to speak but couldn't. She knew she had cholera; she knew that her life was in danger. She pushed the shawl off her but held it tightly in her left hand. Queen Bee prised Zoe's fingers from the shawl and pressed a small, cold metal object into the palm of her hand. 'For luck,' she whispered as she helped Zoe drink again. Zoe quietened and fell into a light sleep, but even though she was asleep her senses were alert and she was aware of voices and the sensation of cold water on her face . . . then everything seemed to fade and she was aware only of blackness all around her . . . and then . . . something else – the sound of a child sobbing. She opened her eyes and looked up at Catrin, but her face started to blur. It cleared momentarily, and blurred again . . .

Detective Constable Ian Dixon stood alone, trying desperately to shelter under his umbrella as he waited by the police car, which was parked outside number 3 Davies Row. Inspector Bowen was inside the house with a criminal psychologist, talking to Zoe's family. The rain drove against him. He looked across the street: the drains were overflowing and bubbling as the water, brown from clay and soil, gushed down the hill. The roadway was strewn with stones, soil, cans and rubbish that was being washed and carried by the force of the water. He glanced down the hill . . . 'Oh no, don't do this,' he breathed, as he saw Emma trudging towards the house. He ran to her. 'No Emma, don't, please,' he begged.

'I wanted to say sorry to you, and I also want to see Bethan and David . . . and Rose . . . to explain. I just want to *see* them,' Emma explained.

'No Em, come on, you'll land yourself in huge trouble. You're off the case and if you're not careful you could end up with disciplinary action . . . Quit while you're ahead,' he urged as he gently guided her away from the house. They walked uphill, through the storm debris, towards the reclaimed area above Georgetown. Ian pulled on her arm as they walked, arguing with her.

Emma stopped suddenly and stared, peering ahead through the rain at an odd shape on the ground. 'What the . . . Is that . . . ? I don't believe it,' she whispered. She pulled away suddenly from Ian and ran.

Ian sprinted after her. Together they clambered over the grass bank and as they reached the shape they could hear a groaning sound and could see a mud-spattered hand moving.

'Quick Ian; your mobile,' Emma yelled as she grabbed the hand . . .

Catrin tightened her grip on Zoe's hand and moved

forward, leaning above her face.

'Come back, please Zoe, come back,' she pleaded. 'Don't go, come back. Wake up, wake up . . . Please . . . '

Zoe could hear the voice but the face above her was out of focus . . . The sound of howling wind started to build in her head, getting louder and louder. Her blurred vision suddenly turned to swirling colours, and then . . . blackness . . . and silence . . . Gradually she became aware of voices, in the distance, and then one voice, louder and clearer . . .

'Wake up, Zoe, please wake up, look at me,' the familiar voice urged.

She opened her eyes and the face slowly started to come into focus. Then it cleared.

'Come on Zoe, look at me. What are you doing lying here?'

'Dad?' she whispered. 'What? . . . where . . . where am I?'

'Thank God, thank God,' her father murmured, his eyes filled with tears.

She looked up at her father as he held her hand tightly.

A crowd of people gathered around, peering down at her. Through the driving rain soaking her face she could see blue flashing lights of fire engines, police cars and an ambulance on the road nearby.

'Zoe, Zoe, where have you been? Were you in *there*?' David was crying, pointing to a gaping hole in the hillside, just a few feet away. 'Did you get stuck in there?'

Bethan arrived with the ambulance crew and ran to where David was crouching beside Zoe.

The police and rescue services were setting up tape and cones to cordon off the tunnel, which, according to the chief fire officer, must have been uncovered by the continuous and torrential rain. 'The whole area's unstable,' he said to Emma, Ian and Inspector Bowen, pointing to an upended tree with its roots torn from the ground. 'The place is riddled with mines and tunnels. There's a rescue team from Aberdare dealing with a problem just across the river, on the waste ground next to the supermarket car park; another hole's opened up there – probably an old ventilation shaft.' He looked around, a worried expression on his face. 'I wouldn't be surprised if we had a collapse . . . and this rain,' he continued, "is making things very dangerous . . . We could have some serious subsidence. We'll need to get everyone away and the engineers in as soon as possible."

Zoe tried to sit up. Stones, plants, mud and soil had washed up against her from the tunnel; her jeans and vest were caked in mud. Paramedics had brought a stretcher and a foil blanket and were checking her for injuries. She couldn't say anything. Confused, shivering, she clutched her mother's hand.

Alison Jenkins and another police officer helped Rose Davies alongside her family. 'We were so worried when you disappeared,' Bethan cried, before breaking down and sobbing uncontrollably as she hugged Zoe. David pulled his wife back gently and the paramedics wrapped Zoe in a blanket and lifted her onto the stretcher.

Zoe looked up at her father and mother and her greatgrandmother. She was frightened, her eyes pleading as she pushed the blanket aside, and finding her voice she begged, 'Please don't let anyone take me . . . please Dad . . . '

He quickly reached forward and touched her face,

'You're not going anywhere without us sweetheart,' he said. 'We're coming in the ambulance with you, and I won't let you out of my sight ever again . . . from now on I'm going to make sure . . . '

'Never mind that now, David bach,' Rose cut in, 'plenty of time for talking later.' She looked at her great granddaughter and asked softly, 'Sut wyt ti cariad?'

Zoe smiled weakly and answered, 'Wedi blino, Nan.'

As Rose placed her hand on her grandson's shoulder, Zoe stared; something jolted in her mind as the flashes of blue light from the emergency vehicles reflected on the small silver torque bracelet that her Nan wore on her left wrist.

David murmured, 'Yes, Gran you're right, time for talking later, and we'll all have the chance to talk together.' His eyes didn't leave his daughter's face. 'I'm sorry Zoe,' he said, 'thank God you're alright . . . '

Zoe lifted her left arm from under the blanket and gazed at the beautiful, hexagonal, metal brooch that she'd been clutching tightly in her hand, the brooch Queen Bee had given her 'for luck'. She looked up at her mother and father and whispered, 'Blessed be.'